THE LAW
OF
BETRAYAL

BOOKS BY TESS COLLINS

FICTION

The Midnight Valley Quartet:
Notown
The Hunter of Hertha

The Appalachian Trilogy:
The Law of Revenge
The Law of the Dead
The Law of Betrayal

Helen of Troy

NON-FICTION

How Theater Managers Manage

THE LAW

OF

BETRAYAL

TESS COLLINS

San Francisco

Casebound: 978-1-937356-12-5
Trade paper: 978-1-937356-13-2
Kindle: 978-1-937356-14-9
EPUB: 978-1-937356-15-6

Library of Congress Control Number: 2011916320

Publisher's Cataloging-in-Publication Data

Collins, Theresa.
    The law of betrayal / Tess Collins.
p. cm.
ISBN: 978-1-937356-12-5
    1. Women lawyers—Fiction. 2. Appalachian Region—Fiction. 3. Melungeons—Fiction. 4. Kentucky—Fiction.
I. Title.
PS3603.O4559 L33 2012
813—dc22

                                                    2011916320

Published by BearCat Press BearCatPress.com

BearCat Press logo by Golden Sage Creative

Design by Frogtown Bookmaker: FrogtownBookmaker.com

This book is dedicated to
Anne Cosby Alwood,
and in memory of
Rhoda Cosby.

Acknowledgments

I would like to acknowledge Jean Patterson Bible's book *MELUNGEONS, Yesterday and Today.* She accumulated the myth and the facts about this most interesting group of people, both of which I have fictionalized. Thanks to Margot McFedries for refreshing my memory of what it's like to scuba dive; Jesse Collins for his research and firsthand knowledge of lake fish; Joddy Collins for the hundreds of details he remembers about growing up in Appalachia; and Helen Latiff Coleman for inspiring those great one-liners that I always feed to Merl Bashears.

1

Alma Bashears offered a slice of pizza to the man pointing a revolver at her. "You'll think clearer on a full stomach," she said. The commonwealth attorney offered him a tense smile, as well.

Sweat poured down Quincy Pollard's face in pencil-thin streaks. His eyes darted from the courtroom door to the oversized windows that formed the west wall, to the four remaining hostages. Willard Yokum and Chester Sanders were jurors; Barry Cage, a state's witness; and Jake Moreland, the bailiff who lost his service revolver to Quincy, a petty criminal about to be convicted of stabbing a bank teller in a fit of rage.

"Why's it so hot in here?" Quincy stated, rather than asked.

"Air-conditioning's been turned off." Alma shifted in her curled-up position on the floor and pushed the pizza box toward him with one hand. "It's only a matter of time before the electricity is disconnected, too, Quincy."

She leaned her head against the wall. Thoughts of all she might have done to prevent this situation filled her head. She was the prosecutor and should have anticipated a two-time county jail escapee with a hair-trigger temper might attempt another break for freedom. If the forty-year-old Quincy had been about sixty pounds thinner, he could have succeeded. He tripped trying to jump the gate separating the defense table and seating section. Had he been able to flee the building and jump into the truck near the rear entrance of the court-house, where his brother was waiting, they both might have disappeared into the Cumberland Mountains, never to be found again. They wouldn't have been the first.

Quincy bit his bottom lip hard enough to leave an impression and then slid opposite her, careful to keep from showing himself in the windows. He fiddled with the tuner of a radio that was propped up on a bench. "They better not kill the electricity," he said, rubbing his forehead and smearing the sweat into a dense forelock of thick brown hair. "I have to hear myself on the radio. I have to know that my side of the story gets out."

"I'm sure Chief Forester is working as hard as he can on getting you that connection," Alma said.

"He'd better. He will. With you here, he'll get it."

Knowing Quincy was counting on her relationship with Police Chief Grady Forester gave Alma a short-term sense of security. At the same time, she was the commonwealth prosecutor, and, to end this situation peacefully, she would have to make him forget her official role and establish a personal connection.

"Why don't you tell me your side of the story?" she asked soothingly and leaned back against an overturned bench that formed part of the barricade in the southwest corner of the room.

"I tried to tell you," he spit out. "You wouldn't hear! That thievin' bank was cheating my ass, jacked up the interest, forged my name, threatened to take my house." He wiggled around in the cramped space between toppled benches and tables. "I don't let people cheat me and get away with it."

Alma shifted and stretched out her legs to unfurl a twitch in her calf muscle. Every time Quincy turned to the radio, she peeked over the furniture that partially blocked the view to the windows and doors. "Don't you think it's time to let another hostage go?" She paused, making eye contact when he turned back toward her. "You promised Chief Forester you would if he brought the pizza and sodas."

"If you'd only listened," he said, pressing his lips together as if holding back a surge of regret, "none of this would've happened." He stared at the four men at the far end of the room located in the witness box where he could control them without being taken out by a sharpshooter. Gripping the revolver tightly in one hand and aiming it at the hostages, he nodded toward the men. "Go ahead. You choose."

Alma stood. Outside the window, she could see law enforcement vehicles spread throughout the parking lot. Sharpshooters on the roof of the building across the street trained their weapons on the courtroom and watched her through scopes. She caught a glimpse of a mirror being lowered to the window ledge so that the police on the roof could see what was happening in the room. Slowly she walked toward the men, knowing that Quincy's gun was pointed at her back. "We're going to send one more of you out," she said, then lowered her voice to a whisper. "Remember what I told you." A deep cut on Jake's forehead still bled and he leaned against the wall to compensate for an injured leg. Alma touched his arm. "You."

"Alma," Jake said through a thinly drawn mouth, "I am not getting out of here before you—"

"Jake, you're bleeding badly and if I can get you out of his line of fire, the rest of us can make a duck-and-cover behind the Judge's bench if we need to." She pulled a bloody rag from his forehead and pressed a clean paper towel in its place. "Patience is not one of the chief's talents. I give this another hour before he storms the place. You need to go out and—"

"Don't even ask me," he pleaded, trying to sound firm, but his voice wavered with the pain of his wounds.

Alma sensed the guilt that coursed through his veins—guilt at having lost his weapon—and she was partly afraid he might try to make up for it with some unnecessary heroics. "You represent authority to him," she explained.

"What about me?" Barry Cage asked. "I was set to testify against him."

"Mr. Cage, you were a bystander. He doesn't hold that against you."

"Says you." Barry shot a fearful look toward the corner where Quincy hid well out of sight of police sharpshooters.

"He'll target Jake. Best that he leaves next."

"And what are you—the fairy godmother?" Jake cynically rolled his eyes. "You're prosecuting him, for godssakes."

Alma tried to smile with comforting confidence but suspected that she was not succeeding. "I have an ace," she whispered, "and as soon as I have you out of the way, I'm going to play it." She squeezed his arm. "You have to trust me on this."

"I'm sorry, Alma," Jake said, unable to look her in the eye.

"You didn't do anything. He did this, not you."

Barry and Willard helped Jake to his feet. "Not the men!" Quincy shouted. "Only you, Alma. Only you and stop five feet from the door."

She anchored herself underneath Jake's arm, helping him walk. All the while, she kept Quincy in sight. Each time he turned to listen to the radio, she took the opportunity to talk to Jake. "Tell Grady to hang tight." She kicked the disabled access unit and the door swung outward. "Give me some time."

Outside in the hallway, Grady kneeled behind a trash container, gun pointed. He stood, holstering his weapon while two paramedics rushed forward to assist Jake. "I know what I'm doing," Alma whispered. Jake nodded and limped the remaining few feet into the paramedics' arms.

As the outer door closed behind them, Alma glimpsed the black helmeted force of men that Grady had been training for the last year for just such an occurrence. Many of Crimson County's local law enforcement agencies had laughed behind his back, taunting that this kind of thing could never happen in their small Kentucky county. Grady had the last laugh, but at what price?

Alma prayed that no one on the force would overreact. As long as she was still a hostage, she was fairly certain they would not. Looking over at Willard Yokum, Chester Sanders, and Barry Cage, she felt relieved that all were in good physical shape. She had talked Quincy into holding them in the witness-box and, when his attention had been diverted by the pizza delivery, she had pointed out to the hostages that there was a route to safety behind the judge's bench, bulletproof since a layer of steel had been installed the previous spring. She hoped that the jump wouldn't be necessary.

The sun dipped lower in the sky causing a blinding glare on the windows and intensified the already-warm temperature in the room. Alma wiped the nape of her neck and returned to the floor between the overturned bench and the defense table that Quincy used as a back brace.

"Quincy, can I tell you something?" Alma asked.

His eyes narrowed, and he looked away from her, but nodded.

"You're not the first person the bank has cheated. There are at least a dozen people that I personally know of—Louise Miller, Johnny Clark, Freddy Nixon, to name a few. They're not stupid people. The bank pulled the same fraud on them."

4

"What?" He twisted to face her. "Why didn't you do something about it?"

"I was." She opened her hands palm up. "I've had an investigation going on for almost a year. We were a month away from arresting not only a few bank tellers, but Vice President Carl Richie. Criminal fraud, embezzlement, grand larceny. Hell, I've even got the Feds looking into racketeering charges. He'll be in jail a long time."

"I didn't know that."

"I couldn't very well announce what I was up to by giving a newspaper interview, now could I?"

He let his head sink to a bent knee and closed his eyes as if he were wishing the situation could all just go away. "I didn't know."

"Quincy," she said, continuing to use his name and nurture the growing bond between them, "if you'd only come to me instead of taking the law into your own hands, I could have helped. Not only that, you could have helped me."

He looked up, not quite understanding, but willing to listen. "What am I going to do?"

Alma reached out to hesitantly pat his shoulder. He jerked at her touch but kept the gun barrel resting on the bottom of an upturned chair. "Maybe there's something we can work out."

"It's too late." He nodded toward the door. "They're going to kill me."

"Not if you're a state's witness."

"What do you mean?" His attention perked up, and, for the first time, his tightly drawn features began to soften.

"No one here has been seriously hurt," she explained. "If this ends peacefully, and you testify for the state, then I'll give the judge a good sentencing recommendation. You'll be out in five years—max." She waited as he processed her words but knew that she wasn't completely forthcoming. It wouldn't be easy to lessen the consequences for a person who had held a courtroom hostage, but as long as he believed her, she might be able to put an end to this without someone dying.

"At the end of the night, you got to be able to sleep," he said.

"My father used to tell me the same thing," Alma mused, letting her lips curl into a smile as if remembering. She watched him carefully, hoping he would relax enough to set aside the gun.

Quincy bit his bottom lip and his eyes took on a dazed look. "I think your daddy was the first person ever to say it to me," he said, his gaze drifting into memory. "Gotta be able to sleep."

"You knew my father?" she asked, her skin prickling.

"Met him in Pollyhollow. Me and Isham Thunderheart was drunk and fightin' over a girl."

"Go on," she prodded, knowing she was creating a firm ground with him. She was equally eager to hear about her father.

He sighed, looking down at the floor. "Things were just so different back then. All that stuff that happened."

"Stuff?" She hardly realized she had said the word. The conversation was taking a different track than she expected. Could he know something about her father's disappearance? Information she had never been able to pry from anyone else? She told herself to play it carefully, not only because of the fact that she was being held hostage, but because this man knew what she'd been trying to learn for over twenty-five years. She would spend the entire night there if it led to information about her father.

"Well," she said slowly and deliberately, "that kind of stuff can't hurt anybody now."

Quincy let out a short hiss and shook his head in uncertainty. "The past can strangle the future, if you let it." His grip on the revolver loosened as he brought it to his chest, and then rested his hand in his lap. "You really think a deal can be worked out?"

"You're looking at the person who made the offer."

He exhaled a long, slow breath. His eyes narrowed and his forehead furrowed deeply in thought, but a look of trust slowly seeped into his expression. "You're a lot like your dad, helping people who don't have nobody to depend on."

She nodded and spoke softly. "Why don't you give me the gun?"

His weary expression gave way to resignation. He raised the revolver and started to hand it to her. "All I ever wanted was justice." Hesitating midway, he stared at the barrel.

"Did you marry the girl?" she asked to recapture his attention.

"Allafair Adair . . . naw, I don't think that girl'd ever lend out her heart."

The name stunned Alma. "Allafair Adair?" she echoed. "I've been trying to find information about her for nearly five years." She held her breath, then forced herself to speak. "What was her connection to my father?"

"You mean, you don't know?" Quincy cocked his head to one side, squinting as he studied her. "You really don't know about them?" Dark shadows swung across the gleaming windowpanes and he jerked around.

"It's a bird," Alma said, hoping to distract him, but Quincy jumped up and aimed the gun. The windows broke in a shattering cacophony, sending glass spraying across the room.

"No!" he yelled, firing wildly into the glare of the sun.

"No!" Alma repeated as a black-suited figure landed on her, knocking the breath from her lungs as they hit the floor. The crackle of gunfire mixed with her screams for it to stop.

The room spun in slow motion before her. Bullets ripped into Quincy's body and sent sprays of blood spattering the room. His arms jerked like a puppet tangled in its own strings; then, in a slow twist, he dropped to the floor.

The officer covering Alma held her down even when the only sound was a single set of boots crunching on broken glass. "Get off me!" she yelled, wiggling out from underneath him. She swung up on to her knees as the three hostages ran past her and the rest of the officers pushed into the courtroom.

The black boots belonged to a husky, six-footer; he was in his forties with steel gray hair that grew back from his strong-featured face. Grady Forester stood above Quincy, aiming his gun at the man's head. He grinned the smirk of a cop who had just taken down his man.

"Damn it, Grady!" Alma yelled. "He was about to surrender!"

His surprised expression was matched only by a defensive spike of anger. "He was pointing a gun at you." He holstered his weapon now that he had secured the scene and moved toward Alma.

She pushed him away and dropped to Quincy's side. His eyes stared straight ahead, a trickle of blood running from his nose as faint breath panted between his chapped lips. "Quincy?" She rubbed his shoulder, the only part of his shirt not gushing blood. "Where are the paramedics?" she demanded and swung her head toward the door.

"Tending Jake," said a voice behind her. "They're on the way back up."

"Stay calm," she urged Quincy, "breathe slow."

His frightened eyes locked with hers. "Too late," he said.

"It's not too late." Her voice dropped to a hoarse whisper as she realized the man was dying.

He reached up to grab her collar, but Grady leaned down to release the grip.

"Leave him alone," she growled.

Grady pulled back, his confusion evident in his furrowed brow. His cheeks reddened, and he glanced quickly at his men, who avoided looking at him.

"Quincy," she said, "tell me. . . ."

He coughed a bubble of blood and struggled to form words. "People . . . know," he said.

"I can hear you," Alma encouraged him. "What do they know?"

His pupils grew wide and dark, then still and flat. His lips moved, but no sound came from his throat as the coldness of death enveloped him.

Alma shook him, squeezing the hand that still clung to her collar. "Come on, Quincy," she said louder, trying to keep him conscious. "What was my father doing with Allafair?" Her voice broke. She leaned her face as close to his as she could. The metallic smell of blood filled her nostrils.

He forced one last word from his lips, *"Allafair."*

2

"Yes, Mamaw," Alma said. "I promise I'm okay." She switched the phone to her other ear as she motioned her assistant, Val Durward, into the office. "Yes, I'll stop at your house on my way home to prove it."

Val came around the desk, tearing open a Band-Aid and positioning it over a scrape on Alma's cheek. "Hold still," she whispered.

"Don't call Momma in Hollywood," Alma told her grandmother. "Let her enjoy her vacation." She winced as Val pressed down on the bandage. After making another call and giving her Aunt Joyce the same assurances, Alma hung up the phone. Despite all she had been through that day, she fought against giving into the stress of the incident. One word pounded in her brain. *Allafair. Allafair.*

Allafair Adair. A name that had haunted her for five years, ever since one of her bitterest enemies, Charlotte Gentry, had hurled it at her from her deathbed. *"Allafair Adair is the one responsible for everything that happened."*

Alma could hear the old woman's voice as if it were yesterday. She knew those words had to be a clue to her father's disappearance, but after an exhaustive search spanning the three surrounding states, Alma had come up with no one who knew this Allafair Adair. In frustration, she had tried to forget, but the past had awakened, and it burned her as hot as a flame. She heard Quincy's voice: *"People know."* *A dead man's last words,* she thought. *Someone out there knows all about Allafair Adair.*

"Are you in shock?"

Alma looked up. Val was still bent over her, and Alma realized she had completely spaced out. "Fine," she managed to say, a flush warming her cheeks. "I'm fine. Are they both still out there?"

"Stamping their little hooves like ponies at an empty trough."

Alma sighed and rested her chin in her hand. "Give me five minutes, then tell Jefferson and Grady to come in."

A moment later, she went through a walk-in closet and shut herself in the lavatory on the other side. She inspected the bandage. The surrounding skin throbbed, and her whole left side ached. Combing her fingers through her shoulder-length black hair, she realized it had several tangles that would take some time to comb out. She tied it all back in a ponytail and headed back to her office.

Inside the closet, she paused to look through the contents of several shelves until she found it—a snow globe. The round glass set in a piece of shiny black coal held the small, eyeless face of a porcelain doll. Its pink cheeks and cherry lips were still bright, but underneath the left eye socket, the outline of a tear had faded. Alma had drawn that teardrop at the age of ten to show her sadness at her father's leaving. Then she had hidden the doll in his car just before he drove away. The snowy flakes settled around the mask as she walked into the light of her office and held the globe up to the window.

Outside, the town's long main avenue bustled with late afternoon activity. The junior high school had let out and teenagers gathered around Bartholomew's Ice Cream Shop. The adjoining Toyota dealership looked like a patchwork of multicolored autos, and waves of heat came off the asphalt. Contrary, Kentucky, had expanded a good half mile in the four years since she had become Crimson County's prosecutor. Its population had grown to nearly 20,000, while many other eastern Kentucky towns were shrinking.

Nearby Kingsley University in Liberty was beginning to rival major Southern colleges as a research center and was a mecca for scholars recording and preserving the mountain culture. Just the previous week, Alma had attended the opening of the Appalachian Museum. To the south of there was Dollywood; you could also go skiing in Gatlinburg and go hiking in the Great Smoky Mountains; to the east of Contrary was Cumberland Gap and the Daniel Boone

National Forest; and to the northwest was Pine Mountain State Park and Cumberland Falls. The tri-state area had everything. It was nearly a perfect place to live, and yet, there in her hand, she held everything that had been evil about Contrary's past. She shook the snow globe and watched the flakes settle, then set it on a credenza underneath the window.

A smashing sound outside the office door jarred her back to reality. She hurriedly opened the door, and a tray of pencils, pens, and paper clips rolled onto the floor in front of her. Grady and Jefferson Bingham, her former law partner and best friend, stood at the end of the receptionist's desk. Guilt masked their faces. Val, stationed behind the desk, had both hands anchored on her hips, and her lips were pressed together in an irritated scowl. Alma realized one of the men had shoved the other.

"Inside," she said, shooting both of them a stern look. Before closing the door, she turned to Val and shrugged her shoulders. "Sorry."

Grady dropped into a chair in front of her desk while Jefferson waited for Alma to come in. The latter rubbed one hand up and down her arm as she passed by. "How are you feeling?" he asked.

Turning around suddenly, Grady shot up and rushed to Alma's side, determined to outdo Jefferson's sympathy. He softly kissed a spot just above her scraped cheek. "That's going to bruise to a color that matches those pretty gray eyes of yours," he said.

"Will you two stop hovering? I'm fine." She moved behind her desk to limit their contact and hoped they would behave like adults, for once. "Have either of you ever heard of Isham Thunderheart?"

Both stared at her blankly. Jefferson brushed his blond bangs from his forehead.

"What about Polly Hollow or maybe Pollyhollow? I don't know if it's a name or a place."

They glanced at each other briefly, then back at her and simultaneously dropped into the chairs opposite her desk. Their puzzled expressions didn't change.

"Well?" she asked.

Jefferson rubbed his chin without taking his eyes off her. "Are you the same woman who just got bounced around a room like a rag doll, shot at by your so-called boyfriend, body-slammed by an armored gorilla under the mistaken impression of saving your life, and all you can do is ask questions about—"

"I resent that," Grady interrupted.

"Well, isn't that just like you," Jefferson shot back, straightening up to avoid appearing so slight next to Grady's muscular frame.

"Stop it!" Alma slapped a hand on the desk. "If I don't see some reining in of the testosterone, I'll throw one of you out that window!" She leaned forward, holding up an index finger to emphasize that she wanted silence. "Now." She reached around to the credenza behind her desk and picked up the snow globe.

"Not this again," Jefferson groaned.

"Alma," Grady stretched out her name in a familiar sound of frustration, "I searched from the peaks of West Virginia to the panhandle of Florida, and I couldn't come up with one person who'd own up to knowing Allafair Adair, much less claim to be her child."

"But someone is out there nonetheless," Alma said. "May I remind you the words *Beloved Mother* are on her gravestone and she only died in 1997?"

"I looked for the paperwork on who might have buried her, paid for the headstone, the cemetery plot," Jefferson said, his green eyes soft with sympathetic understanding. "It's all disappeared. These people want to stay hidden."

"And doesn't that say a lot?" Alma leaned back, clenching her hands on the blotter. "Somebody in this town has a lot to hide."

The quiet that followed wove through the room like a curtain being pulled. She knew they were all thinking the same name—Gentry. Little difference which one they picked—Charlotte Gentry, a town matriarch who had died in 1999 after giving Alma the snow globe and taunting her about Allafair; or her son, Walter Gentry, whose own disastrous past with Alma was a guarded secret which had brought her so much misery. She and Jefferson locked their eyes on each other. He was one of the few people who knew that a teenaged Walter had held fourteen-year-old Alma against a cold, muddy creek bank while two of his friends raped her. Jefferson protected the secret as an unquestioning act of loyalty.

Alma broke the stare and picked up the snow globe, holding it out in front of them. "When I was ten years old, I put a doll in my father's car just before he left town. Five years ago Charlotte Gentry gave me this snow globe containing that doll's face. Before that vindictive bitch died, she told me a woman named Allafair Adair was the reason for all that had happened to my family."

"It's a blind alley," Jefferson said. "One big lie perpetuated by the Gentrys as a way to keep you spinning your wheels." He stood, leaned on the desk, and reached out to lift her chin. "Don't let them do this to you."

Alma turned away and pressed her thumbs to her temples, fighting the memory of Mrs. Gentry on her deathbed, cackling spitefully that Allafair Adair had caused the pain of the past as she gave Alma the snow globe. Alma had been too distrustful of her enemy to listen, and by the time she realized the importance of what Charlotte Gentry knew, it was too late. Charlotte died, knowing her gift to Alma would haunt her the rest of her days.

"Look," she said, standing up and leaning against the wall. "My father left this town twenty-eight years ago to work in a Detroit factory. His children were told it was to earn Christmas money, but he never came home for Christmas—he never came home at all. When I tried to investigate this thing five years ago, Mrs. Gentry's delightful son, Walter, said my father didn't leave to earn money, but rather that he ran away with the town whore—Allafair Adair." She took a breath and realized her tirade had silenced the two men. "You've both read the letters my mother received for months after Daddy disappeared. He loved my mother more than his own life. Something's not right here. Charlotte knew what was going on, and she covered it up. My only choice is to find Allafair's children and hope they can tell me the story."

"Dragged Walter over the coals?" Grady asked.

"More times that I care to recall."

"Let me take a crack at him." Grady balled a fist in front of his face.

"Guys, he was a kid, too. He didn't know what his parents did or why. Look at the cobwebs I've had to clean out since I heard the name Allafair Adair. My poor mother hid those letters for years because she was afraid her husband had deserted her."

"So what do you hope to get?" Jefferson asked.

"My father," she said firmly and certainly. "I want to know if Esau Bashears is alive."

"Are you sure you can handle that answer?" Grady rose, came around the desk, and took her hands in his. "These might be answers that you'll never get—too much is lost in the past."

"Well, it wouldn't have been if you hadn't shot Quincy Pollard." She pulled away from him and walked to the window. Behind her she could hear Jefferson sniggering—a deliberate jab at Grady.

"A man is dead," she said, without looking at either of them. "Maybe a little less sarcasm is called for. Death is not about the two of you and your juvenile squabbles." The heat in the room increased the tension between them, and she reached down to switch on the air conditioner.

"This is not my fault," Grady said, anger lacing his voice. "Quincy Pollard injured a bailiff, held a courtroom hostage and a gun to the head of the woman I love. I don't understand why you'd even listen to the crap he was spouting. He wasn't going to—"

"Walk out of there?" Jefferson said in a smirky tone.

Alma turned just as Grady sailed over the desk to grab Jefferson. She raced to get between them and ended up in a tangle of flailing arms. Only her cry of pain stopped them. She held her arm and both men slowly lowered her into a chair.

"I guess I hit the floor harder than I thought," she said. A knock on the door went unanswered. She shot Jefferson a hard look warning him not to comment. She knew Grady felt guilty about rushing the courtroom too soon, but how could she blame him? From his perspective, it had looked as if Quincy was about to shoot her. The knock sounded again.

"Come in," she called. "Let's get back to the point. I have to find the man Quincy named—Isham Thunderheart."

The door hinges whined as the portal opened, revealing Walter Gentry standing in the late afternoon light. He took in their shocked expressions upon seeing him in what was obviously not his empire any more. "I heard about what happened," he said. "I thought I might be of some assistance."

3

"Come to see if reports of Alma's survival were true?" Jefferson asked with pointed sarcasm and moved to lean territorially against the desk.

Walter Gentry ignored him and stepped inside the office that was once his. He stood erect as his eyes made an uncomfortable sweep of the room. "I admire what you've done with the old home place." He stood less than six feet tall, balding with brownish-gray hair circling his head, and his crooked lips made all the more expressive since recently shaving a full beard.

Alma moved behind him to close the door and offered a chair from a conference table covered with law books. He declined, choosing instead to walk to the window, and take in the view as if reminiscing about his years of rule as commonwealth attorney. "That's an excellent article," he said, pointing to a legal journal on one of the overcrowded bookshelves.

His eyes hardened as they came to rest on the snow globe that sat in the center of Alma's desk. He pressed a hand on the windowsill, and she realized the gesture was to hide the nervous tremor of his fingers.

"Coffee?" she asked. He didn't respond, and she figured he was assessing how open she was toward his visit. Walter had made numerous efforts to make amends for his and Alma's anguished past. She didn't want to be the one to start a new round of feuding. "Thanks for stopping by," she said. "It was an ordeal, but it's over, and I'm coping."

He turned toward her and focused on her bandaged cheek. "If it's helpful to you, I prosecuted Quincy Pollard a number of years ago on assault charges, so I can testify to his unpredictable temper. He spent a year in a state prison."

Grady crossed his legs and eyed Walter suspiciously. "Criminals always seemed to get light sentences during your tenure as prosecutor."

"I simply meant—" Walter began.

"I know what you meant," Alma interrupted before Grady or Jefferson could attack him again. "And your information may be of service. I'll certainly call on you if it's necessary." She shot her two friends an insistent look, warning them to keep their mouths shut. They did, but the awkward silence that followed loomed uncomfortably.

Walter stood halfway between the door and the window while Grady and Jefferson entrenched themselves in the guest chairs. He cleared his throat and stared at the floor before speaking. "I was hoping I might have a moment with you alone."

"No," said Jefferson and Grady simultaneously.

Alma sighed, shaking her head as she made her way to the office door and opened it. With one thumb, she pointed toward the outer office. "Of course," she said to Walter. "These two gentlemen were just leaving."

In an exit as slow as syrup, they slunk toward the doorway. Grady pecked her on the cheek and mumbled that he would return in thirty minutes to drive her home. Both men turned to look back with irked expressions, as if to indicate that they would prefer to wait than be shut out. Alma waved a military salute, then shut the door. "Please sit down," she said to Walter and lowered herself into the opposite chair.

As he stepped toward her, she inwardly assessed the weight of her emotions. At times, a subconscious fear filled her whenever Walter Gentry was near. She clocked her responses . . . nothing. No goose bumps. No sweating palms. No inward trembling. She was okay. Walter Gentry was a horrendous part of her past, but she acknowledged to herself that he had been a reluctant participant, a boy in over his head and unable to stop what had happened.

He drew a deep breath and stared past her. "The local Sons of the Pioneers are holding their annual luncheon on Friday. Members from all over the state and some national representatives will be coming to Contrary to attend."

"I think I read about it," she said.

"At that time," he went on speaking as if quoting a rehearsed script, "they will be honoring my mother and naming a scholarship after her for all the Crimson County high schools."

Alma felt her jaw clench at the mention of his mother, and she massaged her pulsing cheek to keep from showing a reaction. She looked at the snow globe sitting in the center of the desk. "Any scholarship is welcome for a deserving student."

"I'm glad to hear you say that." His eyes held steady on her for the first time and his mouth broke into a half smile, returning just as quickly to a more serious expression. "There's more."

She couldn't fathom what he wanted from her, and leaned back in her chair.

"At the same time, they will be presenting me with an award and putting up a plaque in city hall to commemorate my father."

"He was mayor here for a term or two when we were kids," Alma said. "I remember." She tried to ease the tense tone that she knew was filtering into her voice.

"And state representative when I was a teenager."

"Almost governor," Alma said, her voice losing strength on the ending vowels. She cleared her throat and looked away, unable to meet his gaze. Walter continued talking, recalling all the good deeds his mother and father accomplished for the area—an upgraded utility company, several city parks, the Silver Lake reservoir, and cable TV. It was the governor's race that prompted Charlotte Gentry to run the teenage Alma out of town, afraid the past would come to haunt the state campaign. Alma returned to Contrary six years ago to defend her brother on a murder charge that was made all the worse by inflammatory coverage by the local Gentry-owned newspaper. "So, what do you want from me?" she blurted, interrupting his list of accolades.

He stopped abruptly, realizing he was nervously chattering. "How are your nephews?" he asked. "Larry Joe and Eddie."

Alma nodded and pointed at a picture of two auburn-haired boys of ten and eight. "Fine," she managed to say. "No ill effects from their ordeal a few years back."

"I'm glad to hear it. They must take after their aunt." Walter regarded her with frank admiration. "Look tough situations in the eye and spit."

Alma glanced away, unsure how to respond.

"I am hoping . . ." He stopped, cleared his throat and began again. "I'm here to request that you'll allow these proceedings to take place without any . . . any . . ."

"Interference?"

"I, I," Walter stuttered, "I wouldn't have used that word." His cheeks flushed, and he looked at the floor. "I, I didn't mean to make this visit seem as if—"

"It's okay," she said, deciding to ease his discomfort. "Scholarships are always needed in Appalachia, regardless of who they're named after."

The relief in his expression was mixed with uncertainty. "I'm grateful for your cooperation," he said, then quickly rephrased the comment, "for your understanding, that is."

Alma remembered that he had risked his life to save her nephews three years ago when they were held hostage. His parents were dead. Regardless of the distress the Gentrys inflicted on her life, both she and he must live in the present and face the future. Walter was trying to do his part to overcome the past hostility; now it was time that she made an effort. "Have a good time at the banquet."

She rose, and he followed her toward the door with the quick pace of a man determined not to push his luck.

"The luncheon is Friday," he said, pausing beside her. "You're welcome to come as my guest." Her silence must have alarmed him and he continued hastily, "That is, if you've no other plans that day."

Alma dipped her head and resisted a shrug of her shoulders. "Not such a good idea."

"Think of it as the start of your campaign," he said. "People will see that we've buried the hatchet."

"I'll have to think about it." She looked off to the side, thinking that she might stand at a distance while the Gentry family was praised, but doubted her ability to sit through a ceremony honoring them.

"Let me know," he said, his expression hopeful, and his face almost handsome without the beard. He turned to go, then stopped. "Alma, I'm glad you're okay." After another step, he turned back again. "I know it's none of my business, and I have no right to say this, but . . ." he pressed a hand to his chest as if he couldn't hold the words inside. "You could do better than both those jokers."

Alma tried suppressing a laugh, but could not. "Your blue blood is showing, Mr. Gentry."

"Chief Forester certainly has been a superman to the city . . . and to you," he added, "but even he must have some secrets."

She rolled her eyes. "Whatever Kryptonite the chief might be allergic to is insignificant considering his vast law enforcement talent."

"As well as what he's brought to your life." Walter's expression tightened as if to steel himself for her response.

"He's been a godsend."

"No offense intended."

"Everyone has a right to an opinion." She stepped toward the door, eager to get rid of him.

Walter shrugged his shoulders, appearing relieved, but uncomfortable.

She closed the door, turned back to her desk and chuckled at the notion that Walter might have been flirting with her, perhaps testing the waters. A ridiculous thought. The lighthearted moment melted away as she eyed the snow globe. She picked it up and stared into the empty eye sockets in the porcelain face. *If only,* she thought. *If only I could see into the past.*

4

When Grady failed to show up, Alma went outside to see if he was waiting for her. The main government buildings—Contrary City Hall, the police station, and the Crimson County Courthouse—formed a triangle around the quadrant filled with oak, maple, and dogwood trees. A center fountain sent a musical sound through the air as it sprayed upward with timed regularity. A variety of eateries, boutiques, and produce stands lined the side streets.

Alma looked both ways down the street and across the courtyard toward the police station and the no parking zone, where Grady often parked illegally. Neither his police cruiser nor his off-duty green Blazer, with the dented side door, were anywhere in sight. *Perhaps he went back to the courtroom,* she thought, *or got caught up with processing the paperwork from this morning's incident. But surely, he would have delegated most of that.* She read 3:00 p.m. on her watch, then paced the length of the building. The sun was about to dip behind the top of Jellico Mountain. Just as she started to cross the street to go to her own car in the parking lot behind city hall, Jefferson pulled up in his red Toyota truck and leaned out the window.

"Need a lift?"

"I'm sure he'll be here any minute," she said.

"The old Grad-man," Jefferson joked. "He's in the coffee shop." He pointed at a corner drugstore, which also housed a Starbucks. Grady sat at the window table with Detective Henry Moody and a dark-haired woman of about thirty.

"Elaine Bartholomew," Alma said under her breath. A jolt of surprise shot through her, followed by a jab of jealousy that she instantly suppressed. "Did you arrange for him to sit where you knew I'd see him?"

Jefferson raised his hands shoulder-high and shook his head. "I take no blame for this."

"But you don't mind pointing it out." She forced a grin. "I expected better from you than to try to plant a seed of doubt. Look over there. He's with Henry Moody, the detective who taught him everything about this force. He's going to retire this year—that Elaine is sitting there beside him means nothing. There could be a thousand reasons."

"Uh-huh," he muttered. "A million maybe."

"I don't like you when you do this," Alma snapped. "I trust Grady."

"Then why don't you go over there?"

"And interrupt his business? I think not."

"Still, it seems a little rude to keep you waiting, after all that's—"

She walked away, heading toward the parking lot. She paused to call over her shoulder. "I'll take my own car."

He steered over to the side of the street. "After all you've been through today, don't you even think of driving." He leaned across the seat and opened the passenger side door. "Besides, I promised your grandmother and Aunt Joyce."

"They called you," Alma said, and sighed. "I told them not to worry." She glanced around at Grady. His hands gestured animatedly as if the discussion was important. "What's this?" she asked Jefferson, pulling a piece of paper from underneath the window wiper. "A ticket."

He snatched it from her and cursed. "Courtesy of your so-called boyfriend." He unlatched the glove compartment, stuffing the ticket inside with a dozen others.

"Grady write those, too?" she asked, hoping he would say no.

"You'd think the chief of police would have better things to do."

Alma bit back a sarcastic response, then climbed into the truck feeling both guilty and responsible for the animosity between the two men. Complicating matters was her foolish lapse of an occasional romantic moment with Jefferson, a man who had been her friend growing up in the hollows. But all that happened before she met Grady. Grady had changed everything in her life.

Jefferson drove in silence down the long avenue out of town, making his way toward the hilly hollows at the west end of Midnight Valley. The road narrowed into two lanes and the trees grew so tall with limbs so wide that they formed a natural tunnel over the road. "Do you think you can go a little faster?" Alma asked, a tightness growing in her chest.

He patted her knee without speaking and increased the speed of the truck. After a few seconds he turned on the air-conditioning, even though the August afternoon was cool with a western wind. "This'll help."

Without warning Alma shouted, "Stop!"

Jefferson swerved onto the gravel shoulder and the vehicle screeched to a halt. She jumped out. Every muscle in her body trembled. She stumbled toward the rear of the truck, holding onto the side until she could lean against the tailgate.

He was immediately beside her, touching her shoulder and stroking her back as she heaved in gulps of air. "I was waiting for this to happen," he said. "Deep breaths."

No time to answer. Flashes of breaking glass, the glaring sun, Quincy's face as bullets broke his flesh, his body falling as if in slow motion, blood spreading through the cloth of his shirt, his eyes staring into hers. The images rolled in front of her like an old penny arcade film. They mixed with an old terror that was ground into her bones—running through weeds and briar patches, three boys pursuing her, yelling out that she couldn't get away, every cell in her body screaming that she was going to die. *If they catch me, I'll die.* The voices echoed in her mind and she couldn't stop them.

"I hate this," she said between gasps of air. "I hate being like this." All her life she had mastered delayed reactions. Coldly and efficiently dealing with crises, then falling apart later, usually when no one was looking. "I have to stop and see my grandmother. I can't let them see me like this. I have to—"

"Alma, nobody is going to blame you for having a bad day."

"No," she huffed out. "Can't worry them. Mamaw—too old, too fragile."

"Ursula Bashears has the constitution of a tank."

"Have to focus." She drew in a slow, deep breath. "Focus on Isham Thunderheart." Her muscles began to relax. "He can tell me what I need to know."

Jefferson wrapped an arm around her shoulders, waiting for the anxiety to pass. He looked up the slope of the cliff, then bent down to pick a purple wildflower. "You're amazing," he said, handing it to her. "It's not going to kill you to depend on somebody now and then."

Alma swallowed, trying to alleviate the dryness in her mouth. She knew she was shaking but was unable to stop. "I'm okay." The blood rushed from her head. Jefferson caught her, pulling her into his arms until she rested against him. Every muscle in her body felt drained.

Carefully, he supported her, letting her limbs slowly regain their strength. His lips caressed one of her ears, and he whispered as if he couldn't keep the words from spilling out. "You don't trust Grady. You've never trusted him and that's why you two will never have what you and I share. He's never seen you like this because you don't trust him to know you as deeply as I do." His hands cupped her face, turning it toward him. His forehead pressed against hers and their breaths mingled, familiar and comforting. His lips gently covered hers, tasting them like a man savoring a rare wine.

"Stop," she said, stepping back. She looked deep into his eyes but couldn't find the right words. He pulled her toward him again. She touched her fingers to his lips. "I have to stop."

He hit the side of the truck. "This is wrong," he argued.

"Let's go home." She stumbled toward the front door and pulled on the handle so hard that it jammed. Hesitating, she closed her eyes, willing herself to loosen her grip, then spoke over the hood to Jefferson. "Don't tell anyone about this."

He stared back at her, agitation etched in his features. "The panic attack or the kiss?" He jumped into the truck as if not expecting an answer, waited until she was inside as well, then gunned the engine and skidded in the gravel as he sped toward the hollows.

5

Alma's grandmother, Aunt Joyce, Uncles Ames, and George were circled on the porch of Ursula Bashears' two-story house as Jefferson pulled into the driveway. "I hope you're not out here waiting for me," Alma shouted out the window. They waved, smiled, and shook their heads, but their worried expressions said they had spent the day following the courtroom takeover. She guiltily wished she had come home sooner.

"You just missed Vernon's call," Mamaw said. "He heard the news on the radio and was about to come back."

"Not necessary," Alma said.

"We caught him in time," Uncle George assured her. "He's gonna finish out the week at the dog training school."

"Good. Learning to train those police dogs is going to be a great career for him." A swell of pride shot through her chest. Grady had helped Vernon get into the school and they planned to start a K-9 unit in Crimson County. "Nobody called Momma, right?" Alma asked. The uncomfortable quiet that followed told her that her mother was the first to be informed of the day's events.

"She says she's tired of Hollywood," Aunt Joyce piped up. "And she's got to be back for catering the high school reunion Saturday night, so she's returning a day early."

"You do all the cooking, Aunt Joyce," Alma reminded her. "Momma only does the billing."

The screen door banged and her sister, Sue, stepped out, balancing a tray of glasses and pitcher of lemonade. "I just spoke to your granddad, Jefferson," she said, setting the tray on a nearby picnic table and starting to pour the juice. "He's on his way up. You get the watermelon from the kitchen table and start slicing."

Jefferson looked over at Alma, and the echo of a slamming door from the house at the mouth of the hollow told him his grandfather was already walking. "Well, I reckon the fact that Alma is still kicking is a good enough reason for a picnic," he said.

The intensity of his gaze spoke all the things he would never say to her—that this hollow was their home, that they were linked by a blood as strong as iron, that their destinies were entwined in the way of people who spend their entire lives together.

Alma felt the same loyalty to him, and his people, but she had made different choices. This hollow had touched many lives. The Bashears occupied the far end with Mamaw's house as the main gathering place. Aunt Joyce and Uncle George were across the road and, beside it, Uncle Ames's three-room cabin was spotted with rabbit, squirrel, and opossum skins hanging on the outside walls.

Toward the mouth of the hollow lived her sister and brother-in-law and two nephews who ruled the hillsides, much to the annoyance of the elderly Fletcher and Gilbert widows, who moved in together when their husbands died the previous year. In a house almost a large as Mamaw's, Jefferson and his eleven brothers and sisters grew up on the Bingham spread, playing with the children of nearly twenty families who were once neighbors. Within a decade, nearly all the young people relocated to cities and the remaining residents held onto a way of life that outsiders considered too provincial for the twenty-first century.

Nestled into a raked incline at the peak of the hollow, Alma had built her own house—a large two story with an unfinished office in the attic and a basement full of guest rooms that spilled over with relatives on holidays. In many ways, she thought, it was remarkable that so many of the Bashears had returned to the hollow. The other families who had moved to town or to the cities rarely came back, except for a graduation, a wedding, or a funeral.

When they did return, Alma would see them walking up and down the dirt roads, taking in all they could never purge from their blood—memories of the toilsome life they didn't realize at the time was hard, comparisons with the cities they now needed to survive, and the connections to family, good and bad—that had formed them and made them who they were, good and bad. She had felt so many of the same emotions when returning to Contrary after more than a decade in San Francisco. In some ways, she was still reclaiming her heritage and learning to appreciate her Appalachian and Cherokee roots.

The squeal of Esridge Bingham's fiddle brought Larry Joe and Eddie running from the barn. Her nephews dogged him as he played, clapping their hands and calling out the names of their favorite songs. Sue handed Alma a piece of watermelon and she bit into it hungrily. In spite of the cheerful surroundings, Allafair Adair remained on her mind, and now she possessed a new clue—someone named Isham Thunderheart. With all the activity around her, she couldn't escape to think things through, but her mind wandered to avenues she might pursue to find him.

* * *

The August sun warmed the late afternoon. Eventually everyone pulled chairs into the shade of an enormous maple tree, commonly referred to as the Shade Tree. *There's only one person missing,* Alma thought. *Grady. Was he still with Elaine?* She chastised herself for even thinking it was possible, but the image was difficult to push from her mind.

Esridge Bingham let Larry Joe practice on the violin and moved to the circle of adults. "I got a loose floorboard in my bathroom," he said.

"Is that a hint, Granddad?" Jefferson asked. "Two of my brothers are carpenters and I'd say about five to six cousins work in either hardware or construction; but it's always me, the lawyer, who gets asks to hammer down the loose boards." Everyone shared a laugh, and Esridge spit a watermelon seed at Jefferson.

Uncle George slapped Jefferson on the back. "Ames and me'll come down and hammer it out in the morning, Esridge."

"But it's more fun to listen to Jefferson cuss when he hits his thumb," Esridge said, winking at this grandson.

"I once heard him three hollows over," Uncle Ames claimed.

"Fine, fine," Jefferson snorted, "everybody have a good time at the lawyer's expense—just wait 'til you get my bill."

"Speaking of hollows," Alma said. "I don't suppose any of you have ever heard of Pollyhollow?"

The sudden stillness was marred only by the sound of Larry Joe practicing a tune on the fiddle.

"Or Isham Thunderheart?" No responses, but this time tension filled the silence.

"I guess not," Sue said, giving her a stare to say the fun was ruined.

"Now that's a name I ain't heard in a bundle of years," Mamaw said.

"Which one?" Alma asked, genuinely surprised that, of all the people there, it was her grandmother who replied. The elderly people looked back and forth at each other while Sue, saddled with Eddie around her leg, shrugged.

"Sun sure hot today," Uncle George said.

"It'll start raining in a few weeks," Aunt Joyce continued.

Sue caught Alma's gaze, then looked over to Jefferson who, in turn, looked back at Alma.

"It's at Silver Lake," her grandmother said, disregarding the attempts to change the subject. "I guess the others hesitated because of Kitty." She looked around at the older adults.

Alma sensed there was more to Mamaw's tentative reference to Alma's cousin, Kitty Sloat, murdered a few years ago on the lakeshore. "I don't follow," she said.

"Pollyhollow is Silver Lake," Uncle George said softly, with a touch of apprehension in his voice. "They flooded the hollow back in the seventies to create the lake."

"And you'll find out all about Isham Thunderheart," Jefferson's grandfather piped up, "in Joddy Paradise's old files." Paradise was a country lawyer who had convinced Jefferson to practice in Contrary and partnered with him in his early days of practicing law.

Alma shot Jefferson a curious look. He arched his eyebrows, pleading innocence, "I stored all his inactive files after he passed away."

"Joddy Paradise was the only lawyer in the mountains who'd take Isham's case to try and stop the Silver Lake project," his grandfather said. "He fought old lady Gentry right up until the dam burst, and then—it was too late."

27

"Isham lived in Pollyhollow?" Alma asked.

"Him and about twelve other families," Uncle Ames said. "They give 'em a week to move out. See, they'd diverted the streams and a couple of small rivers all along that ridge of mountains for almost two years. Had dammed it up and only needed to blow up a narrow ridge to flood Pollyhollow. Something happened and the ridge got blown. Isham and the others barely got out alive."

"I bet Joddy Paradise's records would clear up some unanswered questions." Alma shot Jefferson a look to say he had better put on his archive hat.

"I'd be careful stirring up the past, Alma," Uncle Ames warned. "Nobody knows what went on up there. There's always been stories."

"After all these years, it can hardly matter anymore." Alma glanced at her watch. It was 6:00 p.m. "If we start digging through records now, we might find an address."

Mamaw got up and reseated herself in the wheelchair, which she maneuvered to follow Alma and Jefferson toward his truck. When they were out of hearing range of the others, Mamaw asked Alma to wait. She turned around to hear Mamaw's whisper. "He lives on a narrow bluff at the east end of Silver Lake."

"How do you know?" Alma asked.

Her grandmother smiled faintly, with a pensive hold. She pointed toward the top-most ridge of the hollow ridge above Alma's house. "If this hollow were flooded, that's where I would go live. Here is where your grandfather and me started out our lives, where we raised our children, grandchildren, where he took his last breath and where I'll take mine. If somebody was trying to force me to leave, I'd find a way to stay." She raised her hand and indicated the vast expanse of mountain ranges that wrapped around them like the woven strands of a handmade basket. "There are places out there where the human foot has not made its print. There's always a way to be passed by." She took Alma's hand and squeezed it, looking firmly into her eyes. "I didn't know Isham that good, but if he's anything like other hollow folks, I'd bet that's where he's living."

"If you'll come out of retirement, I'll hire you as an investigator," Alma said with a smile.

The old lady chuckled and let go of Alma's hand. "Be wary, granddaughter. Your uncle is right . . . the stories are full of ruin and wrath."

Alma knelt down and wrapped her arms around her grandmother. She knew there wouldn't be many years left before she stood at this woman's grave. Before that happened, Alma would do anything to give her back the son who disappeared so long ago. The heartache of not knowing was worse than the most devastating truth, and too many times she had watched Mamaw touch Esau Bashears' picture and wipe away a tear. Answers were all she ever prayed for when it came to her lost son. "I'll be careful," she promised.

Alma and Jefferson sped back out of the hollows toward town. Neither spoke and both seemed to sense that they were about to stumble, once again, into a cauldron of Gentry intrigue. "Don't go to your storage area," she told him. "Let's go straight to Silver Lake."

6

"And," Jefferson asked sarcastically as he climbed over a fallen cedar log, "the reason we're doing this is what again?" He dusted gritty moss remnants off his trouser leg, then picked a handful of burrs from his sock.

"The reason you're doing it," Alma teased, at the same time hoping he wouldn't suggest they leave, "was some bizarre rationalization about being at the lake, in the moonlight, with me." She shined the flashlight up the hill, finding another slope of ferns and sumac. Behind them was the lakeshore, twenty feet down an embankment lined with smooth-barked swamp privet, cane, and Queen Anne's lace. In the growing smoky dusk, a great blue heron waded in the shallows looking for minnows and salamanders. Its two-foot long legs were twice the length of its body, and its curved neck dipped to feed. Then with an *Awwk!* the bird spread its wings a full five feet to rise into the air. Alma could smell the aluminum odor of lake water, and a nearby creek gave the land a cool, wet feel. "I was sure we'd find him before nightfall."

"Come on," Jefferson said, huffing as he turned toward her. "It'd be easier to go through Joddy Paradise's records than wandering around out here in the dark."

Alma pulled on his arm. "Between the moon and the flashlight we have at least another half hour before it's pitch black out here. Besides, these are paths." She pointed at foot-beaten trails that followed the easiest terrain. "So we know someone is out here."

"Panthers, bears, moonshiners." Jefferson held onto a tree branch.

"There are no more panthers or bears in the Cumberlands," she stated, side-stepping a wheel-size spiderweb spun between two Elder trees.

A flock of passing wood ducks peeped: *Creeeaap, Creeeaap.*

He anchored his weight against the tree trunk. "I am not up for starring in a *Blair Witch* sequel."

"Just one more hill," she begged. "I can feel it, we're close."

"Feel," he exclaimed, exhaling an exhausted breath and swiping at a profusion of gnats swarming around them. "Take a whiff. We're close to something dead." He took hold of her arm and kept her from moving onward. "Alma, let's come back in the morning."

"Wait. That smell. . . ." She pulled away from him and followed the gurgling sound of water. "You recognize that smell? Think back to when we were six or seven, before all the houses in the hollow had water and electricity." A creek rippled down a well-worn crevasse. She stepped forward onto a flat rock and pointed the flashlight upstream. The glow illuminated the gray boards of an outhouse. "There!"

Jefferson lagged several yards behind her. About fifty feet past the outhouse was a shack with a thatch roof and walls of posts and split canes plastered together with smooth clay. It balanced atop the ledge of a rock shelter, where the ground extended in a round plateau. "Isn't that the way the Cherokee used to build their houses—pre-white man?"

"Don't you ever tell anybody how we found him."

Adrenaline rushed through Alma's veins. She was finally about to meet someone who knew Allafair Adair. "You know what's funny?" She pointed at the door with the flashlight. "He lives almost exactly where Mamaw said he would."

"In the middle of nowhere." Jefferson caught up with her. From the front porch, Isham had a million-dollar view. The water, the valley and the land beyond were all lit with the golden dots of fireflies. Below them, Silver Lake shimmered in the reflection of the moon. An owl cooed as they approached the cabin, but otherwise the dense stillness of the forest boxed them in.

"No lights," Jefferson said, stopping about ten feet from the front door. "Let's come back tomorrow. At least we know we can sniff our way back.

Alma continued forward. She shined the flashlight around the porch. The windows were shuttered with cardboard, and poles held up one side of the roof, while the other side was attached to an oak tree.

"At least call out his name!" Jefferson insisted. "You can get shot walking up to somebody's house after dark in the middle of nowhere."

She stopped next to a tulip tree, reminded that she had recently prosecuted such a case. "Be my guest."

"Isham!" Jefferson yelled. "Isham Thunderheart! We need to talk to you!"

They waited. No answer came back.

"Let's move a little closer," Alma said. Furry outlines of rabbit and raccoon pelts spotted the front wall. "Isham!" She called out, hoping a woman's voice might make him appear. Still no reply.

"He might not be at home."

"We've come this far, and I don't want to come back tomorrow." She listened intently, hoping to hear some sound of movement. "It won't hurt to knock on the door."

The concern on his face bordered on alarm. He looked away, then back at her before taking her hand. Holding onto each other, they balanced on boulders to cross the creek, and climbed the rocky bank.

Emerging in a garden in the side yard, they waded through paths of knee-high tomato plants.

"You know what's strange?" Jefferson said, holding her back. "No dog." He scanned the yard and pointed to an iron spike in the ground that might have had a leash attached to it. "Almost everybody in these cursed mountains has a dog."

The weight of his words made the hair on the back of her neck prickle. *No dog,* she thought, scanning the property for signs of life. A shirt and pair of pants hung on a clothesline strung between two trees, cornstalks had been stripped of their cobs, and a basket of green unshelled walnuts sat on the edge of the porch. "Maybe the dog is inside with him." She knew her words were more hopeful than probable.

"Why doesn't it bark?"

The dark house creaked as a breeze blew off the lake and goose bumps sprang up on her arms. Night had consumed the woods, and they would have a difficult journey back down the mountain. "Let's leave a note," she said. "Hopefully, he's not so antisocial that he won't come to Contrary and see me." She dug through her wallet for paper while Jefferson supplied the pen and held the flashlight. On the back of a business card, she jotted down her name and an urgent request to see Isham. As an afterthought, she added that she was Ursula Bashears' granddaughter, hoping the connection with someone he knew would encourage him.

She wedged the card into the door, and it sprang open. Gasping with surprise, she stared at Jefferson. He seemed to be holding his breath. With a trembling hand, she pushed the door until it hit the wall.

"This could be construed as breaking and entering," he said nervously.

"I'm not inside. Give me the flashlight." He held it away from her, and she reached over and took it. "Isham?" she called out.

"Alma, let's go."

"What if he's sick or hurt?"

"I have a bad feeling about this."

She moved the light over bare walls that were lined with newspaper to keep out the winter cold and the summer bugs. A side window was open and a dingy curtain was pulled to the side. A cast iron skillet, a bowl, and a tin cup were stacked on a high shelf. Clothes hung on nails. A vase of wildflowers on the table looked fresh enough to have been picked that day. She stepped deeper into the room, swallowing to wet her dry throat. "Hello?" Resting her hand on a table, she touched something wet and jerked back. A red liquid stained her fingers.

A loud thud clamored from outside, as if two people had collided. "Hey!" Jefferson yelled. "Stop!"

Terror shot up Alma's back. She ran toward the door, then tripped, landing on her knees and jamming the palms of her hands on the floor. The flashlight rolled, coming to rest on open, bulging eyes, blood matted on the surrounding skin, and a deep gash that held a protruding chunk of brain. "Oh God!" She twisted backward, knowing the wetness on her hands was blood, and scrambled up, sprinting toward the door. "Jefferson!" she screamed. She slammed into another body.

"It's me," he said.

"He's dead!"

Jefferson leaned inside and closed the door. His body tightened against Alma's. He took firm hold of her shoulders. "Somebody just barged past me like a truck with no breaks."

No need to ask who. It had to be the killer.

7

Dawn brought calm, except for the loud *Aaannnt!* of blue jays feeding at the top of a beechnut tree. The terror of the night gave way to the clinical investigation of a crime scene. All the human commotion had disturbed the birds and their noisy, constant cries were raised in objection. Alma and Jefferson sat on the bumper of a police van that had plowed over two hillsides of brush to get to the cabin. Dozens of law enforcement officers scoured the yard, porch and house for evidence. A female officer brought jeans and a T-shirt for Alma, so she could shed her bloodstained clothes.

In the light of day, Alma realized why a solitary man would choose to live there. With a cliff at his back and a one-eighty-degree view, he could see anybody coming. It was a strategic choice. *Then why didn't he see his murderer? Or was it someone he knew?* It had been foolish to go out there after dark. She and Jefferson could've been victims, as well.

Grady emerged from the shack with the county sheriff and a state trooper. They stood in a triangle, their gazes inevitably shifting to Alma and Jefferson. The thought of Elaine, and whether or not Grady spent last night with her, tugged at Alma's confidence. She willed it out of her mind.

Grady hammered down the steps toward them, his long strides across the yard causing whiffs of dust to wisp in the air. "Why the hell did you come out here in the middle of the night without me?" he asked Alma.

"Don't blame her," Jefferson started.

"You shut up!" He jabbed an index finger in his chest.

"Just a minute," Jefferson shot back.

"This is not a conversation. This is a police investigation."

Alma stepped between them and patted Jefferson on the shoulder. "He's right," she said. "Go wait down the hill." She took Grady by the arm and moved over to the shade of a hickory tree. In a low whisper, she said, "Don't talk to me like I'm in interrogation."

His stern expression eased to a look of concern. "You could have been killed out here." He squeezed her shoulders and stepped in closer, seeming to want to embrace her, then glared down the hill at Jefferson. "If I appear burned up, you're right."

In her heart she knew his anger came from caring about her. "I got a lead on Isham Thunderheart and I followed it. I waited on you at the office; you didn't show up. I called you, no answer on your cell phone. I didn't want to wait 'til morning. Okay?" She fought with all her might to keep from mentioning Elaine, determined not to drag personal matters into a professional investigation. She waited; he didn't offer an explanation. "So, what does it look like happened in there, and where were you last night?"

"There's a moonshine apparatus out back," he said, avoiding her last question. "I suspect a transaction went wrong. Sheriff says he sold to some old-timers. Nothing big." Grady ran a finger across the side of his forehead. "Beaten with a tire iron all around here." He swallowed and his face took on the hardened detachment of a seasoned lawman who had steeled himself to the sight of death. "Defensive wounds all about the arms and shoulders. He put up a hell of a fight."

"Positive ID?"

"I haven't confirmed he's Isham Thunderheart, but he looks to be full-blooded Cherokee, as was Mr. Thunderheart. There aren't too many of them left in this area."

Alma stared at the shack and the word "Damn," escaped her lips. She hesitated, half-knowing what Grady's response would be to her request, but made it anyway. "I need to go inside and look around. Can you walk me through the cabin?"

"Don't even think about it," he spat out, one hand balling into a fist without his seeming to notice.

"Don't make me pull rank," she whispered. "I am the commonwealth attorney. Eventually I'll prosecute whoever did this to him."

"I'm investigating a murder, but *you* want to go through the crime scene for your own personal satisfaction." His deep blue eyes flashed with exasperation and he was unable to keep from looking down the hill at Jefferson.

"That's ridiculous." Even though Alma knew he was right, and she swallowed her own lie, she couldn't take her eyes off of the cabin that might hold answers.

"You're also a witness, so act like a professional and pass this case off to one of your assistants." Grady stomped downhill toward Jefferson, motioning for a detective to follow him.

Alma figured he took the other man along to keep from losing his temper. She walked down near the creek, but stared at the cabin. Of course she was being unreasonable, but she still felt like a child unable to get at a toy. Grady was also being far more defensive than he needed to be—probably because she was with Jefferson—yet he was in no hurry to explain about Elaine. She rolled her eyes, biting the side of her tongue. Her stare locked on the cabin she wanted so desperately to enter; she wished she had taken more time to look around last night. But something bothered her even more. *Of all the nights to get yourself killed,* she thought. *It might be too much of a coincidence that you get murdered the night I'm looking for you, Mr. Thunderheart.*

* * *

As Jefferson drove her home, Alma sat quietly, half-fuming over how Grady had treated her, half-scolding herself for being so insistent. In her head she replayed the unlikely possibility of Isham Thunderheart's death having something to do with her. "Too farfetched," she said.

"What?" Jefferson asked.

"Just thinking," she replied with a frustrated yawn. "We were so close to finding someone who knew Allafair Adair."

"You know what I think?" Jefferson followed her yawn with one of his own. "I think she's a myth, a legend of convenience created to be the solution to every unanswered question."

"That's wishful thinking and a bit too simplistic."

"Alma, when we first started looking for information on her, I checked with Social Security, the IRS, the armed forces, and the electric company. Grady followed up with the schools, hospitals, the FBI, and all his contacts in law enforcement. No one will claim being related to her. If she had children, this woman would have left a paper trail somewhere, and there is simply nothing."

Alma rubbed her chin in thought. *Except for Allafair's grave, it's as if she had never existed.* They turned onto Contrary's main street and passed a fifteen-foot neon sign reading *Bartholomew's Cafe, Home of Pan Fried Chicken.* A newspaper flitted across the road, swept up into the air and down under the car wheel with a whoosh. Through the ensuing blocks, she kept noticing the same name: Bartholomew's Furniture, Bartholomew's Drugstore, and Bartholomew's Hardware. "An ad," she said, sitting up straight. "It's not too late to get an ad in today's papers."

"Put your seatbelt on," Jefferson said. "Why don't you let me spend some time with Joddy Paradise's records first?"

"And a reward." She clapped her hands, excitement rushing through her veins, knowing she was onto an idea that would yield results. "I'm going to offer a $5,000 reward."

"Let's think this through,"

"If you'd drive a little faster, we can get the ad in both the *Contrary Gazette* and the *Crimson County Sun* today. By tomorrow, we'll have it in every newspaper in the county."

Jefferson shook his head with the resignation of a man who had surrendered. Then he laughed.

"What's that for?" Alma asked.

"I'm going to enjoy how much this will burn old Grady's hide."

8

All afternoon Alma paced around her office. She had managed to get a couple of hours sleep, but dreams of Isham Thunderheart's bashed skull kept jerking her back to consciousness. Finally, she went to work and kept herself busy with details that could have waited till next week. All she could think about was Allafair Adair.

Copies of the *Contrary Gazette* and the *Crimson County Sun* lay on the desk. Her ad was a four by six and offered a five-thousand-dollar reward for information from anyone knowing Allafair or her descendants. Jefferson had hastily arranged a P.O. Box and added his own 800 number, which rang to his office. His offer to screen the responses touched her, but she also knew he was doing it to irritate Grady. Beside her own ad was one for a sale at Bartholomew's Furniture store. She folded the paper so she wouldn't have to look at it. Well, hello there," she heard Val's voice outside the door.

Alma put the papers with her ad facedown as Grady stepped into her office. He closed the door and leaned against it. She stayed in her seat. His domineering attitude toward her that morning still stung, and she was too preoccupied for an outright quarrel. "I sent Craig Carr over to talk to you," she said. "The case is assigned to him . . . for the time being."

"I came to apologize." The lines around his eyes crinkled, as he spoke words somewhat foreign to him. "Seeing you there with that Jimmy Olsen-tagalong, then the busted skull, I overreacted."

She stood up and pulled him over to the table. They sat next to each other. Their knees touched and neither of them moved. "I could have been more professional."

"As I went through his belongings, I kept an eye out for anything that might connect him to Allafair Adair." He leaned closer to her and caressed her cheek. "I didn't find anything, sweetheart, I'm sorry."

Alma touched his hand, pressed it firmly against her cheek, then laced her fingers through his. The tangy odor of his skin was fused with the metallic smell of his gun. "Grady, I don't know that you'd even know what to look for."

"And you would?" Defensiveness returned to his voice, and he pulled back in the chair, severing any physical contract.

She raised a hand chest-high to indicate a refusal to fight.

"Let's discuss this over dinner," he said, frustrated with his own impatience. "It's been the craziest week either of us has had in a while. We need some time together, away from work."

Her gaze returned again and again to the newspaper ad for Bartholomew's Fashions. "We need to talk about a lot of things."

"It's hard," he paused, then covered her hand with his, "working so closely with someone you love."

Her intercom buzzed and Val's voice bounced over the speaker. "Alma, get ready for—"

"A surprise!" The door to the office was kicked open and her mother entered, arms loaded with packages and colorful retail bags. Atop her head was a headband with the Hollywood sign on it and decked with dangling stars on both ends. "Oh, hello, Grady." Merl Bashears dumped her load on Alma's desk. "Just got back and I came here first thing; well, after talking to Vernon. He's coming home in a few days with another two dogs, but here, try this." She held a Disneyland T-shirt up to Alma's chest. "I had the best time and, boy, do I have a true Hollywood story to tell you, but I'm not going to tell it to anybody 'til my half-birthday party next week—"

"Oh, Merl, can I help plan it?" Val interrupted. "You have the best half-birthday parties." She clutched a Cinderella figurine and wore a Universal Studios baseball cap.

"Darn shootin', but I got to get that high school reunion catering out of the way first, so it might have to wait a week. Oh, I don't know. Here." Merl held out a fanny pack imprinted with the logo *The Young and the Restless.* "I got this for you, Alma."

"Thank you." She examined it at arm's length. "It'll hold my cell phone."

Merl scrunched up her face. "I'd never own one of those things." She shook her mane of platinum blond hair, which had just begun to sprout black roots. "Being unavailable just adds to my mystery."

Val showed Alma a *Buffy the Vampire Slayer* pen shaped like a wooden stake. "Look what I got. It doubles as a flashlight and a tape recorder." She clicked a button and they heard the sound of their last few sentences.

Grady slowly edged toward the door and waved over his head at Alma.

"Don't you leave," her mother called out. "I didn't forget you." She threw him a Los Angeles Dodgers baseball cap. "I know they're the team you love to hate—how many times have they trounced the Detroit Tigers?"

"None this century!" Grady called out. "See you tonight, Alma. You look good in horns, Merl."

"Those are stars, Mr. Po-liceman," Merl hollered after him, then chuckled as she turned back to Alma. "Oh, Lord, I just love making his life miserable."

She continued sorting through trinkets and souvenirs.

"So, Vernon didn't pick you up at the Knoxville airport?" Alma asked.

"Cotton Lee picked me up." She wagged a finger. "Don't ask." She cleared her throat and changed the subject. "Vernon's got one more week to finish out his dog-training school, but he'll be here in time for the party."

"It's *my* high school reunion."

"Lord, no, not that, my half-birthday." She stared beyond Alma, then walked past her to the cadenza. "Keep your priorities straight, honey." She picked up the snow globe, staring into the flaky water as she continued on to the closet. For several seconds, her eyes glazed over with a vacant look that hid a pain deeper than she could ever admit. "You know, Vernon's stopping in Claiborne County on his way home. It's his final parole meeting. That's one nightmare behind us."

"You might as well know." Alma held her breath. "I've had some leads on Allafair Adair."

Merl had entered the closet; there were noises of boxes being moved inside, then she emerged without the snow globe. Alma realized that looking at it brought more painful memories for her mother and agonizing unanswered questions. "We can talk about this, can't we?"

"So," Merl acted as if nothing had been said, "what's been going on around here?"

"Not a thing you need to worry about," Alma said, knowing to drop the subject until a better time.

"You're not gonna tell her about being held hostage?" Val piped up. "And finding a dead man?"

"Dead man?" Merl gasped.

"A story for your party," Alma said.

"Well, I have to get out to Sue's." Merl scooped up the rest of the souvenirs. "The boys are waiting on their toys from grandma." She made her way to the door, tripping on a dropped T-shirt, which Val retrieved and placed in her over-loaded arms. "You come by and tell me that story," she said. "I don't want it outshining the one I'm gonna tell, though."

Alma closed the door behind them, tossing the fanny pack up in the air and letting it land on the chair. She went to the closet and found the snow globe, hidden behind a stack of boxes. She hated the pain it caused her mother, but this was something she couldn't lock away in a closet.

She sat at the table, staring through the globe at the newspaper ad, then picked up the phone and dialed Jefferson. "Anything yet?" she asked the instant he answered. She crossed her fingers, hoping.

"Phone calls," he said. "All cranks and psychics. More interested in the money than helping."

She sighed, wishing she had done this a year ago. "How do you think we'll know if it's someone serious?"

"They'll know where she's buried," he said. "They'll know she was a mother. They'll have far more intimate knowledge than what I'm getting so far."

"I'm really glad you're helping me."

"How about we get some dinner?"

She almost said yes, then remembered Grady. "I can't tonight. Momma just got home and you know what a hullabaloo that is." She hated insinuating that she would be with her mother, but mentioning Grady would upset him, even though he would never let on. More than anything, she wanted to make peace

with Jefferson. "Are you going to look at Joddy Paradise's records tonight?"
"Doing it now."

Alma straightened up in her chair, her grip on the snow globe tightening.

"So far," he said, "I found an invoice for Isham's last will and testament, but no copy. I might have to go through years of filings."

"What could he possibly have to pass on? Don't waste your time with that." The silence that fell between them was interrupted by a ringing phone, which Jefferson excused himself to answer.

She sat at her desk for several minutes, wondering why a man with nothing and no one would draw up a will. Looking at the snow globe, part of her wondered about Charlotte Gentry's motives for giving it to her. "Passing on a sphinx," she said, then picked up the snow globe and headed for home.

9

In her driveway, Alma found six dogs and three cats basking in the late afternoon sun. "How did I get this collection?" she asked.

She got out of her car and the pack of critters went into a frenzy of jumping, barking, meowing, and slobbering at her return. She had started with one beagle puppy named Willie and the rest slowly assembled—a tan-spotted bird-dog, a miniature collie, two more beagles and a German shepherd Vernon brought home from the school where he was learning to train police dogs. She pointed at a tan Chihuahua. "You don't belong here." It raised a paw and cocked its head, more eyes than face.

The dogs followed her onto the wraparound porch that let her trace the path of the sun on her days off. The nearby woods offered plenty of shaded escape from the hot August weather. Far more modern than the other houses in the hollow, she could see the breadth of Midnight Valley with its flat base, which geologists believed was formed by a meteor slamming into the Cumberland Mountains. The long strip of town lights at the south end was Contrary. Quinntown and Liberty anchored the eastern side.

Juggling a pie she had picked up for desert, Alma unlocked the door and stepped on an envelope. A gray, a calico, and an orange tabby cat scrambled to get in. She tried to bar them with "shoo" and other firm, ineffective words, then emptied pet food into a variety of bowls and left them to fight it out.

Retrieving the envelope, she ripped it open, kicked off her high heels and collapsed on a black leather couch. A ticket fell out. It was for the Sons of the

43

Pioneers Luncheon honoring Charlotte Gentry. A note from Walter accompanied it: *In case you change your mind.*

She put both in her briefcase, thinking it unlikely she'd attend, but his offer was well meaning. In many ways she felt relieved to let go of so much hatred. Much of the animosity had lessened with the death of his mother, and yet Charlotte Gentry was the person who introduced the mystery of Allafair into Alma's world.

As she showered and touched up her makeup, she continued wondering about Walter's motives. *He could be contemplating another run for political office. If I go to the luncheon, it might seem like an endorsement.* Their paths rarely crossed these days and, when they did end up at the same event, each of them kept a safe distance from the other.

Maybe she and Grady should go. She picked up the single ticket, figuring she could buy another one. It would be good for Grady, get him more familiar with the town's power and social structure, and she was facing re-election in November. Being seen and networking were an inevitable part of campaigning. Another side of her wondered—might she use the occasion to ask Walter again if he remembered any thing about his mother and Allafair Adair?

A car horn blew outside. Alma hurried downstairs to greet Grady, and he breezed out of his Blazer and up the porch steps with the lightness of step of being off work. The minute their eyes met, she felt his same joy; the evening would be full of treasured moments.

"I brought *American Beauty* and *Gladiator* for us to watch after dinner," he said.

"If we get that far," she teased, holding the screen door open for him "Pearl's Cafe is delivering country ham, mashed potatoes with soft butter, and sun-dried tomato biscuits."

"I may roll out of the chair and under the table—and don't you dare wake me 'til morning—but I doubt it." He smacked her on the thigh and pulled her into his arms for a deep, long kiss.

When they reluctantly broke apart, it was more to hold the best for last rather than wanting to stop. He kissed her on the cheek before pulling back and reaching for a package he had dropped on the chair. He pulled the videos from a bag with a Bartholomew's logo. She stared at it, her mood suddenly filled with storm clouds. The bag dropped to the floor, and she continued looking at it as he moved around the living room with the familiarity of someone who considered it a second home.

"A little fantasy, a little reality," he said, popping one of the videos into the VCR. He spun on his heels and stopped like a soldier ordered to halt. "What is it?" he asked, his blue eyes narrowing as he studied her.

Alma clutched her hands in front of her chest, weighing whether or not to say what she was thinking. "I saw you yesterday . . . at the coffee shop."

"I was with Henry Moody . . . he talked about retiring." Grady looked away, obviously aware of what she referred to. "You did spend the whole night on a Silver Lake ridge with Jefferson."

"And you know why I did," she retorted, anger planted in her voice.

"It . . . the coffee shop was nothing." She continued to stare at the large Old English *B* embossed on the bag. "Do you really expect me to let this go?" she asked softly, looking up into his eyes and imploring more from him, but unsure he would give it. She moved toward him, then reached out and stroked his arm, the hard tricep muscle flexed under her touch. She leaned into him, her forehead touching his cheek. She could smell the mint on his breath and the sharp edge of sandalwood soap. Slowly her hands rubbed up over the cotton T-shirt, finally grasping the hem of the sleeve and balling it in her fist. "I need to know." She exhaled long and hard.

His arms came up around her and he pressed his lips to her forehead. "Remember last summer when we broke up?"

"Yes," she said tentatively, her chest muscles beginning to unexpectedly tighten.

"You dated Doug Brewster for awhile."

"I wouldn't say dated," she said. "Only had dinner with him a couple of times. I helped him get a job in Frankfort."

"Yes, but . . . " Grady walked away, dropping onto the center of the couch. He rubbed both hands over his face and stared through his fingers, avoiding Alma's gaze. Then he sat erect with both arms anchored on the back of the couch as if he would have to be pried up from it. His lips were pressed together and, when he finally did look at her, the deep blue of his eyes masked his feelings.

"Go ahead," she said, sitting next to him. "Just say whatever it is."

"I dated someone, too." He scooted closer to her on the couch, letting one hand rub her thigh in gentle strokes.

Alma felt a tingle spread through her body, the kind of sensation she was unsure she could control. She was equally afraid of kissing him and slapping him. "Elaine Bartholomew. Well, she certainly chased you long enough."

"It was only that one time," he said slowly and deliberately.

"It," she repeated. "One time . . . are we talking about a date?"

His gaze dropped to his lap.

"You slept with her." Alma got up and moved to the window. She opened the sliding door to let in some fresh air. The warm evening air now seemed stifling, and only the uncertain flutter of a mosquito kept her from stepping outside.

"I've told her it's over. Many times, but—"

"She doesn't want to take no for an answer?" Alma turned and looked at him, hoping.

Grady was nodding his head. "She'll have to take no for an answer."

"The youngest daughter of the man whose name is plastered on half the town's retail section is not used to taking no for an answer." Alma turned again to the window, sifting through feelings of relief and regret. It was never pleasant to be the cause of someone's pain. "This is a complication."

Grady came up behind her and wrapped his arms around her midsection. Alma turned toward him and leaned back to look into his eyes. His solemn expression spoke of his determination. "I need you," he said, his voice quivering. "I can't breathe without you."

She reached out and touched his cheek. She was not going to lose him. Not now. Not to Elaine. Not to her own stubbornness. Not to anyone. Melting into his arms, her whole world seemed to be in place with him. His mouth closed on hers and, after a long, deep kiss, he picked her up and carried her upstairs.

* * *

The phone rang, jarring Alma awake. She snatched it up. Grady stirred next to her and rubbed his eyes. The clock hands pointed to midnight. She could hardly believe they hadn't left the bedroom, even when the deliveryman from Pearl's Cafe came and left, probably depositing the food on the porch. The dogs and cats must have enjoyed a feast. "Hello?" she said.

"Alma Bashears?" a man's voice asked.

"Yes."

"Don't try to find Allafair Adair."

"What?" The name shocked her. "Why?"

"People could get hurt. People will end up dead."

The line disconnected. Alma sat up, her heart beating with alarm.

Grady reached out and groggily rubbed her back. "For me?" he asked.

"No," she replied. "Wrong number." She looked at him, smiled, and shrugged her shoulders before replacing the phone. Some unrealized fear kept her from telling him the truth. She half-remembered Jefferson saying the reason she didn't confide in Grady was that she lacked complete trust in him. She looked at his resting face, eyes closed, lips slightly parted. His rough beauty touched a savage longing in her. He belonged to her and she would protect him however she had to, even if it meant holding back hurtful truths. She ran her fingers though his hair. "Are you awake?"

"Come back here," he answered, pulling her toward him.

She let him. The safety of his arms was what she needed now.

10

"He sounded young, maybe middle-aged." Alma plopped on a sofa in Jefferson's office. "I don't know, maybe elderly," she added in frustration. "The call woke me out of a dead sleep."

"Sure you didn't dream it?" Jefferson took two deli bags from his secretary, then closed the door.

"Not a dream. Grady heard the phone ring, too." She bit the inside of her mouth, embarrassed by her callousness. "I'm sorry."

He raised his hand and shrugged. "I should be used to it by now." He let his gaze run the length of her body, then stared gloomily at the floor. "Alma, just watch yourself."

"Now, what do you mean by that?" She met his knowing look with newfound confidence. "Elaine? Jefferson, I assure you I would not stay with a man who cheats on me. I'm no Hillary Clinton."

"But you are a little bit Tammy Wynette."

She smacked his arm playfully and pinched his shoulder. Picking up half a tuna sandwich, she hummed a bar of "Stand By Your Man."

"All I'm saying," he explained, "is don't let your sense of loyalty blind you."

She bit into the sandwich instead of responding. He was as true to her as a brother, and an aching sentiment twisted in her chest. "The *69 went to a pay phone on Highway 25E." She swallowed a sip of soda. "Since the ad response was to a P.O. Box or the 800-number in your office, someone had to get an inside connection at the newspaper to learn it was me who paid the bill."

"I'll stop by the business offices and grill the staff at both papers. It's doubtful anyone will admit to it." He raised his voice to override a car alarm outside on the street. "Money probably changed hands."

"That's my thought."

"You want me to bribe them?"

"Increase the reward to ten thousand dollars."

"Alma, that's crazy." He dusted crumbs off his hands and stood up, pacing in a circle. "Half the phone calls I got were from the county jail. Add more money and every inmate in the state will be calling."

"Somebody out there is real nervous. This will raise the stakes."

"That's what I'm worried about. If someone went through the trouble to track you down, I wouldn't take the midnight caller's warning as an empty threat."

She followed Jefferson to the window where he pressed both hands against the panes. "I'm a prosecutor. It's not the first time I've been threatened. I'm prepared to take care of myself."

"Especially with a police chief sleeping beside you." The windowpane reflected his resigned expression, both from trying to talk her out of increasing the reward, and from being depressed by the romantic situation he was not a part of. "I found another two boxes of Joddy Paradise's files. I'll go through them tonight." His flat tone hinted at his mood.

"Let's go out for dessert." She pulled him toward the door. A wave of heat swallowed them as they descended the staircase.

As they walked, she could sense the heaviness of his steps. He stared steadily at the sidewalk, even though they passed two high school classmates. "Coming to the reunion?" Clara Carter asked.

"I'll be there," Alma said, then looked at Jefferson, who seemed not to have heard. "He graduated a year ahead of us," she answered for him, "but I bet he escorts his sister."

She squeezed his shoulder as he held open the door of Pearl's Cafe for her, and Clara nodded that she was going the opposite direction. "I'm going to get you a really good birthday present this year," Alma said, trying to cheer him up.

"You can bring it to Merl's half-birthday party next week," Jefferson replied. "I got my invitation today—a Hollywood sign that opened to the words: 'You are invited to Hollyweird.'"

Alma motioned to the waitress that they would sit at the counter. In her mind, she reviewed steps to track down the caller if he phoned again. Maybe she could talk him into a meeting; if she *69'd the call and it was a place where someone might have observed him, she could get a description; if the location was close by she would try to get there before he left the area.

Straightening her hair in the wall mirror behind the counter, she focused on a reflection that jarred her. She swiveled around on the stool and Jefferson followed her gaze. Grady and Elaine sat in a corner booth having lunch.

"Don't blame this one on me," Jefferson held up both hands. "Dessert was your idea."

Alma's head flushed with heat. At the same time, Grady looked in her direction. Their eyes locked. She fought the sensation of having exposed a secret, and turning away was like tearing tape off her skin. "Let's get out of here." She glanced again at the couple. Grady rose and signaled to her, but she kept walking.

"Alma?" he called out.

She stared at Grady's reflection in the mirror. His face looked stark with embarrassment. Elaine had put a hand on his shoulder.

Jefferson rushed in front of Alma and held open the door. Before she could exit, a strong grip on her arm pulled her around. Grady towered over her.

"I called your name," he said firmly.

"I'm humiliated enough," she said. "What are you doing? Telling her all about last night?"

"As a matter of fact, yes." He squeezed her arm again. "Listen to me—"

"Let go of me!" She jerked out of his grasp and stepped backward, bumping a table. A cup hit the floor and shattered, and the silverware followed in a jangle of noise. She was sure her face must be as scarlet as Grady's.

"My fault, Pearl," he called back toward the kitchen. "My nightstick got out of hand."

"You can say that again," Alma whispered, then walked toward Jefferson and out to the street.

The hot August breeze was no match for the growing confusion she felt. Jefferson draped an arm over her shoulders and led her back to her own office. She got through the next hour with a series of slamming doors and snapping at coworkers. When a copy of the ad came through the fax, the increased reward made her angry. *There are people out there who can help me,* she thought. Their deliberate refusal was as close to a crime as she could imagine and she wished she could prosecute them for it. "Keeping secrets gets you a life sentence," she said out loud.

She continued staring at the ad copy and searched around the office, wishing there was something she could do to make events happen faster. Her gaze came to rest on the ticket to the Sons of the Pioneers Luncheon. She looked at her watch. The event would start in ten minutes. She bit her lower lip, arguing with herself. *If Walter really wants to put the past behind him,* she rationalized, *now would be the time to tell me anything he's holding back about his mother and Allafair Adair.*

She picked up the ticket, weaving it through her fingers. One hand on her full stomach, and feeling somewhat sick from seeing Grady and Elaine all cozy in a booth, she weighed the consequences of dining with the enemy. *One thing is for sure,* she thought. *This is going to shock a lot of people.*

11

When Alma stepped into the banquet room of the Queensbury Hotel, a wave of murmurs sounded toward her like a well-rehearsed choir. Publicly, the feud between the Gentrys and Alma had its roots in her brother's murder trial, which cumulated in her defeating Walter for the office of commonwealth attorney; but none of these politicians, socialites, or town leaders knew the darker secrets of the past.

Alma thought they must be shocked down to their socks that she would attend an event honoring the Gentrys. She waved to the Mayor, who signaled back that he would catch up with her as a slew of matrons crowded around him, giggling like girls. Most of the city council members were there and she made her way through the crowd offering pleasantries and campaign promises. She felt surprised to fit so snugly into the role of elected official but had learned that the biggest part of being a politician was being accessible to both parts of her constituency—the hollows and downtown.

The scents of marjoram and basil swept around her, and she chose a fried hush puppy as a waiter dipped beside her for a view of the platter. Many of the men wore name tags indicating a pioneer ancestor, but with so many Daniel Boones, Thomas Walkers, Isaac Shelbys, John Finleys, and Rebecca Bryans in the mix, it stretched credulity.

A group of about fifty high school students seated in front of the podium squirmed impatiently, obviously forced to attend the event during their summer vacation. Alma surveyed the room, looking for the one odd absence—Walter

Gentry. Finally, she spied Clayton Foster pacing nervously in an outer foyer. He spoke frantically into a cell phone, then clipped it shut and slapped his forehead in the same motion.

Alma approached him gently and asked, "Anything I can do, Clayton?"

"I can't believe it, I simply can't believe it." He huffed an exasperated breath and looked about to cry. "Lunch is getting cold and no one can find the guest of honor."

"Walter Gentry isn't here?"

"Or in his office, or his home, not answering his phone, pager or, or, or—"

"He wouldn't miss this, Clayton. I'm sure he's on his way."

"Nothing worse has happened in this county since five city council members got stuck in an elevator on swearing-in day." Clayton threw up his hands and, with various assistants in tow, went to the hotel entrance to watch for Walter. Alma stopped a waiter for a glass of water, amused by the affair's disorganization and Walter's absence at probably his biggest event of the year. She lingered near the door, chitchatting with acquaintances and introducing herself to a few others. Clayton returned, ordering the crew of waiters to begin serving lunch. Alma took a seat at an empty table near the exit. She was actually beginning to enjoy the festivities when a voice behind her turned her blood to ice water.

"And have you seen that bruise on her face?" asked a woman. "If she's bitchy enough to make him punch her, then it spells trouble for that bogus relationship."

Alma peered over her shoulder at where Elaine Bartholomew and Lee Ann Rogers sat about ten feet away. Elaine had changed clothes since Alma saw her with Grady earlier in the day and now wore a more conservative shirtdress with a matching headband. Alma touched the scrape on her cheek and, with a fervent growl in her belly, pushed her chair back and turned around with a deliberate smile. "Lee Ann," she said, holding out her hand. "I haven't seen you since we rang bells for the Salvation Army last Christmas." She glanced at Elaine, who blushed even though she gave Alma an up-and-down bat of her eyes. "Elaine," Alma said, with a nod of acknowledgment.

"Good Lord, Alma," Lee Ann said, pointing at the purple skin on her cheek. "What caused that?"

Alma circled a finger around the bruise. "That little tussle at the courthouse the other day. I got caught in the crossfire."

"Ahhh," Lee Ann smirked toward Elaine. "It must have been terrible for you."

"Not easy," Alma said, "but my hero came to the rescue."

"Ahhh," Lee Ann said again with another knowing glance at Elaine. "I'm glad to hear no one is smacking you around."

Alma dared not look directly at Miss Bartholomew, but her stony silence indicated that her gossip had been trivialized. If there was one obvious insight, it was that Elaine would stir up as much trouble as she could to keep herself in Grady's sphere.

Clayton Foster sprang into the room at a trot and clapped his hands. "Our guest of honor has arrived!" On his heels, Walter Gentry entered in a navy blue Zegna suit and tie with a large diamond clip that matched a college ring on his right hand—the image of success, but something about his face was severe and anxious. An older man followed him, not so smartly dressed, and with an equally apprehensive expression. He was maybe sixty-five, with gray hair and stooped shoulders. No one was more surprised than she when Walter circled around Clayton, took Alma's arm, and pulled her along with him. The other man waited at the door, staring intently at a phone in his hand. The crowd stood and applauded.

"You two sure make a cute couple," Elaine called after them.

"What the hell do you think you're doing?" Alma snapped at him out of the side of her mouth.

As the audience clapped, Walter whispered, "You've got to help me, I didn't have time to write a speech." He smiled and waved. "Just introduce me, keep talking, so that all I have to do is go up there and say thank you."

Clayton Foster took the podium and began making preliminary comments before awarding the scholarship. Alma sat beside Walter, while waiters put plates of food in front of them. She leaned into him. "And why would I do that?"

"Because the only reason you'd be here is because you want something."

She smiled playfully and looked intently into his eyes. "Is there anything . . . anything, even the slightest thing, you can tell me about Allafair Adair?"

His face reddened, perhaps with anger, but he looked at her with softer eyes. "Can't you let go of the past? It serves no one."

She leaned forward until her face was inches from his. "Two awards away from the one they want to give you."

"Let's bury the hatchet, not start new wars." He stared out into the audience, just above their heads, not looking at them, but past them as if they were on a movie screen. When Alma didn't respond, he picked up his fork and pushed the rice and green beans around on the plate. "Okay, I was eight, maybe nine. A babysitter lived in a guest room in our basement." He paused, putting one hand on his chin and looked at her. "Mind you, I don't know if it was the same Allafair."

"It's not a common name," Alma said, astounded at his admission. "The only time I've found it was in a historical reference to the sole female killed in the Hatfield-McCoy feud."

"This girl was . . . very pregnant, even though she couldn't have been more than fifteen, sixteen."

Beloved Mother, Alma thought, remembering the epitaph on Allafair's gravestone. "What was she doing at your house?"

"I don't know." He opened his hands, palms upward. "She stayed two months, I would guess." He shifted in his seat, his back awkwardly straight. "I remember my parents having a fight about her. She'd sneak out. I supposed it was to meet the boy who'd gotten her pregnant. Anyway, one day I came home from school and she was gone."

"Didn't you ask your parents about her?"

Walter's features twisted, the memories of his childhood evidently not pleasant. "Even at that age I wasn't crazy enough to ask mother about her and Dad's fights." He cut into a filet of catfish but pushed it aside. "That's all I know. I'm sorry."

"What did she look like?"

Walter's eyes rolled upwards. "Long black hair, parted in the middle, it reached down past her waist. A handsome face, not exactly pretty—Cher, no, Angelica Houston-ish."

Alma saw the picture in her mind, wondering if she might have passed Allafair on a street and not realized who she was.

"She was . . . " He hesitated and stared down at his hands, clasped in his lap. "She was very kind to me."

"How?"

He looked at her with a guarded expression, which quickly transformed into a gentler expression of reminiscence. "Sweet, the way a kind person is to a lonely boy."

"Do you have any idea where she went, where that child might be?"

He shook his head. In the back of the room, the man who had entered with Walter signaled to him. He held the phone to one ear and shortly afterward was joined by a younger man of similar stature with the same stooped shoulders. Alma thought they looked like muscle from the old days of gangsters and land barons. Walter rose, seemingly unaware that he had done so, and stared at the men, then sat back down when he noticed everyone looking at him. "There was one other thing . . . " He turned back to her, but kept his eyes fixed on the two men. "It's silly, and I'm certain it's not relevant."

"Yes?" Alma asked.

"I remember that she kept insisting that there was no father."

"No father?"

"Go figure," he chuckled. "A virgin birth."

"There's got to be something else," she whispered. "Could your father have been—"

"Do me a favor," he said through gritted teeth. "Leave my parents out of this."

"And I'm going to say such nice things about you," she smirked, rising to take center stage. She stared down at the high school students and cleared her throat. "Many of you here today have traced your lineage back to the days of the pioneers. Those pioneers walked through Cumberland Gap to open up a new country. I'd like you to consider that they followed an Indian Trail that came to be known as the Warriors' Path. This route was carved into a passage, which came to be called the Wilderness Road. Soon individuals, families and even armies traveled this road, which eventually became Highway 25E. But now it carries tourists and commerce and still more settlers into the area. That highway leads to Interstate 75. The roads that many of you young people will travel will be just as exciting as those the pioneers walked. Perhaps one of you will be the ancestor of the first person who will walk on the planet Mars. Not so farfetched a thought in retrospect, considering the Wilderness Road was carved out in the mid-1700s. In another 250 years, the roads into space will be the paths of your descendants, but always remember that the roads that lead away also lead back. As you chart your destinies, make it a path that counts. If you're a doctor, find a disease and cure it; if you're a teacher, learn a subject and make it new again; if you're a writer, find the untold story and tell it; if you're a lawyer, find inequity and seek justice."

She looked over at Walter and let her right eye closed in the slightest wink. "One man among us, who left the mountains and came back, is Walter Gentry." She hesitated, swallowed, and mentally told herself not to choke. "He left a monolith of a law firm in New York to serve as this county's commonwealth attorney for twelve years and has since been in private practice. He's made himself a leading citizen of Contrary, not because his family name demanded it, but because it was his path. His bloodlines run deep in this community, and he is a man who has reclaimed his land and will serve it. Accepting your award on behalf of himself and his mother, the late Charlotte Gentry, I present to you, a man who became a lawyer and wants to make his destiny count . . . Walter Gentry Jr."

A roar of applause followed as he stood to receive the award. He spoke only a few thank-yous. Alma noticed him glance more than once toward the back door, where the older man continually made phone calls. "With such a wonderful speech as Ms. Bashears has given, I will not take up further time," Walter said, posing for photographs. "Please enjoy your meal." He returned to sit beside her, his eyes on the rear of the room. "Thank you," he said, nodding toward her, but watching the two men in back.

"Who is that?" she asked.

"An emergency with my son. An old family friend, Mr. Burke, is helping me."

"I'm sorry to hear that."

"I was hoping it would shut you up."

Alma studied his face. Walter's wife had left him a few years earlier and taken their two children to her home state of New York. "I hope everything will be okay."

"I think so," he said. "It's hard being away from them; no father, you know."

"Yes, I know," Alma said coldly.

He looked at her, caught off guard by his own words and their meaning. "I'm sorry," he muttered. "I didn't mean any reference to your own father."

"Well, your family had a lot to do with that," she said and rolled her eyes.

"You're obsessed." His fork dropped onto the plate with a clank. "Why can't you let go of the past? It's the only way to any peace in this town, short of one of us dying." He scooted back his chair in one stroke and rose to leave.

Alma caught his arm. "Are you sure there's nothing else?"

He leaned down next to her, putting his lips against her ear. "She had a crescent birthmark just behind her left ear and told me that was how she talked to the Devil." He jerked from her grasp, but leaned back long enough to add, "It was the only way she could blackmail me into going to sleep—so don't read too much into it."

She watched Walter walk over to the two men and get into a vigorous discussion. They ignored various people who wandered by, expecting him to acknowledge them. Abruptly, Walter and the two men left, leaving both his hosts and the majority of the audience wondering what was going on.

"He had a family emergency," Alma whispered to Clayton Foster. They stared at the award abandoned on the table between the bread-sticks and the ice water. She wondered if more was going on than a problem with his son. At any rate, he had told her all he ever would about Allafair. Looking out at the audience, Alma's gaze landed on Elaine. Subconsciously, she curled her hair behind her left ear and pressed on the skin of the lobe. Still staring at Elaine, she wished she could whisper to the Devil.

12

The Sons of the Pioneers luncheon raised more questions than it answered. Alma's gut told her Walter knew still more about Allafair Adair. That she had once been his babysitter and lived with the Gentrys seemed too outlandish to be untrue. Could Walter's father have had his mistress living in the house? A fifteen-year-old? Charlotte would not have been able to hide that forever.

The two strangers who abruptly pulled Walter away during the lunch also nagged her thoughts. Could it be exactly as he said—old friends handling a personal problem with one of his children? Still, he was as nervous as a kid caught in a lie. Maybe apprehensive because of the circumstances—his late arrival, the forgotten speech, the honor bestowed. *His conscience.* At the very least, she had gotten a description of Allafair, even though it was over twenty years old.

After a second lunch of the day, Alma put on a baggy T-shirt and stretch shorts; then, with a stack of work that included Isham Thunderheart's autopsy report, she curled up in a backyard hammock hung between two elm trees. Caesar, Bud, Sadie, and the Chihuahua were sacked out in the shade with no sign of Willie or the cats. The sun began to pinken the sky and streams of white clouds laced the horizon. The phone rang from inside the house and she heard the machine pick up. She wondered if Grady was calling again. She had ignored all ten of his previous messages.

The autopsy report was as expected. Cause of death was blunt trauma to the head. She looked over preliminary police reports and noticed Grady had

59

made a note that Thunderheart had a driver's license, but no vehicle was found at the scene. She considered that for a moment. He was not within walking distance of any store, nor was his living arrangements such that he could be completely self-sufficient. He would have needed a way to get around. *Good thinking, Grady,* she thought.

Now, if she could only figure out the relationship between Thunderheart and Allafair. She pulled the ad copy from a folder and studied it, eager for tomorrow's paper to hit the street. A ten-thousand-dollar reward ought to bring real results. The phone rang again, and she fought the urge to answer. At least one other satisfying piece of information had come from the banquet. Elaine's attempts at stirring trouble indicated that the little vamp was more insecure than she acted.

Alma giggled with a snide pleasure worthy of her mother. There was no doubt that Miss Bartholomew was still after Grady, and her anxiousness about his relationship with Alma bled right through her self-assured act. Still it didn't explain Grady's actions. He had assured her that there was no longer anything between them. Perhaps what she saw that morning wasn't as serious as she had first assumed. *But lunching together,* she thought, *is not nothing.*

Willie's high-pitched howls were followed by the grinding of tires on gravel. The other dogs jumped at the sound and raced toward the front of the house to form a pack. Alma twisted around. Grady's cruiser plowed up the hill. Eager for an escape route, she considered running up into the woods, but he was as familiar with them as she, and she had no doubt the dogs would give away her location.

A car door slammed. She shot out of the hammock, sneaked inside through the kitchen door, and hoped the sliding door to the patio was locked. His heavy-footed steps thundered on the side porch. As she rounded the staircase, he rapped on the glass.

"Go away!" she yelled.

"I will not." He slid a pocketknife into the crack between the patio door and the jamb to spring the lock.

"That's breaking and entering." She trotted halfway up the stairs and heard the door slide open.

"I told you to get that fixed last week," he yelled. "Anybody could break into this place."

"Get out of my house!" she hollered back. She caught a flash of him out of the corner of her eyes as he came up the stairs after her. She swung the bedroom door closed as hard as she could, but his quick hand stopped the impetus, and he followed her inside. "Do I have to call the—"

"I am the police."

"My uncles."

Grady stopped in his tracks. He looked around, embarrassment seeping into his stance as he stepped back into the frame of the door. His shoulders sank a trace.

Alma let out a malicious laugh. "Figured that would glue your boots to the floor."

One hand came up to his hip, and he looped a thumb through his belt. He couldn't look her in the eyes. "I'm sorry," he said. "If you'll hear me out, I'll leave; and if it's what you want, I won't come back."

"Ever?" she asked coyly, not meaning it, but part of her relished his discomfort.

His lips pressed together and struggled to form the word. "Ev . . . Ever. Maybe . . . No, if you want that . . . okay. Ever."

Alma jumped, landing on the center of the mattress with a bounce. Lying on the bed, still unmade from the night before, the smell of their lovemaking wafted upward as she tangled her bare legs through the silk sheets. He shifted uncomfortably, and she knew his desire was getting the best of him. She motioned for him to tell his story. *Let him suffer,* she thought. "I'm listening."

"I went into Pearl's Cafe with Lou Mills. You can ask him; he has no reason to lie for me." Pacing the length of the bed, he resembled a teenager rationalizing to his parents. "Elaine came in and said she had to speak to me."

"I bet she did." Alma rolled her eyes and stared at the wall.

"She started begging," Grady insisted, the uncomfortable memory marking the edges of his eyes with deep lines. "Got down on her knees. Right there in front of Lou. It was embarrassing."

"But wonderful for your ego?"

"She cried. Ask Lou. He'll tell you." He held onto the bedpost, letting the fingers of his other hand caress the silky sheet. "So Lou excuses himself, and she sits down. When you came in, I had her to the point where she understood that she had to move on with her life." Grady leaned forward, his thighs pressing

61

into the mattress. "Alma, you would have done the same thing. There is no reason to be deliberately cruel."

"That's ironic considering the way you treat Jefferson."

"That's different—"

"It's not different," she interrupted. "Jefferson and I have never slept together. We're best friends, not lovers."

Grady raised a hand and patted at the air as if to say he did not seek an escalation. He looked up at the ceiling, exhaling several breaths before speaking again. "I'm not asking you to forgive me because I didn't do anything wrong." He peered down at her, his cobalt eyes penetrating hers. "I'm asking for your help with this situation."

Alma's warming gaze scanned the full length of him. Black uniform pants tight on the muscles of his thighs; his large hands, scarred from years of street work in the roughest neighborhoods of Detroit; the police badge—like a sheriff's star—on his chest; the hardness of his face, like a bust of a Roman senator. His rough exterior was so opposite to the person who asked for her help. She slid down a bit, letting one leg hang off the mattress. "And Elaine is clear that there will be no more lunches?" she asked.

His lips formed the trace of a smile. "A clean break."

Letting her heel caress his calf, she pushed back on her elbows and drew her other foot up the length of his inner thigh. She stopped at the crotch and pressed slightly, "Gotcha," she whispered.

Grady stared down at her. His lips parted and his fidgety words came out in gasps of breath. "Though I did tell her that, when she got married, we'd attend her wedding."

Alma's toes wiggled underneath his belt and she pulled him toward the bed. Pressing the heel of her foot into his groin, she teased him, controlling how close he could come to her.

He unhooked his belt and it dropped to the floor with a thud. He traced the arch of her foot with his index finger, wrapping his hand around her ankle and pulling it harder into his belly. Leaning forward, he brought her leg around his side until it encircled his back.

Close enough to reach his shirt, she pulled him down on top of her. His mouth closed on hers, kissing her deeply, hungrily, and with passionate gratitude. She pushed him back and over, flipping herself on top of him at the same time.

"I can't reach my handcuffs," he said.

She bent down and gently sucked his earlobe as she whispered, "Restraint is the last thing I have in mind right now."

"Sticking in my back . . . " He repositioned himself pulling the handcuffs from a pocket and dropping them on the floor. "You're not going to believe this," he sighed between heavy breaths. "But I have a meeting with the mayor in thirty minutes."

She kissed his neck, bit his shoulder, and then let one hand wiggle inside his pants. "Cancel it."

"I'll call," he said, reluctant to leave her embrace. He reached for the phone and she loosened her hold. His head jerked up from the pillow. "What's that?" He pointed at a torn ticket and program on her bedside table. She tried to knock it onto the floor, but he grabbed it first.

"It's nothing."

"Only one?" He looked at the program. "To that banquet honoring Walter Gentry." His muscles tightened, the passion of the moment dampened. "And only one ticket."

"He sent it to me," she said, unbuttoning his shirt. "I wasn't going to go, but thought he might open up to me about Allafair."

"I'll bet he did some opening up."

"Be quiet," she said, kissing his neck.

"I can't put my finger on it, but that guy has an agenda."

He tried to sit up, but Alma pushed him back down. "Not now," she whispered in his ear.

He grabbed her by the arms and pushed her back. "He's got the hots for you."

"Grady, don't overreact."

"Oh, no," he said sarcastically. "A trait you're unfamiliar with."

She untangled her legs from his and sat beside him. "It means nothing."

"There's something about him. He's always watching you."

"Walter Gentry is not a discarded lover."

"It's not even that," he said, sitting up. "You went to this stupid event to get back at me."

"You don't know what you're talking about." Frustration filtered into her voice as she tried to explain. "There's a history here that you don't understand."

Grady swung up from the bed and zipped his pants in the same motion. "I've always known there was something between the two of you. Something you won't tell me." He picked up his gun belt and wrapped it around his waist.

"It's not what you think."

"Then tell me about it."

"Not now."

"When?"

"I don't know," she said, his insistence sending a frightening sensation shooting through her body. She was being forced again. Commanding phrases ripped through her mind as if they were guardians telling her what to do. *Too much to reveal. Too much to hide.*

"Seems there's a lesson here about ganders and geese," he said mockingly. "If not now, when?"

"Maybe never!" she yelled back.

"Fine!" he shouted back. He picked up a picture of them encased in a silver frame that sat on the bedside table and threw it with all his strength out an open window. "Never!"

He stormed from the room then, his boots heavy on the steps. A few seconds later, Willie barked as his car squealed down the driveway.

Alma sat on the side of the bed, staring at the Sons of the Pioneers program and torn ticket. She walked over to the window and watched Grady's car peel out of the hollow. The picture had no doubt flown down the mountainside; there was no telling where. Why did she refuse to explain her past to Grady? Other than her brother, Vernon, Jefferson was the only other person she had allowed to share her secret shame, and it had almost taken the loss of her career for her to tell him. Logically, she knew what happened all those years ago was not her fault; but, inside, in her deepest self, she could not keep from feeling the shame. And now, the past, that awful day when she was raped, had put a wedge between her and the man she loved at a time when they least needed it.

She lay back on the bed and closed her eyes. Pulling the sheets up around her, she savored the smell of Grady's body. It was on her skin, her clothes, her hair. She sat up and started to pick up the phone, but paused when it rang. *Let it be him,* she prayed.

"Hello?"

"You got the money?" a man's voice asked.

The faint, familiar tone shocked her to alertness. "Yes?" she said, uncertain, but hoping it was the man who had called her the night before. "How do I know this is legitimate?" she challenged.

"I need the money," he said.

"You haven't said anything to prove that you have information."

"Midnight," the man said. "Bring the money to *her* grave."

13

"Do you know how hard it was to get Bill Crocker to open up the bank?" Jefferson let the kitchen screendoor slam behind him. "He almost called the police—thought there'd been a kidnapping."

Alma reached for the bag that Jefferson dropped on the table. She released a sigh of relief when she peered inside at the neatly bundled bills. Her mind raced. She was about to meet someone who had known Allafair Adair. Based on what happened to the last person who had that information, it seemed that she had better hurry.

Jefferson sat in the chair opposite her, his lips drawn tight. "Don't do this." He reached across the kitchen table and lifted her chin with one finger. "I know that look." He threw up his hands and let them slap down against his thighs. "I'm coming with you."

"He told me to come alone." Alma tightly wound the opening of the paper bag with a rubber band.

"This could be more about reward than information."

"Possibly, but what else can I do?"

"It's a con," Grady said as he approached the screendoor and let himself into Alma's kitchen. He was in uniform—*obviously called by Jefferson,* she thought—*to try and put a stop to my meeting.* The weight of his service revolver on one hip and baton on the other caused a slight swagger as he walked toward her. Whatever animosity there was between them earlier that evening had been put aside for the moment.

"Well, you two must have suppressed a lot of testosterone to join sides." Alma looked hard at one, then the other, expecting them to gang up on her. "Now, I appreciate everything both of you are doing. I know you're concerned, but this is the first break I've had since I began investigating my father's disappearance."

"This man will take your money and give you nothing!" Grady's fist slammed into the table, jarring the salt and pepper shakers. The orange cat sitting on a nearby counter jumped and scrambled off.

"I'll know what he has to offer soon enough."

"I have a bad feeling about this." Jefferson rubbed his forehead and swiped back his blond hair. "Alma, do this for us," he pleaded. "If this man can't meet you during the day, then everything is all wrong."

"I don't have a choice. Can't you two understand that?" She stood and paced the length of the room, then turned toward them.

"Alma, I have some interesting leads from Joddy Paradise's files," Jefferson said. "Let's see if they pan out."

"If I'd known it was going to lead to this, I would never have found that woman's grave for you," Grady said.

"Well, you did," Alma said, her voice full of determination. "And we both read on her tombstone the words: 'Beloved Mother.' Allafair has children out there who might know the connection between her and my father."

Jefferson was silent. He watched her with worry, care, and a love he would never speak of, but also with intimate knowledge of her determination. Grady anchored his hands on his hips, staring up at the ceiling with a fixed expression. "Your going alone is out of the question," he said with finality.

"I won't be alone." She slipped her hands into the deep folds of a loose jacket and opened it enough to show him a bulletproof vest. Next, she pulled the handle of a pistol from the pocket. He didn't look impressed. She stared at the floor, wishing she could give him more confidence. "You can wait here if you like," she pointed at Jefferson, then Grady, "but don't either of you dare try to follow me."

"Alma," Jefferson pleaded, "if something were to ever happen to you . . . "

"Don't worry," she said. "I have a plan."

* * *

Alma double-checked the magazine on the Colt Mustang .380 automatic. Full. She studied the dark rolling mounds of the Rose Hill Cemetery, then snapped off the safety, jacked a shell into the chamber, and slid the gun back into her coat pocket. With the bag of money under her arm, she picked out a path with the flashlight that cut across the faces of tombstones, some from the 1850s.

Lanterns sporadically placed throughout the grounds gave the graves a golden glow. She moved silently through them, stopping at the crest of the hill beside a six-foot marble angel with one arm pointing toward the heavens, and the other open to the earth. The graves beneath it belonged to Charlotte Gentry and her husband, Walter Gentry, Sr.

Alma hesitated, knelt down, and shined her flashlight on the inscription: *As Above, So Below, Come Walk With Me On Streets Of Gold.* She had repeated the words to herself many times since Charlotte died. Whatever the meaning, she knew it was more than a simple verse. Mrs. Gentry was far too cryptic for a simple *Rest in Peace.* Those words were her final joke on the people she hated in the world—and Alma was one of them.

As a guide, she tilted her head in the same downward angle as the angel's, looking for the tombstone of Allafair Adair about twenty feet away. Two departed women who obviously shared a secret that involved Esau Bashears. Her eyes came to rest on the other grave. Alma gasped when she saw the lit candle planted in the ground. He was there!

She looked back at her car, parked close enough that she could make a run for it, and her hand unconsciously rubbed the handle of the .380. "Where are you?" she called out. She made her way down the hill and stood at the foot of Allafair's grave. Someone had planted honeysuckle at the base of the headstone and it now wound around it so tightly that it obscured part of the name.

Alma shined the light around, catching the red reflection of a rabbit's eyes—nothing else. An owl whoo-hawed, followed by the sound of flapping wings through tree leaves. Insects chimed out their familiar calls of kay-tee-did-it, kay-tee-did-it. Low throaty frogs burped from a nearby pond. An engine started and headlights blinded her. A truck, parked on the same service road she had used, turned around and headed in the opposite direction, then it stopped and its horn beeped twice. She crossed the uneven ground and paused beside the truck.

A dark figure wearing a wide-brimmed gray hat sat in the driver's seat. "How do?" he said, staring to the side as he whittled on a piece of wood that he held out the window. His lean hands moved the penknife across the wood with the smoothness of one who did it for a living. "Appreciate it if you'd kill the flashlight and hold yourself about where you stand."

Alma complied, wishing she could get more than a three-quarters view of his profile. "My office would have been more comfortable."

He scratched through whitish whiskers on his jaw and grinned, but didn't turn toward her. "Some things are best told in the dark."

"Things like Allafair Adair?"

"You forgetting something?" He sat up, bristling with irritation.

"I'm sorry." Alma held out the packet of cash, but not close enough for him to grab it.

He turned just enough to see the bag, then averted his head and tugged on the hat, bringing it lower on his ears. He held out his hand for the money.

She stepped closer but didn't give it to him. At this distance, she could see that the truck was painted a primer gray. It was battered, as if several decades old. "How did you know Allafair?"

He eyed the envelope but kept his face either turned or shaded by the hat so she was unable to get a good look at him. "She cursed me," he spat out. Scraping the penknife against the wood, he continued his whittling.

"Where will I find her children?"

The man looked straight ahead. Alma judged him to be in his late sixties, if not seventies. "Give me my money," he growled. "I didn't promise nothing about her young'uns."

The truck puffed out gassy exhaust and his foot pressed on the accelerator, revving the engine so it ground even louder. "My ad said Allafair and her descendants. Why the secrecy? I only want to talk to them."

"You don't want to find 'em. They're Melungeons—spawn of a shadow."

"Ma-lunj-un," she repeated phonetically. "Is that a surname?"

"Go talk to a crow or a mountain lion or a hare on a full moon night, and you'll have talked to a Melungeon."

"You're playing word games with me. Unless you start being more forth-coming, I'm leaving and so is my money."

The driver's side door creaked open. One leg exited the truck, but the elderly man obviously couldn't move as quickly as he wished. Seconds later, a siren began to wail.

Damn! Alma thought. Her eyes picked up the police car on an adjacent road and she stepped toward the truck. "Don't be alarmed," she said.

He kicked the door wide open, knocked her to the ground, and grabbed the bag. She held onto it tightly.

"You!" he said, getting a look at her face. He drew back. "Didn't count on it bein' you."

"You know me?" She sat up, still unable to see enough of his face for iden-tification. The police car turned onto the cemetery road.

He reached down and fastened a hand around her wrist. "Hurry up," he yelled. "We got to run." He pulled her toward the truck as his other hand clamped onto the bag.

"Stop!" she yelled, struggling to back away, but the only way she could break his grasp was to let go of the money.

The old man clutched it to him, jumped into the truck, and sped off past the police car.

Grady emerged from the cruiser, and Alma had to fight the urge to slap him. "He was about to tell me!" she shouted. "He knew me!"

Grady clicked on a flashlight and dropped to one knee beside the spot where the man had gotten out of the truck. He ran his fingers through the grass at the edge of the road, pushing aside the wood shavings that had dropped from the whittling. "I was watching with night goggles," he snarled. "There's a reason why he could tell you everything you wanted to know *and* let you identify him." He held up a wooden device with a thin wire strung between the handles. He let it sway before her eyes like a pendulum. "He was about to strangle you."

As stunned as Alma was, she couldn't let herself give in to Grady. "You don't know that was his." She turned away and looked down the road after the disappearing truck.

"You should have listened to me. Coming out here by yourself was stupid."

"Stupid? I just learned more about Allafair than you've been able to turn up in years!" Her fury erupted. "I might have learned more if you didn't have such a Lone Ranger complex!" She put two pinkie fingers at each side of her mouth and whistled. Over the hill galloped the silhouette of a pack of dogs. Within seconds, Caesar, the German shepherd, stood at attention, ready for orders.

"Sitzen," Alma said in German, the language used to train police dogs. Caesar sat and looked up at her, awaiting a command. The other dogs followed suit, except for the Chihuahua, who took some extra time to figure out what was going on. "Those dogs will take down a man at the sound of my voice," she growled. "You should know. Vernon was training Caesar for you."

Grady laughed out loud at the motley crew. "Yeah, until we found out he was terrified by the sound of gunfire."

His amusement infuriated her even more. "Stop it," she said, but his laughter continued. "Vernon's worked with Caesar. He's as brave a dog as . . ." She curled her small hand into a fist, ready to strike the amused man before her, but the trembling Chihuahua approached and rubbed against her leg like a cat. "You're not supposed to be here," she said, picking up the dog and petting the top of its head. "One thing is for sure; I'll never see that old man again or the money."

Grady moved to stand beside her, and she noticed that his expression was more hopeful than relieved. He pointed to the night goggles hanging around his neck. "I got the license number." He smiled. "We still going to the high school reunion tomorrow night?"

"This is a big joke to you, isn't it?" She didn't wait for him to answer, but instead headed for her car with the dogs in tow. "That truck will be dumped and set on fire by dawn. Next time, help me a little less!"

"Fine!" he called after her. "You don't want my help, I won't give it!"

The pain in his voice shot through her like an arrow. She halted. *Turn around,* she told herself. *Turn around and talk to him.*

71

She walked on.

"You don't need me at all! You don't need me anymore than all these dead people out here!"

She had been too hard on him. A line had been crossed, and she knew it. She felt it in her gut like a punch. *Reach out to him,* a voice inside of her said. She walked forward again, and again, continuing until she reached her car and loaded all the dogs into the back. She couldn't make herself turn around or reach out to him. She couldn't let herself need him.

Grady trailed behind her in his cruiser until she turned into the hollow. She breathed a sigh of relief when he didn't follow her. She was still fighting the anger; anger that shouldn't have been directed at someone who had probably just saved her life. At the same time though, his determination was equal to hers. She loved him for it as much as she hated him.

After telling Jefferson about the night's events, Alma fell into bed and into a kaleidoscope of troubled dreams. In all of them, she followed Esau Bashears up a mountain trail. She kept the back of her father's head in sight but could never catch up to him, and, despite her frantic calls, he would not turn around.

14

"Eureka!" Alma shouted. After an hour on the Internet, she had found it. She had checked every possible spelling in databases for the yellow and white pages and determined that "Melungeon" was not a proper name. After several hours of clicking icons and tracking links that led nowhere, she tried a spelling that produced a website and a few thesis abstracts about a group of people who inhabited a mountain ridge in Eastern Tennessee.

"At least I'm in the neighborhood," she muttered to herself. Sheba, the calico cat, jumped onto her lap, and Alma plunged on with her detective work.

After another hour of reading, she was left with a potpourri of legend and fact. As early as the 1750s, an ethnic enclave had occupied Hancock County, Tennessee, and by the 1890s, they were pushed to the top inferior lands of Newman's Ridge. Once classified as "free people of color," they were disenfranchised and, thus, could not testify against Caucasians. The ruling made their valley easy pickings for white settlers. The origin of their unique bloodline couldn't be linked to Native Americans, Africans, or white Americans.

That was where legend began. Reports of reddish-brown complexions, as well as white skin, caused their contemporaries to consider them inhuman, if not demonic.

"Spawn of the shadow," Alma whispered, remembering the old man's words. She stood up and stretched, sending the cat scampering. Checking her calendar, she realized she wouldn't have time to go to Newman's Ridge for at least another month.

The information didn't bring her any closer to finding the old man, but it did give her a direction for finding out more about Allafair. *Keep focused on the prize,* she thought as she padded down the stairs, still in her slippers and robe, even though it was nearly 6:00 p.m. She made a peanut butter and jelly sandwich, then checked the answering machine. No messages.

Picking up a glass of milk, she carried it, along with the sandwich and the phone, out to the deck. The cats followed. She settled into a lawn chair wishing she had some ice cream.

Chocolate. Ben and Jerry's Cherry Garcia. Damn it!

She bit into the sandwich and told herself to *stop thinking about Grady. He'll call when he calls. If he calls,* went through her head. The phone rang and she nearly spilled the milk as she dumped her food on the picnic table and hit the speaker button.

"Hello," she said nonchalantly.

"I thought you'd be in the office today," Jefferson said.

"I can take an occasional Saturday off if I want," she shot back, holding in her disappointment.

"Just as long as you're not out trekking through graveyards."

When she didn't laugh, he cleared his throat and the sound of flipping pages followed. "I found what a Melungeon is," she said.

"So did I. Seems Joddy Paradise had some dealings with them, too. His great-grandfather was a clerk to Lewis Shepherd."

"I was just reading about that," she said. "1872, it came to be known as the 'Celebrated Melungeon Case' and thereafter affected the laws involving them."

"It was a long shot, but brave, even genius to argue that these unique people were descendants of early Carthaginians."

"He won his case and the Melungeon girl kept her land, but let's come forward a century," she prodded. "What do Joddy Paradise's files have for me?"

"Well," he drawled as if about to tell a long story, "it seems that Isham and many of his relatives were part of a group who lived among the Melungeons."

"At Newman's Ridge?"

"No, they were a more cloistered group. By the 1970s, the Newman's Ridge Melungeons had begun to spread out—even mixed with the races that lived in the valley below, if I may generalize. The Pollyhollow sect was organized around a doctrine."

"Are you saying they were a cult?"

"No, not exactly." He inhaled a deep breath as if trying to understand at the same time he was explaining. "They brought in like-minded people to live with them, but whatever it was they believed isn't in Joddy's notes."

"Could be as simple as banding together to protect their land interests."

"Considering what ended up happening to Pollyhollow, that makes sense."

"But you think there's more?"

"I'm not even sure Joddy understood it. Listen to what he wrote in 1975." Jefferson shuffled some papers, then read: " '*The more I learn about them, the more arcane they become. Isham sits there on the mountainside like a gate-keeper; no, a guardian, a guardian of the entrance. The mystery behind the gate stays out of reach to us common folk—and we are that in their eyes, despite our superior proclamations—that's the way their land retains its power. There will be no reassurances of fact here, only the allure of enigma, but when I look into their eyes, I see a wisdom I cannot articulate.* '" Jefferson huffed out a cynical breath. "I knew Joddy Paradise like a father. He never spoke of these people to me."

"I don't suppose he left directions to Allafair's kinfolk."

Jefferson yawned. "Tomorrow's mission; another six boxes. Right now, I've got to jump in the shower and get dressed."

"For what?" she asked.

"For what?" he repeated incredulously. "I have to take Trina to your high school reunion. Don't tell me you're not going."

She hawed and moaned. "I forgot, and I don't really feel—"

"You can't do this to me. Every time I escort my dear sister, Trina, to one of these things, she tries to fix me up with Okie Lee Clover."

"She's cute," Alma said. "She had a nose job."

"I'll remember that when we christen our son Pinocchio."

She heard him knocking his fist on the desk and looked at her voice mail light. Still no messages. Grady hadn't called. "I think maybe I'll stay home."

"I'd even put up with seeing you and Grady dance close."

Her silence must have alerted Jefferson to a problem because he blew a long, slow whistle that said he knew something was wrong. "He's still a little peeved about last night," she admitted.

"He'll get over it," Jefferson said in a totally bored tone of voice.

"I don't know," she said. "Maybe not this time. I was pretty quarrelsome."

"That's what he likes about you."

She smiled. "Jefferson, I might have gone too far this time."

"You want me to talk to him?"

"That's the last thing Grady would respond to. We have to work this out ourselves—I mean, *I* have to work it out . . . I have to let myself trust him a little more."

Jefferson held his silence, but seemed to understand. "Come on," he said softly. "It he doesn't show up, you can dance with me."

"Just like high school."

"Can you do one thing for me?" he asked.

"Of course."

"I left my favorite cummerbund at Granddad's after Sheila got married last month. Can you bring it?"

"Sure. See you there," she added and hung up. All three cats had milk mustaches and the peanut butter that had oozed over the edges of the bread was tracked across the table in paw prints. "How did this happen to me?" she asked.

* * *

Alma showered and changed into eveningwear, then checked her messages again. Nothing from Grady. She finally called his number and got the answering machine, but left no message. She called the police station and discovered that he had left the office around 4:00 p.m. She tried his cell phone. No answer. A nervous wave twisted in her stomach. She deserved this. She should have been more understanding with him last night. After all, everything he did, he did for her.

She got in the car and drove away from the hill, deciding to go by his apartment. If he was there, she would beg like a desperate defense attorney and talk him into a slow dance. She bypassed Jefferson's grandfather's house by accident, then backed up and parked. She found Esridge Bingham and Uncle Ames target shooting in the backyard.

"His mother picked up his cummerbund a week ago," Esridge said. "Jefferson doesn't know, but she hates that color of lime and he's worn that rag for the last fifteen years. It's probably found its way to the trash heap by now." He held up a .357 magnum and pulled the trigger. A teardrop-shaped orange flash erupted from the muzzle and the pressure wave spread over Alma's face.

"That packs a little power," she said, wiping her cheeks after the blast.

" 'Course it was his favorite, but she didn't listen."

"Then I guess he's bund-less tonight."

Uncle Ames held up his own .44 magnum, aimed at a target, and fired. A whitish cloud wafted around them like cigarette smoke and dissipated. Alma batted her hand through it as she inhaled the acrid smell of burnt powder.

"I just love your guys' 'Dirty Harry' night."

She turned back toward her car. "Have a good time," Esridge called out. Uncle Ames waved before taking aim at the target.

15

A Phil Collins rendition of "You Can't Hurry Love" blared from the Contrary High School Auditorium. Alma tried to remember if that was the class song. In many ways high school was a blur to her. About all she could think of at the age of seventeen was getting out—not only out of school, but out of town. From the distance she read a sign over the east doorway: *Class of '82, Yearly Reunion.*

She hesitated at the corner of the building and looked at her reflection in a chrome window frame. Her black hair in a French twist suited her lean features, but the blush makeup only enhanced the growing purple bruise on her cheek. She took a tissue from her purse to blend in the plum color. For a few seconds she stared directly into her bloodshot eyes. *Great,* she thought, and considered going home. She had waited outside Grady's apartment for an hour. She had called his cell phone and got his voice mail. She called the police station, but he hadn't returned. Where was he? Guilt flooded her. How often could she criticize his every decision and not expect a backlash? "No," she whispered to herself. "We'll work it out." She looked down at the cracked sidewalk and realized she was standing in a muddy puddle that wet the toes and heels of her silver suede shoes. *It's dark inside,* she thought. *No one will notice.* She sucked in a deep breath as she smoothed the folds of her lavender dress and headed toward the reunion, ready to step into the past. Grady would meet her there and they could discuss the future.

"Alma!" Trina Bingham squealed as she entered. "I drive all the way from Pineville and you don't show up until 9:30." Her arm circled Alma's shoulder and she steered her toward a long table filled with sodas and bottled water. "You're not going to believe how skinny Nora Hinley is. It made me feel so bad I ate an extra slice of Derby pie." She held out the last piece, offering it to Alma.

"Upset stomach." Alma smiled and also declined a glass of punch.

"It was so good of your mother to do the catering."

"Aunt Joyce does the cooking. Momma's better at the presentation." Alma felt a swell of pride at the compliment. "She does seem to have found a niche for herself."

"Look over yonder at her. She's just the queen bee."

Merl wore a low-cut pink smock and darted behind the tables to ensure all the food trays were fill. Her hair was dyed a soft ash blond for the occasion, so light it matched Trina's natural color. Alma quickly surveyed the rest of the room when Trina looked the other way. Grady was nowhere in sight.

They strolled toward the auditorium, where a strobe light made the dancers appear to move in slow motion. Willie Nelson's "Always on My Mind" began to play, and the lights clicked into wide spotlights of pink and blue. Alma peered through the darkness but didn't move into the crowded areas of the room. Trina noticed her hanging back and leaned into her.

Alma spoke before Trina could pull her toward a ring of alumni who motioned for them to join their group. "There's a lot more people here than last year," she said to interrupt the awkward silence. "It was a good idea to do this every year rather than every ten."

Trina was quiet, sipping an iced tea and studying Alma. "Call me nosy if you want, but you look like you'd rather be at an IRS audit."

"Headache," Alma pointed to her forehead and waved her hand as if to dismiss it. "Where's Jefferson?" she asked quickly to cover a nervous shiver. "I have bad news about his cummerbund."

The music swelled with an eighties rock beat and Trina spoke loudly to be heard above the din. "Jefferson said he'd be here in time for the speeches, but he's late as a snake . . . again."

Alma smiled to reassure Trina but sensed something was amiss. She hoped Jefferson wasn't out searching for Grady to talk about her problems. "Probably too embarrassed to be seen with the class that graduated behind him. You remember how they were."

"Arrogant, mean-spirited, and little quick on the trigger." Trina laughed, taking aim with her thumb and forefinger. "Uh-oh," she said, the sounds slipping out her mouth unexpectedly.

"What?" Dread filled Alma like a mountain slide bearing down on her.

"Elaine sighting."

"What's she doing here?" Alma said under her breath and turned her face toward the wall.

"I guess she's somebody's date," Trina said sheepishly.

"Grady's?" Alma asked. "Tell me, did she come with Grady?"

"Honey, I don't know. I haven't seen him all night. Besides, why would he be here? He graduated from some podunk place up north."

"Trina, don't you leave my side." Alma took her arm. "I have an irrational fear that I might slug Elaine."

"I'm sorry, Alma; this is one triangle I can't take sides in." Trina shifted away to distance herself. "You know her daddy owns the company I work for, and they don't think a minute about using that."

"Maybe I'll go to the lobby and see how Momma's doing."

"Good idea. I can at least run interference." Trina moved behind Alma and raised her voice to a high-pitched squeal. "Elaine Bartholomew, what in the world are you doing here? You graduated at least two years behind me."

"Five," Elaine said as Alma safely stepped out of the auditorium.

The fluorescent lights tinged the lobby with a green haze and the loud beat of the music from inside filled her hearing with white noise. Her mother was at the end of a long food-filled table issuing orders to white-coated workers.

"But Merl," she heard a teenage girl say, "if we put the cakes out now, nobody will finish the food."

"Mrs. Bashears when we're on duty," her mother instructed and wagged her finger underneath the girl's nose. "Save Merl for when we're slicing carrots, understand?"

Rather than argue, the girl nodded and headed toward the other end of the table, balancing a platter holding a pink icing cake.

"Momma," Alma called out. "Can I talk to you?"

"Can't you see I'm busy?"

Alma nodded and nervously looked behind her. "Just wanted to say you're doing a terrific job."

Merl stopped as though she had jammed on car brakes and whirled on the heels of her shoes, adjusting her dress in the same motion. "Okay, what's wrong?"

"Nothing."

"Don't you nothing me. The day you give me compliments, you either need your house cleaned or somebody's slipped you a Mickey."

"That cliché went out with twentieth century detective movies." Alma smiled. She fidgeted with a strand of hair falling on her forehead and pressed her lips together. "Seen Grady?"

"He's not with you?"

Alma hesitated and glanced around to make sure no one was listening. "A small disagreement. I hoped he'd calm down and meet me here."

Merl glanced at her watch, then concentrated on Alma. "It's only 9:45." A clash of dishes from the other end of the table distracted her and she gestured at the workers to clean things up. "Stop worrying. He'll show up. You know how a police chief's schedule is." She stepped closer and took hold of Alma's arm just above the elbow. "Now, go in there and dance. Let him see you can have a good time without him. He'll see what he stands to lose."

Alma halfheartedly smiled as her mother strutted away with a bowl of potato salad balanced in one hand and a basket of biscuits against her hip. She picked up a handful of sliced celery, amazed at how simple Merl could make relationships sound, as if it were only a matter of manipulation. Her and Grady's bad times were as intense as their good times, and their fights were the stuff of legends. Yet one of them would always call the other and it seemed that, whoever picked up the phone, the other was sitting there hoping for the call. She bit into a celery stick, strolled down a hallway filled with displays of sports trophies, opened an exit door, and stepped outside.

The brisk mountain air gave her a shiver. A deep breath filled her senses with the smell of misty rain mixed with green pine, a relief from the hot days. The parking lot lights shined on the road leading up to the high school. She moved away from the building and the beat of the music faded, replaced by a gentle hum of the building's air-conditioning system. The shadow of a man appeared on the far wall and she watched it, biting into her lower lip. *Please, let it be Grady,* she thought.

Aaron Fletcher, the school's security guard, rounded the corner. She waved at him and he slowly paced toward her. "I just finished reading the *Crimson County Sun* article about the Luftin trial," he said, referring to the case she finished just before Quincy Pollard took her hostage. "You did a heck of a prosecution."

"With a lot of help," she said. "Chief Forester and his detectives didn't let anything get by them."

"Yeah, well," he hawed, "you're the best commonwealth attorney in the state and a lot of us are afraid we're going to lose you."

"Lose me?"

"I suspect you been eyeing the attorney general slot."

Alma shook her head vigorously. "No, no, no, no, no. There're enough politics in Crimson County to do me for the rest of my life. The last thing I need is state shenanigans."

"Well, I guarantee people have noticed you." He smiled and shook his finger in the air. "Don't be surprised if some state bigwigs come calling."

Alma chuckled, flattered by the praise and, for a few seconds, her ambition sparked as she envisioned herself being Kentucky's attorney general. Her reverie was interrupted when she stared over Aaron's shoulder. Elaine Bartholomew emerged from the lobby; her head swung in both directions.

Alma turned quickly to Aaron. "Is the upstairs deck open?" If Elaine came out there to meet Grady, she would see it firsthand.

"Use that side staircase," he said. "The moon's half-full and looks like a wide-toothed smile."

Alma thanked him and shot up the staircase that twisted around the building. She paused at the first landing, stared blankly at dark towering mountains. *What am I doing out here, spying like a woman scorned?* Above her the stars reflected like sugar sprinkled on the deep purplish sky. A colossal half-full moon resembling a huge Christmas ornament tipped the mountaintop. *I have to trust him,* she thought.

"There you are," a voice said from behind her.

Alma's throat constricted as if someone had grabbed her. She turned halfway as Elaine climbed the stairs and circled round to face her.

"I'm surprised you showed up for this," Elaine said in a singsong voice as she ran her hand through her deep brown hair, cut in an early Princess Diana style. She leaned on the banister to stare up at the moon. Her angular horsy features were the kind that photographed well, but seemed cartoonish with her toothy overbite. "I'm here with Grady."

"No, you're not," Alma said calmly, determined to avoid the trap.

"Seen him out here?"

"Grady didn't graduate from this high school, so why would he be at a reunion unless he came with someone from the class of '82?"

Elaine's eyes darted back and forth as she swallowed and bit down on her full lower lip. "He's doing the security," she said. "I'm supposed to meet him here 'cause it's faster than us catching up with each other at our little dance joint."

"I don't believe you, Elaine." Alma walked away. She halted after a few steps, unable to resist the impulse to turn back. "If Grady wants to be with you, I'm not stopping him."

"You act like I don't know who I'm sleeping with." Elaine's lips curled into a slight sneer.

"When you're down on your knees in public places as much as you are, I'm surprised you can keep track." Alma turned to leave, but Elaine grabbed her, jerking her back. "Let go of my arm."

"What are you going to do? Prosecute me?" She pushed Alma backward, ripping the bodice of her dress, and in the next instant, Elaine raised her fist.

Alma blocked the blow with an upraised arm and caught Elaine by the hair, twisting her backward so she couldn't strike out again. "Are you ready to stop this?"

"Alma!" Aaron Fletcher yelled from below. He flew up the stairs, followed by two policemen, Detective Henry Moody and Officer Todd Weaver.

They arrived at the top landing, and Elaine took the opportunity to hold one arm against her chest, put one hand on her forehead and pant in short distressed gasps. "Did you see what she did?" she demanded.

"Oh, save it," Alma mumbled out of the side of her mouth. To her surprise, all three men pushed past Elaine, posed so obviously as the victim.

"You need to come with us," Detective Moody said.

Alma's brow wrinkled in a frown when she realized the police were there for professional reasons. Moody was the senior detective, the first to be called on homicides; it must be a very serious crime scene if they wanted her right away.

Todd Weaver stood back, almost teetering on the top step; it was obvious that he wanted to keep his distance. "How could you do it?" he asked.

Alma looked at him, thinking she must have misheard. "Do what?"

"Not now," Detective Moody growled.

Hair on the back of Alma's neck spiked. "What happened?" she demanded.

"Boy, you're one to ask," Weaver said. The distraught tone of his voice wavered until it broke. "The best police chief this town's ever had, and you had to shoot him."

"Grady's . . . " Her own voice disappeared as she processed the man's words. "Take me to the hospital."

"We can't," Detective Moody said.

"Now!" Alma insisted.

"He's dead!" Weaver announced.

Elaine screamed an "Oh my God," backed up against a wall and slumped onto the stairs. Her sobs pierced the evening like the call of a distressed bird.

Alma's muscles cramped head to foot; she was sure they would shatter if touched. She held to the railing to steady herself. "How?" she managed.

Henry Moody moved to stand beside her and rubbed her arm. "You know I hate to do this," he said. "I'm just doing my job, Alma. You know I have to ask some questions."

"Of course, I know," she said between gasps of breath. "I insist on it. We must, you have to . . . eliminate suspects so . . . find who did this."

"Where have you been tonight?" he started.

"You might as well tell us," Weaver said before she could respond. "We're checking your wheels right now—if you've been some place off the main road, we'll know it."

"What are you talking about?" Alma asked. She wished desperately that she could turn away from them; her face showed too much emotion. "Does this have something to do with someone I prosecuted?"

Detective Moody pushed the younger officer back with a stern look that acknowledged the turmoil of the situation. "We need you to clear some things up," he said, keeping his voice calm, almost mellow.

"We know about the fight with Grady in Pearl's Cafe," Weaver said, "and we all heard about how you treated him at the Pollard crime scene after he saved your life."

Moody put a hand on his shoulder, prompting Weaver's silence but not affecting his own focus on Alma. "We know you didn't arrive here until after 9:00 p.m. They were shot between five and eight o'clock and I need to know where you were because—"

"They?"

The men glanced at each other as if her surprise was disconcerting, then Weaver's eyes narrowed as he scrutinized her. "We've seen this charade as many times as you have," he said as if she were a con artist. "Don't act like you don't know Jefferson Bingham was with him."

Alma's hand covered her mouth and her chest muscles contracted, an explosion of shock invading every part of her body. "Don't say he's—"

"He's critical," Moody said, "before he went unconscious, he said, 'Alma, Alma, no, don't do this.'"

"No," Alma said, hearing her voice as if it were far away. She realized she was holding her breath and, with some effort, exhaled. The smiling moon cleared the top of the mountain and she stared into the massive half-disk as if it were a broken mirror. Then she turned to Aaron Fletcher, who stared downward. The two police officers followed his gaze. She looked down as well. All of them were staring at her muddied shoes.

16

Alma leaned her forehead against the cold metal bars of the Contrary jail cell. A night in prison left her exhausted and sore from trying to sleep on a single-layer foam mattress. One odd thought kept playing in her mind: how much bail she might be worth? She stared at the brown tile floor, unconsciously making patterns out of the scuff marks. When she checked the clock mounted high above the door of the guard station, only twenty minutes had passed. Breakfast—scrambled eggs, grits, biscuits, four slices of bacon, and watery black coffee in a Styrofoam cup—remained untouched as she waited for her attorney, Bob Krauss, to arrive.

Why had this happened? Her mind hadn't accepted the fact that Grady was dead—gone forever, and that Jefferson might die, also. What details she knew were sketchy and, she suspected, more rumor than fact. Jefferson and Grady were at Isham Thunderheart's cabin. A camper heard yelling, gunfire, and then found the bodies when he investigated. Grady was shot in the chest. It looked as if Jefferson was running when a slug to his shoulder took him down. The critical damage came from a second bullet—a fragment that was lodged in his brain.

She pressed a hand to her forehead. How could this have happened? From the beginning of her relationship with Grady, their lives burned in a passionate tangle. The last week had built to a point of no return, and it all focused around her past . . . a past that kept her from building a future.

A low humming came from the opposite cell. Wanda Luftin raised her Styrofoam coffee cup as if to toast Alma. "Want some?" she asked, leaning forward on the top bunk and offering her drink.

Alma prosecuted Wanda for poisoning her mother-in-law. She was now awaiting transport to the state women's correction facility but seemed more curious than vindictive at seeing the commonwealth attorney of Crimson County in a jail cell.

"Hey," Wanda said, jumping down from the bunk, "my wig's off to you. You did something I didn't manage." She pushed her face between the bars. " 'Course my mother-in-law deserved a killin'. I ain't sure what them two fellas did to you." She held onto the bars and swung herself to and fro. "The cops say unrequited love." Leaning her head back, she released the bars, then twirled around playfully. "Family stuff, it's what gets all of us in the end."

Alma moved to the far side of the cell and stared out the window. Resting her chin in the palm of her hand, she leaned as far into the window as she could. The anguish of her situation ached like scalded skin. *How could this have happened? How could it have happened to her?* When she first came back to her hometown of Contrary, Kentucky, her family needed her. Now, she needed them.

Accused of shooting two people she would have given her life for— Jefferson Bingham, her lifelong best friend who now lay in a hospital clinging to life; and Grady Forester, the man she loved, soon to be sent home for burial in a faraway state—a funeral she wouldn't be able to attend. She went through the reasons why the two men might have been at Isham's cabin. Maybe Jefferson found something in Joddy Paradise's files. No. He would have come to her first. Why would they have gone there together?

Grady questioned how much I loved him, she thought. The bitter memory of him throwing the silver framed photograph of them out the window was burned into her memory. He died thinking that she didn't trust him. She drew in deep breaths and tried to hold back tears. But inside, every bone, muscle and nerve seemed fractured. It wasn't a dream. She had been arrested for murder.

The blue sky breaking through a thick white fog gave her spirits a small lift and, beyond, she could see the side of the mountain erupting through a tightly-woven forest of pine, poplar, oak, and maple trees. Maybe the town wouldn't believe it of her. Maybe they would know that she could never be responsible for such a heinous act.

Just past 8:00 a.m., shop owners began sweeping the sidewalks. A yellow school bus stopped to pick up some grade school students waiting on a corner. Donny Preston stood in the center of the intersection waving his arms frantically as he did every morning and, though Alma couldn't hear him, she knew his speech by heart: *It's the end of the world. Come now to the Savior and repent your sins. The end is at hand and you who are not clean of spirit or pure of heart will know the fires of hell. Burn! Burn! For you will suffer. It's the end. The end of the world.*

The solid clang of metal doors startled her and she turned to see Bob Krauss approach her cell. He was a stout man in his late fifties who walked with a deliberate sense of purpose. His stunning blue eyes peered beneath heavy eyebrows; a lionish mane of slate-colored hair framed his face. Krauss was a maverick, the best criminal attorney in the southeastern United States. He represented every kind of client, ranging from corporate informers to war crimes retaliation and had argued in front of the Supreme Court three times in his thirty-year career. Although he lived in Knoxville, he assured her that he would stay in Contrary until her situation was cleared up. Alma couldn't thank him enough.

The chains on her wrists clinked as she accompanied him down the sterile hall. Those on her ankles caused her to take small steps; she stared at the floor.

Bob glanced away, sensing her humiliation. "This'll be over soon," he said in a low voice. "Don't worry. I'll have you out of here today."

Wanda called after her. "I'll save you some shelf space at the state pen, Alma!"

* * *

Alma stared out the window of the courthouse holding room as a guard unlocked the ankle cuffs. Three floors below, a crowd of journalists and camera crews jockeyed for position around the front of the building. They reminded her of minnows who darted for the fracture in the rocks when a heavy-footed hunter crossed a creek. They didn't know she was already inside, brought through the rear entrance to avoid representatives of every TV, radio, and newspaper in the state; members of the media sent to get copy on what they expected would become the trial of the decade. "Do we have a commonwealth attorney who practices murder on the side?" a morning editorial had already speculated.

She changed from the prison jumpsuit into a camel-color suit and combed her ebony, shoulder-length hair. The female guard handed her a makeup kit. At first she declined, and then decided a bit of blush would cover the hollows in her cheeks. As she waited, she pressed her hands deeply into the jacket pockets. So much of the last week felt unreal—like a parallel world where everything was the antithesis of the one she knew.

"Ready?" the female officer asked as she nodded toward the door. "The staircase is clear. Let's get up there."

Policemen lined the hallway—all there to get a look at her, she realized. Her cheeks burned as she passed them, taking in their hesitant stares trying to assess her guilt. She nodded at each group, but was disheartened when most looked away, unable—or unwilling—to meet her gaze. Relief spread through her as she entered the back stairwell.

The two guards paused on the landing outside the door while a policeman checked for reporters who might be hiding in the corridor. Several staircases below, footsteps began running toward them. The pounding sent an adrenaline rush up Alma's spine. She and the officers exchanged glances, and one of them descended to stop the intruder. As the man turned the corner, Alma recognized her brother, Vernon. "It's okay," she said to the policemen, then realized that she was in no position to tell them what they should or shouldn't allow.

"I thought I was gonna be late," he said, huffing up another set of steps. "My last trip to Claiborne County today," he added proudly. "I'm a free man. Probation is over."

She motioned for him to come stand next to her. The guard though, kept him one staircase down. "It's as much as I can allow, Ms. Bashears."

Alma nodded and indicated for Vernon to stay put. "Just in time to trade places with me, I'm afraid."

Her brother looked sporadically at the floor, and then up at her. His shoulders hunched, making his six-foot frame seem large and uncomfortable in the linen suit. He was a man unaccustomed to dressing up, and his large hands showed ragged scars from working with the dogs. "You know better than to compare," he said, struggling to hold a slight smile. "You ain't nothing like me."

Alma returned to Contrary five years earlier to defend Vernon on a first-degree murder charge engineered by Walter Gentry and his mother. Alma and Bob Krauss forced the case to another jurisdiction and argued that the death occurred as a result of self-defense, drawing only an involuntary manslaughter charge for which Vernon received probation. Her brother was the wild one in the family, but he was no murderer. "You look real good, Vernon," she said awkwardly, wishing she could reach out and touch him.

"The whole family's in here, Alma; even Mamaw. We'll stand behind you, no matter what."

Alma felt a tremble in her chest as she continued toward the courtroom. Not so much from nervousness, but from Vernon's *"no matter what."* Did they doubt her? Could her family possibly think she might have done this?

17

The acting commonwealth attorney stood. Craig Carr unbuttoned his jacket as he rounded the table, with a slight nod in Alma's direction. "Your Honor, the state is here today only as a matter of due process. Because of Ms. Bashears' connection to this county's office, the police thought it conscientious to hold her. After assessing the evidence just this morning, I am dismissing charges pending further investigation." He handed Judge Mary Dulaney a manila file.

A swell of relief roared through Alma, even though she knew there was still a long road to travel. Bob Krauss stepped forward, his leonine mane of silvery hair shimmering under the florescent lights. His face, with its expression of wisdom and worry, made him seem more like a concerned grandfather. Alma knew different. Krauss was thinking every minute, and it bolstered her confidence. He cleared his throat before he spoke. "I would also ask Your Honor to consider that the evidence in this case points directly, succinctly, and a bit too conveniently to my client."

Judge Dulaney looked up from the file and even Alma held a small breath. "You're saying?"

"That somewhere in this town is a cold-blooded murderer." Bob pointed out the window at a side view of the main boulevard. "It looks so safe. But walking down that street is a person who struck down Jefferson Bingham, a good friend of mine and the best friend of my client since primary school, and took the life of a much respected police chief, who was also Ms. Bashears' partner."

A pathetic wail came from the back of the room. Alma recognized Elaine's cries. "She killed him! He didn't want her so she killed him!"

The crack of Judge Dulaney's gavel struck sharply. "Order."

Alma didn't dare look back, knowing direct eye contact would spur Elaine on to more histrionics. She knew what Bob was doing. Even when she walked out of here today, public sentiment would be against her if it weren't stressed that the police overreacted. He was infusing some reality into the situation, so it would not appear as if her own office was letting her off the hook. Another of Elaine's wails pierced the air.

"Shut your stupid mouth." Alma heard her mother's voice.

Elaine continued to sob, and Merl snapped. "Why don't you go down to the Harrogate Playhouse and tell 'em you want to audition for Ophelia?"

Alma turned in her seat. If no one in her family would hush Merl up, then it was up to her. Despite trying to defend her daughter, the outburst would only hurt Alma in the long run. Aunt Joyce though, had already wrapped an arm around her sister-in-law's shoulders and forced her around in her seat.

The sight of her entire family taking up two rows touched Alma like nothing she had ever experienced. Uncle George and Uncle Ames sat stiffly and stoically against the wall; next to them, her sister, Sue, and brother-in-law, Jack; then her cousins, Rodney, Mark, John, and Emma. Finally, there was Mamaw, her tiny frame almost hidden in the sea of people.

Her grandmother ignored the commotion behind her and looked directly at Alma. Mamaw's eyes looked so sad, but her lips parted with the words, "I love you." Alma wanted to cry.

Elaine wheezed and blew her nose exceptionally loudly.

"Remove that woman from the courtroom," the judge ordered.

Elaine didn't wait for the bailiff. She ran toward the exit, sobbing into a tissue.

As usual, Judge Dulaney tolerated no hysterics. "Place an officer at the door," she instructed the bailiff. "I don't want her back in here."

The rustling of the audience filled the room as people shifted in reaction to the judge's stern tone. Merl stared after Elaine with a tight expression that meant she would like to claw her eyes out. Alma knew it must have taken a lot for her mother to remain in her seat; Merl was doing it for her.

"As I was saying," Bob Krauss continued, "from my client's perspective, all that is required is her explanation of what the police have submitted as evidence. Once that has been clarified, I assure you, Your Honor, she will be completely vindicated. Ms. Bashears is the third victim of this horrendous incident. One man dead. Another still unconscious from the attack. Alma has lost the most important men in her life and, if they could, they would be standing here before Your Honor defending her case."

Despite the agony that tore through her at the truth of his words, Alma hid a wry smile. Bob was making sure that everyone knew she had been singled out by a traumatized police department who had lost their respected chief. The need to blame someone was an emotional necessity for them.

Judge Dulaney motioned both lawyers back to their tables and looked at Alma. Her eyes were sympathetic, even though she had never given Alma any special leeway with cases pleaded before her court. She followed the letter of the law, and Alma knew to present her arguments that way. She was unsure if that helped or hurt her in this particular instance. "Mr. Carr, what is the prognosis on Jefferson Bingham?"

Craig handed Judge Dulaney a medical report. "Still critical. He was operated on late last night."

"And his words before he slipped into unconsciousness—'Alma, Alma, no, don't do this!'"

"We simply don't know what the words mean, Your Honor." He hesitated, and then continued. "This was a crisis situation, and I believe the police read more into the statement than Mr. Bingham intended."

"I see your predicament, Mr. Prosecutor. Obviously, Mr. Bingham can settle many issues here."

"All the issues," Bob Krauss joined in. "He will completely exonerate Ms. Bashears."

For the first time, Alma began to feel hopeful. *Of course,* she thought. *Jefferson isn't dead. He'll recover and clear all of this up.*

"I can't see that this matter warrants any more of the court's time." Judge Dulaney looked at Craig, "You can refile if—"

A loud crash against the door caused the entire room to erupt. Alma expected to see Elaine barging in with more accusations.

"Get out of my way!" a female voice said authoritatively. It belonged to a tall, striking woman of about fifty. Her silver hair brushed the top of her shoulders; it looked prematurely gray with a bluish sheen to it. She walked to the front of the courtroom, followed by a male assistant who carried her briefcase. "Your Honor," she said. "I apologize for halting this proceeding, but I will be taking charge of the prosecution."

18

"Judith Drake, Your Honor," she added in a self-assured voice with an edgy timbre. "Special prosecutor appointed by the attorney general." She motioned to the young, brown-haired man behind her and he stepped forward with a handful of documents for the judge.

Craig Carr dropped his pen on the desk with more force than was accidental. "I know nothing of this and object to turning over this case until—"

"Shhh," the judge said as she studied the papers.

"Your Honor," he continued as he stood. "This is Crimson County's jurisdiction, not the State of Kentucky."

"I said, hush," the judge stated harshly.

Bob Krauss stood at the same time as Craig, but the stern admonition made him sit down slowly.

"What's happening?" Alma whispered to Bob.

He shrugged his shoulders and watched the proceedings with the intensity of an eagle spying on small prey.

As the judge read, the stillness of the courtroom held like the upswing of an amusement park ride about to peak and fall with a ferocious velocity. Alma glanced back at her family. Their worried expressions were laced with confusion and she hoped that she was able to hide her own—at least for their sake. A young, petite blond woman with a mass of unruly curls scooted into the row beside Mamaw and busily wrote in a notebook. Alma glared at the reporter, hoping the girl was decent enough not to harass an elderly woman.

She turned forward again and saw Judith Drake scrutinizing her. The woman's caramel-colored eyes narrowed—not the way they might if assessing an opponent—but more like someone whose mind was already made up.

"I don't like surprises," Judge Dulaney said, continuing to study the papers.

"I expected to be here before court went into session," Ms. Drake said. "The drive through the mountains took longer than I expected, so I apologize for the abrupt interruption, but I won't allow you to let this woman walk out of the courtroom."

"You won't allow?" Judge Dulaney looked over her glasses.

Ms. Drake hesitated for a moment, appearing to realize that her state authority wasn't going to be as easily accepted as she expected. "This woman shot down two unarmed people—one a law enforcement officer." She stepped closer to the table and used both hands to point out Alma. "Your Honor, Alma Bashears is supposed to represent the best of our state. She *is* the law and yet she has defiled it in the worst way. Her actions mean to show there is one law for you and me and another for herself. The evidence in this case is undeniable—her fingerprints are on the murder weapon."

"What are you taking about?" Alma stood up, her hand slapping the table without meaning to. "If the case against me is going to be argued here and now, I demand to be allowed to defend myself."

"Your Honor," Ms. Drake said, "the state attorney general received, by special messenger, a Winchester .22, model 63 with a note stating it was the murder weapon used by Ms. Bashears." She pulled a weapon from a box held by the male assistant and held it above her head.

Alma studied the weapon. Something about the rifle puzzled her. It was an old pump-action model, high quality, lots of hand-fitted parts. The Winchester Company stopped making them after World War II; too expensive. She had even fired one the previous week at the Appalachian Museum. Grady stood beside her and their picture was snapped with the museum rifle between them. There was a dent on the side just like the one . . . she stood up.

"I shot a rifle like that nearly a week ago at the Appalachian Festival. If it's the same rifle, of course my fingerprints are on it." Alma stepped forward as if she were a defense attorney advocating for a client. "There's even a picture of me in the *Contrary Gazette* holding the darn thing."

"She's telling the truth, Your Honor," Craig Carr said. "As I intended to tell the court today, my office is prepared to wait until Jefferson Bingham recovers. As the other person at the scene, he can obviously tell us who shot him—"

"Mr. Carr ignores the fact that her hands tested positive for nitrite." Ms. Drake turned toward Craig with a whisper. "And who signs your paycheck?"

He backed away, stunned by her insult.

Alma moved to his side, while Bob positioned himself between Drake and her assistant. "Mr. Carr has a sterling reputation, Your Honor," Alma said. "He doesn't need to impress anyone." She tossed Judith Drake a glare that could have cut through ice. "I explained to the police that the nitrate on my hands and clothing came from the meeting with my uncle and Jefferson's grandfather. They fired guns while I stood behind them. Both have signed a statement attesting to these facts."

"That there was little nitrite simply means Ms. Bashears made a feeble attempt to wash it off," Judith Drake said. "How convenient that she managed to walk by when relatives were firing guns. It's a manufactured alibi by family members."

"Jefferson's grandfather is not related to me," Alma stated. The *"Amen!"* that came from the back of the audience indicated that some Bingham relatives supported her.

"It is only common sense," Bob continued, as if enjoying the sparing match, "to want to see the ballistics report before considering any further legal action." He gave Alma a supportive glance as if to say Judith Drake was on the run.

"I have no reason to ask you to hold Alma Bashears," Craig said. He turned toward Ms. Drake and offered a slight sneer.

"I can have an office in operation by the end of the week." Judith clasped her hands behind her back and held her breath. "If Your Honor could see yourself delaying this decision until then, and holding Ms. Bashears in custody, I will give you a more complete argument for—"

"I've made my decision," Judge Dulaney said. "Everyone return to your seats." The shuffle that followed was quick and quiet.

Apparently realizing she was in trouble, Ms. Drake turned toward the seating section and spoke to the people as if they were an audience. "We also intend to ask you to excuse yourself from this case . . . " Several people gasped in reply. She hesitated and her expression froze for an instant before she turned back to the judge. "You have sat as judge for nearly all the cases Ms. Bashears prosecuted and she won more than two-thirds of them—"

"Those were jury trials," the judge interrupted.

"You were also her junior high history teacher, were you not?"

The judge didn't answer, but the cherry color of her cheeks indicated her displeasure at being cross-examined in her own courtroom. She shifted in her chair, but did not take her gaze from Judith Drake. "Yes, you could pressure me to remove myself from this case, Ms. Drake, but in the meantime, my ruling is to release Alma Bashears and dismiss the current charges. You can have a grand jury hear your case if you wish, but no charges are going to be filed in this court as a result of the current evidence." She removed her glasses and stared at the special prosecutor, then waved her hands in a dismissive gesture. "Out!" she said harshly. "You have an office to set up."

19

Alma hurried to a waiting car, Bob Krauss on one side of her and Vernon on the other. They managed to avoid most of the press, except for the young blond with the unruly curls and an older man who trotted after them. The girl, faster and more agile, caught up with them.

"Ms. Bashears," she cried out between huffs of breath. "Maggie Armstrong, the *Crimson County Sun . . .* " She gasped another breath. "A quote, can you give me a quote? Were you surprised that all charges were dismissed? Did you know about the special prosecutor?"

The older reporter scrambled up behind her and aimed his camera as Alma dove into the car. "Move it, sister," he told the younger woman, bumping her out of the way. "This is *Gazette* territory."

"Can you tell our readers why we shouldn't believe Elaine Bartholomew?" Maggie Armstrong yelled.

"Wait 'til I get her under oath," Alma snapped back and slammed her car door.

The flash of the camera blinded her as she held up a hand. Bob shoved his way into the rear seat. Vernon floored the gas and drove erratically through a massive traffic jam of more TV vans than she had ever seen in the county. She crouched down on the seat to keep from being recognized. "What are we going to do?" she asked. "This is turning into a nightmare."

"Get your gumption up, Alma," Vernon said. "You don't look good dressed like a crybaby."

His sharp words stunned her, and she sat up straight. *Right,* she thought, *I'm not going to putter around and act guilty.* "Bob," she said over her shoulder. "I want to go to Knoxville, to the hospital. Jefferson is going to need me."

* * *

Coming in out of the heat, the cool corridors at Baptist Hospital of East Tennessee were a welcome comfort. Alma stood with Bob and Vernon beside a wall-size window that looked out over Fort Loudon Lake. Barges slowly maneuvered up the waterway in view of the Sunsphere, a large, gold orb that was built for the 1982 World's Fair. The authentic sun still tipped the top of several buildings, including the historic Andrew Johnson Hotel that now housed Knoxville's local government. Below them, flowering linden trees lined the sidewalks leading in the direction of Neyland Stadium where the University of Tennessee Volunteers played their home games. Alma found herself staring jealously at the relaxed figures on a houseboat as it lounged near the Volunteer Landing. To some people, today was still a normal day.

Behind them the clicking of heels sounded on the linoleum floor. They turned to see Trina approaching, still wearing her party dress from the night before. "Alma," she said, some hesitation in her voice, "only family is allowed in there."

Alma fought off a wounded feeling upon hearing the suspicion in her friend's voice, but told herself not to take it personally. "I'll wait as long as I need to," she said. "I have to be here."

Trina moved to the window. She fought back tears and Vernon put his arm around her as Bob offered her his handkerchief. "I was supposed to pick him up," she said. "If only I'd done that.'

"Why didn't you?" Alma asked, then realized the question sounded accusatory. "What I mean is, I can't figure any reason Jefferson or Grady would go out to Silver Lake."

"All Jefferson told me was that he needed a half-hour to 'tame a lion and find a Maltese falcon,' like he was some knight in shining armor."

Alma looked away, the words reminding her of their conversation earlier that day when she told Jefferson not to talk to Grady on her behalf. What lion would he take on other than Grady, who stayed hidden the entire day like an object of mystery? *Oh, no,* she thought, *he was out there for me.* The guilt that filled her was only increased by more questions. "Do you think—"

"Get out of here," a voice interrupted from behind.

Alma turned to see Jefferson's older sister, Sheila. Her eyes were nearly swollen shut and she squeezed a worn tissue tightly in her hands.

"How are you doing?" Alma asked, her voice lowered to a whisper.

"The last person I need to see today is you."

"Sheila . . . " Trina placed a hand on her sister's arm.

The other woman jerked away and glared at Alma. "His heart stopped three times on the operating table," she said through gritted teeth. "His heart stopped . . . do you understand what that means?"

"Of-of course," Alma stammered, unprepared for the litany of anguish directed at her.

"His heart stopped," Sheila repeated again, this time with a sob of grief.

Trina quickly put an arm around her shoulders and pulled her down the hall. The older sister glanced back only once, a furious expression that couldn't be misinterpreted: *go away.*

20

The August heat filled Mamaw's living room, and open windows only increased the sweltering temperature. Alma scooped the last few ice cubes into a glass of lemonade and handed it to Bob Krauss, who held the telephone with his other hand and listened intently. "Widow of an ambassador," he said loud enough for Alma to hear. One of her nephews peered in, eyed Bob on the phone, then slunk into the next room like a suspicious and curious cat.

"Twelve years with the Department of Justice before moving to Kentucky," Bob said. "She's a little old to be taking on a job like this, don't you think?" As he thanked his informant, Alma rubbed a piece of ice back and forth along her neck.

The stagnant, hot air made her long for her own home up the hill, but when they arrived at the hollow, Judith Drake had already secured a search warrant from another judge, and state investigators were combing through her belongings. "What's this woman's angle?" Alma asked. They stared out the window toward her two-story house high atop the mountain.

"I was hoping you would tell me," Bob said. "She's a little long in the tooth to be a rising star, but she's sure somebody's quarterback."

"I've never heard of her." Alma opened her hands and let them drop to her sides. "What I hate is, I'm sure Jefferson would know her. He knows everybody at the state capitol."

"The word on him is not what we hoped. Doctors induced a coma to try and get the swelling in his brain to go down."

A surge of grief filled her. "Bob, he's got to be all right. He just has to get better." Bob put a hand on her shoulder and Alma sniffed as she struggled to

102

control her emotions.

"Excuse me," said a young boy's voice.

They turned to see her ten-year-old nephew, Larry Joe, holding a pan of crushed ice. "Mamaw says Vernon fixed the fuse so the air conditioner will come on in a minute."

"Thank you, sweetheart," Alma said and petted the top of his head.

"In the meantime, you're supposed to eat this." He held out the ice.

She took it from him and noticed him eyeing the telephone that shared the table with the lemonade pitcher.

"Don't suppose the phone's rung while you've been in here, has it?" he asked shyly.

"No," Alma said, wondering about the curious question as she filled a glass of crushed ice with lemonade. He turned to leave, holding his hands behind him.

Bob wiped a film of sweat from his forehead and loosened his tie. "I've got some calls in to a few Lexington contacts. I'll know more of her story by the end of the day."

"Let's not even wait for that. I want an investigator on her."

"I'll take care of it," he said, and made a note on a legal pad.

"Do you sense something personal about the way she acted today?"

"What do you mean?"

"I don't know exactly," Alma tried to explain. "When she looked at me, it was as if she knew me—well, maybe as if she were after an enemy, not merely prosecuting a case; it was as if convicting me was personally important to her."

"Some prosecutors have to personalize a case in order to be cutthroat. I wouldn't read too much into it." He finished the last of the lemonade as the phone rang.

Alma picked it up. At the same time pounding footsteps hurried up from the basement. "Hello?"

"Is L. J. there?" a young female voice asked.

"There's no one here by that name. You must have the wrong number."

A slight huff of irritation was followed by, "You know—L. J."

"No, I'm sorry." Larry Joe and his younger brother Eddie raced into the room. Both were wide-eyed and expectant, standing so close to Alma that she stepped back.

"L. J." the girl said insistently. "Larry Joe."

"Oohh," Alma said, looking down at the boys. "Yes, I'll get L. J." She handed the receiver to her nephew, who grinned so wide that his face could barely contain it.

Bob Krauss cracked a smile and gestured at Alma to follow him outside. Heat waves shimmered in the distance as dragonflies flitted atop the waist-high bank of honeysuckle that bordered the road and lifted a sweet fragrance into the air. "It's good that some parts of the family stay normal," Bob said. "Alma, the press is going to jumble this like tossed salad. You don't say anything to them unless it goes through me."

She bit her lower lip and blinked several times. "I still can't believe this is happening to me. I'm just so embarrassed."

"It's good you've got the hollow to hide in. I doubt very many reporters will be able to find your place."

"I want so much to see Jefferson and, Bob, how can I not go see Grady's family?"

"Because Judith Drake will take advantage of your devastation." Bob looked down at the floor, his eyes moving back and forth in thought. "There's more at stake here than a simple murder for which you'll be vindicated. Alma, the rest of your life is at stake."

"We both know Jefferson will clear me, right?"

"We have to prove you're innocent rather than waiting for them to prove you guilty." He looked up at the hillside on the far side of the hollow and weighed his words. "Assuming even the best case scenario, where Jefferson recovers a hundred percent and says you didn't do it—the damage is already done. Your career is lost, your reputation crucified. And let's not even discuss the people who will say Jefferson lied because he's in love with you."

His words sent a hurricane of distressing thoughts spinning through Alma's mind. The accusation would cost her everything she had worked for since returning to Contrary. Most importantly, it would taint her good name. "I . . . I guess I've been too preoccupied to think like a lawyer."

"Alma, you haven't even had a chance to grieve for Grady." Bob took her by the shoulders and bent down to gaze into her eyes. "You need to trust me. I'm going to have to do some things that might not make sense to you, but I have my reasons for doing them."

She nodded, hating that Judith Drake, a stranger, had frozen her out of an investigation that she would have overseen like a lioness. One thing was for sure: she wasn't going to waste time waiting for the special prosecutor to convict her. Finding the monster who committed this crime was her first priority. And when she had hold of them, they would pay a high price.

At the mouth of the hollow, Alma's two uncles built a gate to keep out the press and curiosity seekers. Jefferson's grandfather and a brother were helping them. Alma watched, glad they were working together. Neighbors for over sixty years, they sat with each other through births, deaths, and World Wars. In a state caricatured for blood feuds—the Hatfields and the McCoys; the Howards and the Turners; the French-Eversole war—how lucky they were that murder had never crossed their property lines, until now.

After the clash with Sheila earlier that morning, she only hoped the rest of the Bingham family would have a softer view of her. She turned to Bob. "Do whatever you have to. I want this over, so I can find who did this to my friends." He nodded, then exited the house and walked to his car. She watched him drive out of the hollow, passing her mother's car just as it entered.

Alma leaned on the gate across the sidewalk and waited for Merl. Her grandfather had built the house with his own hands. Each of the ten Bashears children left as young adults, and most had also found their way back to the hollow. The roof of her own house, about three-quarters of a mile up the mountain, could be seen above the trees. She tried not to think of what the state police were doing as they went through her possessions. Sometimes she wished she could live like Vernon and have as little personal property as possible. His brown and white trailer sat in the side yard next to Mamaw's house, adjacent to an old barn where chickens, hunting dogs, feral cats, and other assorted animals lived. Grapevines hung from the eaves of the barn, and Vernon's pet possum, Albert, swung from vine to vine, eating all the fruit he could cram into his mouth.

Merl's car pulled into the driveway, with Sue in the passenger seat. Larry Joe, Eddie, and Vernon exited the house at the sound of the slamming car door. Sue called the boys over to help unload groceries. Alma's mother hurried toward her, a determined look on her face and, at the same time, waving for Vernon to come closer.

"Larry Joe's got a girlfriend, Momma!" Eddie shouted.

"Eddie! You promised!" Larry Joe turned and smacked his brother on the arm. "Momma, did you see that?"

"See the sort of refereeing you have to look forward to?" Sue told Alma. "When you have little ones of your own, don't say I didn't tell you so."

Alma knew her sister was trying to be encouraging. They all avoided the subject of her alleged guilt and the consequences. As improbable as a conviction seemed, justice could go wrong and the state could win for all the wrong reasons. Appeals had been known to fail. Occasionally, the innocent were convicted.

"I'm taking Cindy Jane Collier to the Labor Day Dance," Larry Joe said, looking up to his mother for permission.

"Are you going to drive or go by horseback?" she asked, half-teasing.

The obvious anxiety in his small face made Vernon step in. "I'm chauffeuring the lucky couple," he told his sister. "We have a proud tradition of Bashears manhood to uphold." He picked up his nephew, while Eddie ran around in a circle making a noise like an airplane.

"Remember, you said it." Sue pointed a finger in Vernon's face. "And when you're still chauffeuring come senior prom, just remember—"

"I told you so!" Alma, Vernon, and Merl said in unison.

After the laughter ceased, Merl pointed to the car. "You all help your momma with the groceries. I got to talk to Alma and Vernon on important stuff."

Larry Joe squirmed out of Vernon's grasp and stepped up to Alma, taking her hand. "Aunt Alma," he said. "I sure am sorry about your troubles." He heaved out a deep sigh of puppy love and strutted toward the car, holding his head high and proud. "I wouldn't take ten million dollars for Cindy Jane Collier."

Alma was glad to see some normalcy return and the scene lifted her spirits. Even the threat of Judith Drake seemed unable to penetrate the strength of the family's solidarity.

Merl pulled her and Vernon close on either side of her. "I got us an appointment with Aunt Hester. We've got to get there in twenty minutes."

"Oh, Momma. No!" Vernon's face twisted into a scowl. "Not that crazy old lady with the pie-cats?"

"I've never heard of an Aunt Hester," Alma said.

"We're not related to her," he said. "Thank God."

"She kept you from marrying Diane Merts," Merl pointed out, "didn't she?"

"You almost married Diane Merts?" Alma asked, her voice bubbling with amusement.

"Long ago, far away, big mistake," Vernon said as his mother pulled him toward the car. "No, I'm not going." He dug his heels into the ground. "And you better not either, Alma."

"Well—" Alma paused, unsure what was going on "—my lawyer did tell me to stay out of the public eye."

Merl and Vernon looked as if they were playing tug-of-war with his arm. "I'm not going!" he said. "I'm not going!"

21

"Where are we?" Alma whispered out of the side of her mouth. She and Vernon sat next to each other on a couch covered with a frayed chenille blanket. After all of her mother's begging, they had finally consented to see Aunt Hester, and now she wondered what she had gotten herself into. The scent of frankincense was so strong in the room that it could have filled a medium-sized church. Competing with it was the unmistakable stench of cat box odor. She took small breaths and tried not to cough.

Merl occupied a recliner opposite them and petted a large orange cat. Another tabby wound a path around the legs of a couple on a side couch, and calicos, Siamese, and a variety of gray, black, and tiger-stripped alley cats draped themselves on every piece of unoccupied furniture. An elderly woman on the opposite side of Vernon sneezed and quickly apologized.

"No problem," he said. "It's a wonder anybody can breathe in here."

"Shhhh," Merl said, pointing toward the next room, which was closed off by a lace curtain. "She'll hear you."

"Aunt Hester, I presume." Alma covered her mouth with a hand.

"I did warn you."

She was glad to be on the end of the couch next to the door. From time to time, she turned her head and inhaled outside air. She took another deep breath just as music consisting mostly of chimes and bells began to play. Vernon exchanged a tentative glance with her as the lace curtain was pulled aside and in stepped a bone-thin woman with long brown hair parted in the center, dressed in a full-length blue robe. She carried an urn with smoking incense, which she positioned in the center of the room before seating herself in a comfortable looking recliner. A white cat jumped up on the arm of the chair and the woman leaned in and kissed at it. "Hello, Sweet-as-pie, how's my baby?"

"I can't stand this," Vernon whispered from beneath his hand and shifted uncomfortably on the couch.

Alma shot a glance at her mother, mouthing the words *what have you gotten us into?* Merl nodded curtly, as if saying, *pay attention.*

"How's my Cutie-pie?" the woman said to another cat. "And here's Sweet-as-key-lime-pie and Precious-Pie, come to see their momma-cat." As she spoke to each feline, offering it a snack that smelled like raw beef, her speech became slower.

Alma leaned back for another whiff of outside air; the smoky incense seemed to heat up the old house even more. She wiped sweat from the back of her neck; Vernon, on the other hand, had given up. He slumped in his chair, with his arms crossed over his chest, dripping sweat, and a frown on his face that closely resembled a captured bullfrog.

Yes," the woman said, her hands now resting on the arms of the chair and the cats circling at her feet, crawling onto the back of the recliner and all around her. "Yes, I hear you. This is Aunt Hester." Her body became limp. A half dozen cats sat in a semicircle at her feet.

They must be trained, Alma thought suspiciously. The couple opposite Alma leaned forward and the woman nudged the man. "Aunt Hester," he asked, "do you see our child, our little girl?"

Alma looked quickly at Vernon, and a jolt of anger rose in her chest; they were in the hands of a con artist. She wondered how much money Merl paid for the charade.

"I see honey," Aunt Hester said.

"She loved honey," the woman said, clasping the man's hand.

"She wants you to know how happy she is, and that she's well taken care of."

"Can she tell us what happened?" the woman asked.

"She wants you to know that there was nothing you could have done."

The woman stifled a cry, and the man circled his arm around her.

"Let me finish it," Alma said, unable to listen any longer. "She's near water, the number four is somewhere nearby, and train tracks figure in somewhere, but you're unsure how. Does this make sense to you?"

"Our daughter drowned," the man said, looking at Alma. "How did you know?"

She leaned forward to explain why she thought Aunt Hester was a fake, but paused when the psychic's eyes opened wide and she sat upright. "Oh, oh, oh, yes, I see it; she is here."

Aunt Hester swung toward Alma. "There's a man who's passed over. He says to tell you that the other people aren't to blame." She paused, as if listening to words spoken from another world. "It was too late. He just couldn't stop what happened. Does this make sense to anyone?" She repeated the last sentence, then bit her bottom lip, realizing that Alma had previously said the same slick words.

The elderly woman next to Vernon began hacking and wheezing. "Got to go get my inhaler," she said and rose to leave.

Alma took the opportunity to follow her out of the room. "I'll just make sure she's okay," she murmured to Vernon. He grabbed for her, but Alma was already helping the woman through the door. The elderly lady paused on the steps and tried to control a coughing fit. "Are you going to be okay?" Alma asked.

She nodded, holding to her throat. "Just need to get my inhaler from the car. Oh, my Lord, I waited three months to get this appointment with Aunt Hester, and I just can't miss it now." She hurried toward a tan Oldsmobile parked on the side of the road.

Alma walked into a side yard filled with yellow dandelions; a few purple irises grew next to the house. Honeybees darted through the flowers and she carefully stepped through them. She wiped sweat off the bridge of her nose and sought the shade of a maple tree. A bird feeder hung from a limb, but she doubted birds would dare fly into the yard with so many cats around. She lowered herself into a lawn chair and closed her eyes. *A backwoods psychic. My mother brought me to a psychic. What was she thinking?*

"Hello, Sister," came a voice from behind.

Alma turned to see a black-haired little girl standing in the shadows near the corner of the house. She grinned a half smile, her teeth bright white against her brown skin. "Hello," Alma said. "What's your name?"

The little girl shrugged her shoulders but continued to smile shyly; Cherokee, probably, at least half. She held a doll to her chest with equally black curls cascading down its back.

"Well," Alma said, "maybe your doll has a name?"

The girl clutched it tighter and her eyes sparkled as she watched Alma closely. "Sister?" she asked.

Alma cast her a level, nonthreatening look. She had only been called that by people who grew up either in the forties and fifties, or those who still lived in very isolated hollows—like Aunt Hester. In the backwoods, nearly every older person was referred to as Aunt or Uncle and anyone younger was Sister or Brother. "My name is Alma," she said, remaining seated to keep from scaring the child.

The little girl skipped closer to the woods. Her shy smile remained mysterious. "Sister, the answer ye seek is in The Streams of Tyme."

"The streams of time?" Alma repeated.

"The Streams of Tyme."

The front gate scraped across the concrete walk, and Alma turned as the woman returned with her inhaler and made her way back into the house. Startled by the sudden sound, Alma jumped up from the chair so quickly that the blood rushed from her head. In combination with the heat, she staggered dizzily, then steadied herself and, for a moment, fought the sensation that she had been dozing. *No, I was talking.*

She swung back toward the woods. The little girl was gone. "Hello?" she called out. No answer. She walked to the edge of the forest and looked around. There was no sign of the child, although the rear door of the house was ajar. The girl must have gone inside. *Psychic-in-training,* she thought, then she moved into the front yard just in time to meet her mother and Vernon exiting the house.

"I swear to God, I can't take the two of you nowhere without you embarrassing me to death," Merl fussed.

Alma and Vernon stood silently, taking their dose of lecture and knowing it would be a waste of breath to try and convince their mother of the futility of psychic predictions.

"If you'd stayed a little longer, you would have heard," Merl said. "It was about the man who shot Grady and Jefferson, and according to Aunt Hester—"

"Mother!" Alma interrupted. "How can you take someone like her seriously?"

"Listen to me," her mother pleaded. "He wasn't after Jefferson or Grady. He wanted to—"

"Enough!" Alma said, the pain of Grady's death flooding into her voice. "Vernon, take her home. I need to be alone." She shuffled off, glad she had driven her own car.

Merl called after her. "Aunt Hester says he's not done yet, Alma! Listen to me! He's going to kill again!"

22

Alma drove aimlessly. The jewel-green mountains grew taller and deeper. Memories of Jefferson and Grady filled her mind, overflowing the banks of her self-control. The blare of a car horn shook her back to reality. The center line rapidly disappeared under the middle of her car as she swerved back onto her own side of the road.

Pulling into a lot at a restored iron furnace in Cumberland Gap, Tennessee, she opened the car door into a wave of heat and the tangy smell of pine. The forty-foot high pyramid from the mid-1800s was built of gray cut rock. A stream of cold air flowed from the squared-off door. She wiped sweat off her neck as she entered the cave-like opening. The interior stones were burned black. Iridescent streaks of red, green, and blue from limestone, ore and charcoal, shot up toward the chimney stack. The dramatic colors reminded her that metal produced that way had supported early pioneers who couldn't easily transport iron products through the steep mountains. Jefferson and Grady had been such iron to her. She had depended on them for advice, clarity, strength, or a shoulder. She needed them more than she even realized, and their absence sent a barren sensation through her that she couldn't quite define.

She closed her eyes as if to ward off the bubble of emotions. It wasn't grief anymore or heartache, but an awful sick feeling she had felt before—somewhere in her past, a little girl's feeling that life was out of her control. If only she could recall the exact memory, she might be able to deal with the present. Grady and

Jefferson's absence created a loss, a trap with no lifeline, a sense of abandonment. Without them, the world did not feel quite so safe anymore. It came down to a feverish impression that something terrible was about to happen. For a few seconds, she thought of the day her father left home. *Yes, that was the last time I felt this lost.* Shaking off the memory, she got back into her car and drove.

On the winding road back to Contrary, Alma stopped only once in Middlesboro to refill the gas tank. She could not appreciate the lush view at the top of the mountain. All this land, rich with vitality—trees, plants, birds, rabbits, squirrels, foxes. Each new horizon changed like a sunset but only increased the sadness within her and solidified into a sickening knowledge of the waste of life. *This should never have happened,* she thought. *Who could have done this?*

She checked the odometer as she waited at a red light and saw that she had driven almost fifty miles. The idea of facing her empty house was too much. She parked and walked through the courtyard between Contrary's government buildings. The sun was setting and colored the western horizon with a splash of pink. Sitting at the edge of the fountain, she listened to the musical sound of the water jetting into the air and hitting the rock base. The cool spray helped with the heat, but not the fear bubbling inside of her. There was a killer walking the streets.

She could see her office window from the fountain. What she would give to be inside there right now, turning over every piece of evidence she could get her hands on. A figure walked past the window. She straightened her back. *Who was that?* Too tall to be Val; she only stood about five two and weighed almost one fifty.

Alma bit the side of her mouth, looked around, then raced toward the building. She went in a side entrance to avoid being noticed and sped up the three flights of steps. Val stood in the hallway that led to a rear entrance of the commonwealth attorney's office, wolfing down a handful of M & Ms, a habit when she was nervous.

"I thought you gave that up," Alma said.

"Son of a gun," Val exclaimed, dropping the candy. They bounced on the floor, scattering like rolling coins. She grabbed Alma's arm, glancing back at the office door, and gestured toward the staircase. "Get out of here now."

"Val, relax. It's still my office, even though I'm on leave. I don't think Craig will mind." Alma pulled loose from Val's grip and started toward the rear entrance to her private office.

"Alma, don't go in there."

She opened the door and stared in disbelief. Judith Drake stood at an open cabinet, rummaging through files, and the preppy-dressed man who stood beside her in court, sat behind the desk with his feet up. The curly-haired *Crimson County Sun* reporter, who chased Alma from the courthouse, was sitting in a chair, her writing pad open and pen working feverishly.

"A conspiracy of three?" Alma asked, hoping her face did not show the feeling of violation that consumed her.

Only the reporter looked down at the floor in embarrassment. "Your friend, the judge," Judith said, "didn't leave me many options, so it seemed prudent to set up in an office that was already operational." She pushed a file down into the drawer and stepped back to observe Alma fully. "I'm sure you'd have done the same in my situation."

"That assumption is questionable."

A wide sweep of Judith's arm encompassed the office. "I can't compel you, especially without your attorney, but if you'd like, please come in. I've got a few questions."

Alma's brittle gaze settled on several of her family photos. Usually on her desk, they were now scattered on a side table. She stepped forward, biting the side of her tongue to keep irate words from tumbling forth.

The special prosecutor stood like a centaur, then pulled back her shoulders to emphasize her stature. Alma noted that Judith used her height, a couple inches taller than her own five foot six, to intimidate and decided to use the opportunity to seem more vulnerable, especially in front of the reporter. "I think you'll find everyone in my office to be cooperative. They want this over with as much as I do."

"Cooperative," Judith repeated, and a snaky, closed-mouth smile spread on her lips. "You know the people I always find to be the most cooperative?"

"Who would that be?" Alma asked.

"The guilty ones."

Alma crossed the office and, with one hand, shoved the man's feet from her desk. He stood, shocked, and looked over at Judith. Alma picked up as many family photos as she could balance in her arms and ignored whatever reaction took place behind her.

"Those are evidence," he said. "Put them down."

Slowly revolving, she met his gaze with as much contempt as she could summon. "You want my family photos?" she asked incredulously. Then toward the reporter she added, "This reeks of harassment, not investigation."

Judith nodded at her assistant to back off. "Philip is my little bulldog investigator," she said with a chuckle. "He can be overzealous." She indicated the pictures. "Of course you can take your family photographs home, but leave the ones of Grady Forester."

"If I could take this opportunity . . . " the reporter said, bursting to speak as she wiggled on the edge of her chair.

Both women ignored her and maneuvered toward the open space between the desk and a conference table. Alma held out the picture of her and Grady, arm in arm, standing in front of her house. "Yes, I'll leave them." She set the photo on the table with a thud. "You look real close at this picture. You study and memorize it. It'll show you what you need to know about me and Grady."

"Obsession is what it shows me."

"The same drive I see in your eyes."

The reporter jumped up, combing her fingers through her unmanageable curly hair. "Is this to say the two of you might work together?"

"Curious offense." Judith laughed sharply. "You see, I understand the elements of a vigorous defense."

"I don't think you understand at all," Alma said.

"Did I introduce you to Maggie Armstrong?" Judith asked in a condescending tone as she indicated the reporter.

"We've met." Alma didn't acknowledge the girl.

"She and I have discovered we've much in common."

"Should I be surprised—offensively, that is?"

"Both of us were Tri Deltas."

"Different years, I hope."

Judith lost her self-satisfied smile. "Turns out our fathers worked together on a few political conventions. My father was a mentor of sorts."

"If you continue this budding relationship, you may find out you're related."

"Can I ask a question?" Maggie tried to interrupt.

"I think that sort of fooling around only happens in the mountains," Judith smirked. "We're getting our dads together for lunch in Washington."

"I've been up against cheerleaders before," Alma said with a good dose of ire. "Go ahead and call in all your well-connected friends in the press. When Jefferson Bingham straightens this out, you're going to be very embarrassed." She turned to leave, but Judith's words halted her in her steps just as she reached the door.

"Mr. Bingham's family brought him home late this afternoon."

Alma turned back to Judith, trying to assess her sincerity.

"He's been transferred to Contrary Miner's Hospital."

"Then, you'll know soon that focusing on me is a mistake."

"How does this make you feel, Ms. Bashears?" the reporter asked, looking back and forth between the two women.

"Whatever your personal opinion of me," Alma again directed herself to Judith, "I loved both these men dearly, and I'm going to see to it that whoever did this to them . . . "

Judith eyed her suspiciously, letting her tongue wipe her upper lip, which curled just the slightest. "Jefferson's being brought home to die."

The information stabbed through Alma like a knife. She reached out and grasped the file cabinet to steady herself, then inhaled a deep breath. "You seem to enjoy cruelty."

"I only state the facts."

"Is there a particular reason why you're so vindictive? Have we met before? Did I cross someone you know? I can't, for the life of me, figure out where your hostility comes from?"

Judith crossed her arms over her chest and leaned back on one leg. "I don't like seeing people get away with murder."

"How does that make you feel, Ms. Bashears?" The scrapes of the reporter's pen on paper were the sole sound in the room as Alma and Judith glared at each other. When Alma turned to leave, the reporter inserted herself in front of the door. "Just one reaction?"

"That's about as stupid a question as I've ever heard." Alma jerked opened the door and it struck the reporter's backside. "You'd do well to go back to your privileged D.C. lifestyle, because here in Contrary, Kentucky, you're going to find out how the world really works, and I doubt you'll ever be the same again." She let the door slam behind her.

23

"You shouldn't have come here," Sheila Bingham told Alma while she was still a good twenty feet away from Jefferson's hospital room. His sister marched down the hall and put both hands out in front of her. "This is the last thing our family needs right now."

Trina came up behind her older sister and placed a hand on her shoulder.

"Please, Sheila," Alma said. "I heard Jefferson was transferred here. I could never stay away."

"Mom and Dad went home to rest," Trina told her sister. "It should be okay."

Sheila stared sternly at Alma, shaking her head.

"We all grew up together," Alma said, spreading her hands in a hopeful gesture. "You can't possibly think I did this." Both women were silent and it filled Alma with such futility that she could only plead. "Please, please let me see him."

"Sheila," Trina said, "when Jefferson wakes up, do you really want to tell him you acted this way?"

Sheila sniffed and covered her mouth with a hand. "He might not wake up," she said shakily.

"All the more reason to let Alma visit with him. I'll go with her." Trina's eyes darted off to the side and Alma followed her gaze to a state trooper guarding the door.

"Nobody but family on my watch," he said, letting his chair come forward from its backward tilt against the wall. He stood and anchored himself on the frame of the door.

"I *am* family," Alma said. "I pulled his first tooth, and he cut my pigtails off on Valentine's Day. I was the one who smeared soot on his face for a Halloween costume that he couldn't remove for days. He used to cheat from my algebra tests, and I let him hide in our barn whenever he had a fight with his parents." She stepped up and tipped her face right into the trooper's. "He was the first boy who ever kissed me. I was nine and he was ten. I am family."

The trooper looked at Jefferson's two sisters, then stepped aside. "It's up to you," he said.

"We'll both go with her," Sheila said, then looked directly at Alma. "I don't know if you did this to him, but I'm sure not taking any chances."

Alma nodded her head and touched Sheila's arm. "Don't take that chance with anyone."

Inside the room, Alma had to steel herself at the sight of her best friend lying motionless in the hospital bed. He had been so strong for her so many times, that to see him clinging to life seemed unreal. His left shoulder and arm were bandaged, as was the left side of his face all the way down to the neck. His head had been shaved and a brownish stain colored the edge of the dressing. Alma held his hand and spoke softly. "Come on, Jefferson. You have to wake up." The readings on the hospital machinery filled with lines and beeps were a language she couldn't read. She leaned down and whispered in his ear, "I wouldn't take ten million dollars for you."

Trina came up beside her. The awkward silence all the more painful because they knew each other so well. Trina pointed to her brother's head. "The doctors got the bullet, but they had to induce a comma, hoping the brain swelling would come down." Her breath shivered out of her. "Alma, if you're looking for Jefferson to come out of this and be your savior, you better not count on it."

Alma squeezed Jefferson's hand, wishing she could give him vitality from her own body. "I will never, never stop until I know who did this." She looked over at Sheila, who stood at the far window looking out at the mountains.

"Don't you understand that that's the reason Sheila is so against you?"

"I don't understand."

Trina indicated the door and stepped back.

Alma touched the right side of Jefferson's cheek before following her out. "Jefferson and I have always been best friends."

"For you, maybe," Trina said. "But our whole family has noticed though the years how you send him running around in a dither trying to please you and, Alma, you're unpleasable."

"Trina, no, Jefferson and I have always helped each other."

"We don't like how you've treated him all these years."

"We were law partners."

"He's in love with you."

"Jefferson and I made our peace with that. It wasn't to be."

"He even took crap from Walter Gentry for you."

"I would have done the same for him. Don't ever doubt our loyalty to each other."

Trina looked away and tears spilled over onto her cheeks. "Alma, maybe it's best if you don't come again." She pulled a tissue from her pocket and wiped her eyes. "I don't mean to hurt your feelings, but it my brother dies, some of our family will think that one way or another—you're still the cause."

Alma walked slowly out the exit. Her chest burned inside. She crossed over to a fountain and stared into the pooled water that was lit up in a rainbow of colored light. In the soft reflection she saw a mass of curly blond hair behind her. "There is a fine line between reporting and stalking," she said in a low voice.

"You gave me no choice," Maggie Armstrong said. "I had to follow you."

"And why was that?"

"To tell you I'm not a fool."

Alma's spontaneous burst of laughter went on so long it forced her to sit down on the edge of the fountain. Maggie's face was cherry red from embarrassment and Alma gave her no chance to recover. "Forgive me for being the one to ask the questions, but what would you expect me to think of a spoilt rich kid doing her summer internship in the uncivilized hills of Appalachia? It'll make a good book report when you return to Washington, but this is my life."

"I chose the *Crimson County Sun* because of Vera Cleary."

"Who is?"

"Not that many people remember her." Maggie stepped closer and bit her bottom lip as if trying to assess whether or not to trust Alma. "She was from Washington DC, just like me; did her internship at the *Crimson County Sun* in the 1950s and eventually became its lead investigative reporter. She won two Pulitzers and so many other journalism awards I couldn't name them all."

"I see. Well, I'm glad to hear you've a better role model than Ms. Drake."

"Vera Cleary was just like me . . . I mean, I'm just like her . . . starting out. I know the people here aren't ignorant hillbillies who have no shoes to wear and marry their cousins. Vera proved herself again and again. Advocacy journalism was pushed into the mainstream because of her coverage for national magazines. Not many people remember that the *Crimson County Sun* was fire bombed for its investigative stories in the forties, fifties, and sixties." Maggie stopped speaking, perhaps realizing that she was rambling, or that her blond, blue-eyed sorority-looks might lead people to treat her flippantly. "After Vera Cleary suddenly retired in the mid-70s, the newspaper was never the same. I'm going to instill some of the same blood back into journalism. People like her understood what these mountains are about. That's why you need to know that I don't take Judith Drake at face value. My mother could be her carbon copy and that's why I see through that blue-blood facade."

"Hmmmm," Alma said, somewhat amused, but deciding not to patronize such an energetic, but naive young woman. "Then why do you care what I think?"

"I want to prove to you that I mean what I say." She brushed down her unruly curls, which sprang back, and looked around as if to check that they weren't being watched. "This is off the record."

"I think I'm supposed to say that."

"If I tell you something I heard, promise that you'll do an interview with me." She stood completely still and appeared to be assessing Alma's skeptical expression. "When your attorney approves it, of course."

Alma rolled her eyes and nodded. "I think I can agree to that."

"Okay." Maggie smiled, then quickly reverted to a serious expression. "I overheard Ms. Drake and her investigator talking about hiring a co-prosecutor to work on this case."

"That's not unusual."

"They were very excited about this and seemed to think it would not only upset you, but keep you off-balance."

"That's it?" Alma said. "All prosecutors try to keep defendants unsettled. I do it myself—selectively, of course."

"They want to hire a man named Walter Gentry."

Alma bit down, her jaw clenched, but she stared straight ahead, determined not to show a reaction.

"I'm on my way back to the paper now to research Walter Gentry. If you like, I could send you a copy of what I find."

"No need." Alma turned away and stared up at the range of mountains that seemed to take up the entire sky. "I know all about Walter Gentry."

24

Alma dialed Bob Krauss's phone number the moment she entered her house. "Walter Gentry," she whispered to herself as she stood in the dark living room. "Just when we had started getting along."

She snapped on the desk lamp and her eyes widened in shock at the sight that met her gaze. Drawers had been emptied onto the floor, cushions from chairs and couches thrown around. The leather couch had been ripped on one side and several paintings and photographs taken from their frames.

Bob's answering machine picked up and Alma disconnected the call.

She walked through the study, a downstairs guest bedroom and the kitchen, finding the same mess. Part of her wanted to cry and the other part wanted to find special prosecutor Drake and beat the tar out of her. She opened the refrigerator and noticed several items missing. A jar of mayonnaise, ham, pickles, and a carton of milk sat on the table. She bit back her irritation and returned them to the cooler. Her eyes shot upward when a scraping sound jarred the ceiling. Someone was moving the bed.

The state investigators? she wondered. The clock read 10:00 p.m. Her heart rate rose. She took a butcher knife from a drawer and went halfway up the stairs. "Who's in there?" she called out from down the hall.

"Just me," Vernon replied.

"Oh, me." Alma repeated, continuing up the stairs and throwing open her bedroom door. A half-eaten ham sandwich lay on the side of her dresser.

Vernon sat on the floor, tools scattered around him. He stared at the knife in her hand. "Cut my ham sandwich in half, will ye?"

Alma could only stare at the disarray. Dresses and suits torn from hangers and dropped on the floor, makeup drawer dumped upside down, a small shelf emptied, and the books riffled through as if it were a drug dealer's home.

"I got your bed put back together," Vernon said, rubbing one eye as he followed her gaze. "Momma said she'd come up tomorrow and help clean up."

Alma leaned against the wall. If any more energy had drained from her body, she would have been left a shell. "What could they possibly have been looking for?"

"They took your computer, all the disks too." He rose and took a bite out of the sandwich. "I hid your gun and your bulletproof vest underneath the closet floorboards. Figured you might need them."

"And to think you were the one who told me I'd need a secret hiding place."

"Uncle Ames said most of the cars left around 6:00 p.m."

"Both my uncles should get trophies today for holding their tempers and not pulling guns. I, however, may ask to borrow a few."

"Some of the local police—the good guys—are telling me they think maybe drug dealers are behind this. Grady run off a bunch of 'em last year."

"Well, if Aunt Hester was any kind of psychic, she would have warned me."

Vernon waved his hand in a dismissive gesture. "Momma meant well. It's the only way she could think to help."

"I should call Grady's brother." Alma went toward the window and looked down into a clump of woods. "He's the only family Grady had and . . . " She bit down, an involuntary shiver spreading through her body. As much as she dreaded making the call, part of her felt obligated. She exhaled a half chuckle laced with anguish. "My last fight with Grady," she said, pointing down at the grove of trees. "He hurled a picture of the two of us out the window."

Vernon came up behind her and stared out the window. "You two always smooched and made up." He touched her shoulder, paused, then turned to leave. "Call me anytime of night if you need anything." The sound of his shoes on the staircase was light, as if he were trying to be as soft with the house as he was with her.

Alma wondered if she could truly be acting so fragile. Looking down, she saw one hand gripped into a fist, the nails stinging the skin of her palm. *No,* she thought. *I'm not frail. I'm angry.* Fury was the emotion she struggled to hide; the one sensation she resisted, but no more. "Let it come. Let it wake," she said to herself. "Getting real pissed off—that's what always makes you win."

She picked up the phone and dialed. Facing the unpleasant would fuel the hardness she needed to take on Judith Drake. When a man's voice answered, she confirmed the identity of Joshua Forester, Grady's brother. "I know you've probably heard a lot of things about me from the police and the newspapers. I'm calling to tell you about your brother and me. I wanted you to hear it from me. Any questions you have, any questions . . . I'll answer."

* * *

After an hour of talking to Grady's brother, Alma lay down on the bed and stared at the ceiling. She started to get up and put on pajamas, but the ache in her bones sent her sailing back down onto the mattress. Pulling a blanket up over her, she thought of Walter Gentry. If he became a part of the prosecution team, she needed to be ready for a fight. He would play to win and sending her to jail would give him enough exhilaration to last a decade.

The snow globe sat on the bedside dresser. She stared at the eyeless porcelain doll face; it seemed like a soulless entity. She reached out and shook it. The flakes swirled around in the water and came to rest on the base of black coal. She and Walter were captured in a snow globe they could not escape. But on some level they shared a trust— that their secret past must stay hidden. Surely, he would not take the job of prosecuting her. It would be like another rape.

She turned over and stared out the window at the indigo-colored sky. One hand rubbed the wrist of the other and she shook off the image—a teenage Walter holding both her hands above her head, telling his friends to stop; they ignored him. The boys laughed. They laughed at her. They laughed at Walter. And he could not release Alma's wrists. He kept pressing them into the gravel as the boys raped her. All the fear from the terrifying incident clutched in her throat. *"Are you cold, Alma?"* he'd asked afterwards, his voice soft and regretful. But remorse came too late. The damage was done, and they had been skirting around the wreckage ever since. In their hearts though, both knew a final reckoning was yet to come.

Alma squeezed her eyes shut, drifting in and out of sleep. The doll's face in the snow globe floated before her and slowly turned around becoming the raven-haired moppet she placed in her father's car so many years ago. Then, it was no longer just a doll; it was the dark-haired little girl standing in Aunt Hester's yard. "Hello, sister . . . " she said, and then her voice and her face faded away.

* * *

Vernon moaned like he might fall over. "I'm gonna die if I don't get some coffee." He slouched down in the passenger seat of his Jeep Cherokee. "I'm gonna die if I—"

"I heard you," Alma said. "Can't you wait an hour?"

"It's cold."

"It's August, it'll be ninety degrees in two hours."

"Fog won't burn off until—"

"Just stop complaining!"

"Sun ain't even up yet."

She huffed and signaled to turn into a gas station with a coffee shop perched on a roadside cliff. They were halfway between Liberty and Quinntown, using a back road on the Tennessee side to get up to Silver Lake.

Vernon raised his head and pointed at the restaurant built on the overhanging cliff. "Hey, the Hog's Wallow. Me and Van Lambdin used to bungee jump off the roof there." He indicated the back roof that looked onto a deep ravine. "Swan dive off the top with a vine looped on your ankle and grab that little birch, it'll ride you down to the prettiest mossy mound you've ever seen."

Alma got out of the jeep without speaking, rounded it and opened his door. As he slid out, she pointed up at the sky. "There. The sun, okay?"

Vernon followed her quietly as they went into the restaurant. He slid onto a center stool at the counter and his gaze strayed to where several coal truck drivers sat in booths. A waitress poured coffee and nodded that she would be with them shortly. A dance floor and a small stage took up the middle of the room. At the other end, rocking chairs were crowded around an empty potbelly coal stove with a kettle of daffodils on top of it. Four elderly men sat in a circle, overlapping laughter cackling from them until one hacked into a coughing fit.

"They was brothers, I'm a'tellin' ye," said a bearded man wearing a faded blue coverall, "one as white as you and me, and the other'en as saddle tan as a grocery bag."

"Melungeon," said another old man, nodding his head.

Melungeon. Alma studied the old-timers just as Vernon raised his hand and shouted, "Howdy, Martin." None of the men responded. Vernon whispered to her. "They either got their hearing aids turned down low, or Momma ain't paid the down payment on her party."

"They'd wait," said the bearded man, " 'til a family homesteading West come crossing the Cumberland Gap and the white one would sell the dark one."

The other men nodded their heads with the courtesy of lifelong friends who had heard the tale countless times but listened as if it were fresh news. "That night," the man continued, "the one brother would sneak up and free the dark one. Then they'd work their way back to the Gap and pull the scam again."

The men laughed, two of them pounding their knees with a fist. Only the waitress seemed irritated as she approached the counter and poured coffee for Alma and Vernon. Her almond-shaped black eyes flashed toward the old men as if they were an annoying gaggle of geese. She pushed a strand of brown hair behind her ear and glanced toward the mirror, checking that the braid around her head was still in place.

"Reckon them two swindled 'til Lincoln freed the slaves," one of the old men said.

"Yep," said another, sipping coffee from an oversized mug. "Then they started with outright robbery. That was 'til they set upon the Wintergreen cabin and found it haunted by the meanest ghost in the hollows."

"They was drunk," one man argued. "It was all in their heads."

A knowing laugh came in response. "I'm a'tellin' ye that Wintergreen ghost was real. I seen it at least a dozen times in my life, running around Silver Lake causin' all kinds of meanness."

"Old man Wintergreen was kilt by a Melungeon back in the twenties, that's why he's so mad."

The waitress snapped her towel on the counter, hands anchored on her hips and loudly proclaimed toward the men. "If some people don't start washing the dishes, then I might have to put in some overtime."

"I'll be right back," Alma said to Vernon. He was gulping down her cup of coffee and paying little attention to the conversation. She walked over to the group. "Excuse me." She sat on one of the barrels fashioned into a stool.

"Well, pull up, little lady," replied a man holding a spit cup. He offered her a pinch of snuff

Alma politely waved it off. "I heard you mention the word Melungeon. Can you tell me more about them?"

"I'll tell what a Melungeon is—they're descendants of the Portuguese pirates."

"No," the man next to him disagreed, "you got it all wrong. They's older than that. Melungeons are ancient Phoenicians."

"You listen to me," said another man. "They're part of that lost colony of Raleigh. The Croatan Indians kilt the men and took the women. Live way up on the high ridges, hard to find 'em."

"So they're a multicultured people, something like Mulattos or the Cajuns?" Alma asked, comparing their folklore to her online research.

"No, their bloodline is pure. A Melungeon parent can bare a dark child and a light one, not a brown one the way a mixed race couple might. They're a lost tribe of Israel."

"They can change their shape on full moon nights," said the snuff-dipper. "Wolves and panthers mostly."

"And they read minds. Witchery runs in their veins."

"Their dark blood calls out to each other and they recognize others of their blood, even if it's just a smidgen."

"But don't trust 'em, not one of 'em tells the truth."

A clang of pots and pans hitting the floor silenced the room. The waitress twirled around, her rubber-soled shoes squeaking on the linoleum floor. A squint in her eyes flashed a dangerous fury. "I've just about had it," she said through gritted teeth. "I'm part Melungeon. Do I look like a wolf or a panther or a lost anything?" She held a skillet shoulder-high as if about to use it like a baseball bat.

Her outburst stunned the old men into silence. Their eyes opened wide, their mouths gaped and one sat with his hands trembling in front of him.

"Melungeons are bankers and teachers and lawyers and war heroes and even waitresses!" She stepped closer even as they leaned backward. "And this is one Melungeon waitress that's gonna bust some heads if I hear one more word of disparagement."

The old men rose like matching sets and split apart, two toward the front door and the others out the side. One asked, "Why are you running, don't you own this place?" The door slammed on the answer. The waitress turned and looked at Alma, the skillet still held waist-high.

"We're leaving too," she said quickly, and hurried to get Vernon, whom she found sound asleep with his head on the counter.

25

For all its beauty Silver Lake looked like a hibernating demon. The ripples on its glassy surface mimicked the wavy special effects of a time travel film. Despite its splendor, the lake had a troubled history. Formed by diverting the headwaters of rivers and creeks into a dammed-up valley, neither the people who made their living along the waterways or those living in the valley's hollows were happy about the lake's formation. Alma was so young when it had happened, she barely remembered the public outcry.

She disliked the lake, not because of its politicized past, but her own anguished connection with it. She had lost a cousin to murder on one of its distant shores, and now Grady and possibly Jefferson. As she surveyed the rim and the clear water that alternated in shades of green and blue, an insight infused her thoughts. *If any place on earth might be called cursed, then this is it.*

She and Vernon drove around the shore on a one-lane road and parked under a leaning apple tree. "There," she said to her brother, pointing to a path. "That's where Jefferson and I climbed up." The weeds on either side of the path were flattened and she wondered if Jefferson and Grady had followed the same trail. "The police came in where the land is more level, but that way takes longer."

Vernon stretched and rubbed his eyes, looking out at the water. "See the rings in the lake?" he asked. Half a dozen spots on its surface expanded in concentric circles. "Fishin's good here. Means a lot of people could have been around this way."

"No stranger did this," she said. "No druggies either."

"And is this based on anything stronger than the same spooks Aunt Hester talks to?"

"I feel it in my gut."

"I figured."

They hiked less than a quarter mile up the hill to Isham Thunderheart's cabin. In the bright morning sun, it appeared to be a broken-down shack, having lost the charm of a solitary cottage that Alma saw the first time she was there. Walking onto the land where a person she loved had breathed his last breath sent a chill through her body, despite the sun beating hotly on her back. She wished she could dip her hands into the earth and pull out a vision of Grady— *just one last touch,* she thought. She paused to study a laurel thicket splashed with blood. "Vernon," she said, "do you think Elaine could have done this?"

He wrinkled his brow, looking out toward the lake. "She's got bananas for brains."

"It'd make sense that she'd want to pin it on me."

"Yeah, but she couldn't help but open her big mouth to somebody and brag about how clever she'd been."

His words made sense, but she disliked hearing them all the same. "That I have an enemy is a given. That Grady or Jefferson also had one, I can understand. But it's unlikely that we'd all have the same enemy."

"What were they doing out here," Vernon asked. "Together?"

"Jefferson must have discovered something in Joddy Paradise's records." She tried to connect the dots. "His secretary couldn't find anything in his office, but it's just like Jefferson to keep it all in his head."

"But why come out here, and why have Grady with him?"

Alma wondered why as well. She sat on the porch steps, looking at the spread of cinnamon-colored blood that washed out onto the grass. *This must be where Grady fell,* she thought, an ache shooting through her chest.

"I'll tell you why," Vernon said. "They wanted to talk about you."

"They could do that in town." She dismissed the idea with a wave of her hand. "And did on too many occasions."

"I think they came out here to settle it between themselves once and for all."

"They didn't shoot each other, Vernon." She began to get irritated with herself for bringing him along.

"Look," he said, pointing at an overturned chair, a row of stomped tomato plants and the clothesline pulled out of the tree where it had been nailed. "If what my police buddies are telling me is right, they were standing close together here. Grady was shot in the chest and knocked down." He walked the area, and then moved downhill to where Jefferson fell. "Jefferson was trying to get away. The campers found him down the hill, so the shooter was standing up there on the left. He or she didn't destroy all that stuff in the side yard." He looked at Alma, as if waiting for some understanding. "The boys were fighting before this happened."

"I don't want to hear this." Alma covered her ears with both hands. "Even if it's true, why would Grady's department believe I could do such a thing?"

"Well, maybe because you're acting a little bit too guilty."

"What?" She jammed a hand down on one hip and turned toward him.

"Alma, more than once the whole hollow heard you and Grady screaming at each other about God-knows-what. You've never explained nothing to any of us—even Sue, who knows the Grady/Alma romance inside out."

Alma huffed. "And no doubt has told all of you . . . "

"Only the good parts," he said, and grinned. Then he hesitated, looking at the ground, and reached inside his jacket pocket to pull out a palm-sized picture frame—the photo Grady had thrown out her window. He held it out, the silver frame reflecting the morning sun. "I went and found it."

Alma took it from him and stared at herself and Grady, arms around each other at a July 4th picnic the previous summer. A strong smile filled his face, outlined by a thin mustache and sapphire eyes that sparkled as they looked beyond the camera. He had often been kidded by friends who called him 007 because of his resemblance to the young Sean Connery. She imagined him thinking of all the work he had left undone at the office—as he often did, even when they were trying to relax. She wiped sweat from her upper lip and walked into the shade of a hawthorn tree. Blinking back tears, she looked at Vernon and mouthed the words, *thank you.*

"So, come on," he said. "Tell me what Isham Thunderheart's connection is to all this."

She hesitated and looked out at the lake. Heat waves curled up from the water. *Yes,* she thought, *mine isn't the only loss to happen on this land. This is a cursed place.*

"Vernon," she said, "what I'm about to tell you isn't for anyone else's ears."

He regarded her uncomfortably. She ignored his obvious unease and plunged into her explanation, knowing he would hate it and might even refuse to make connections that she had reluctantly accepted as true. The sun climbed higher. Gnats rose in stinging clouds but she kept on, relentless, telling him everything about their missing father.

"Stop," he finally said.

But she continued. "The worst of it is . . . he might be alive."

* * *

"I don't want to hear anymore of this," Vernon said, turning away from her. "And you're right, don't tell anybody else."

"Have you been listening to me? Momma got letters from Detroit for four months after Daddy was reported missing."

"I can't believe this."

"If our father is alive—"

"I don't want to know," he interrupted harshly, turning toward her and grabbing her arm. "I barely remember Esau Bashears, but I tell you what, if he ran off with Allafair Adair or Granny Goose, I'd just as soon he stayed gone."

"But Vernon—"

"You really want Mamaw to find out about this?" He took the picture of Alma and Grady and shook it. "This could kill her. Let go of the past. Let it die right now!"

"I can't," she said, the words sticking in her dry mouth. "I have to know."

"Well, here's something nobody's told you . . . " He walked a wide circle around her, his hand running through his hair. "You know all those wooden what-nots on Mamaw's shelves, the little animals?"

"Yes," she said.

"Daddy whittled those and now you tell me a whittling man stole your money." Vernon stopped circling and stared out at the lake. "Oh, God. Don't let him be alive, not like this."

"You don't mean that, Vernon." His words strangled her. She didn't know what to say to him. The old man who had claimed her reward money was a whittler . . . her father was a whittler. *What if the old man is actually our father?*

"You've got to promise not to pursue this," Vernon said, taking her by the shoulders. "It's a legacy that could stain our family for generations."

"He's our father, Vernon." She faced the lake and squeezed her fingers through her hair. "I can't let it go."

"Even if you find out for all the world to see, for Mamaw and Momma, Sue, Uncle Ames, Aunt Joyce—think about Larry Joe and Eddie—what if they learn their grandfather is a half-crazed, violent thief who haunts graveyards and steals from his own family!"

"The truth is that he'd still be our father!"

"If that sorry son of a gun is our father, he could destroy us all!" Vernon heaved the picture of her and Grady as hard as he could into a grove of swamp-haw trees. It landed with a thump that mixed with the tinkle of glass. "I know exactly how Grady felt," he raged at her. "I'll wait in the jeep. If the music is on real loud when you come back, don't speak to me."

She marched toward where he had thrown the picture and stomped a path through the cinnamon fern. Part of the foliage was already flattened from investigators canvassing the area for evidence. She bent down and pushed back the ferns.

Seeing the silver shine of the frame, she reached past the knobby roots of a nearby tree and picked up the photo. She dusted wood flakes from the glass, then froze when she picked up a curved fragment and examined it. It was a light brown, curled like a pencil shaving. She had seen one like it before.

Alma inched forward, trying to disturb as little ground as possible in case the wood shavings became evidence. Just beyond where the picture landed was a small heap of whittled wood—the very same kind the old man dropped in the graveyard. "My God," she whispered. "He was here. That old man had something to do with this!" At the same time, Vernon's words repeated in her head. *"If that sorry son of a gun is our father, he could destroy our family."*

135

26

Alma hit the door of Bob Krauss's hotel suite like a wrestler slamming the mat. She pushed past the stunned secretary, who exclaimed, "He's with someone."

"I know who did it," Alma blurted, falling into the part of the room he'd set up as an office. "I know who shot Jefferson and Grady."

Bob was standing behind the desk looking down at a seated figure. The person stood, but didn't turn. A tall, wide-chested man, brown hair rimming his head above his ears, blocked her view.

"Walter Gentry," she said, the words sticking in her throat. "What are you doing here?"

He slowly turned, his cheeks flushing a slight pink as their eyes engaged. He looked away quickly.

"I asked him to come," Bob said, stepping around the desk and motioning the secretary to wait in the adjoining room.

When the door snapped shut, Alma fought the urge to turn and leave. She moved toward the left, putting a chair between her and the man who might be prosecuting her. "Judith Drake plans on hiring Mr. Gentry as co-counsel," she announced.

"I know that," Bob said.

"We would be wise to limit our contact with him." She struggled to keep her emotions even and detached.

"I just offered him a job."

Alma's leg muscles trembled and she hoped shock didn't seep into her expression. She leaned against an air-conditioning unit, letting the cool air blow up her back. Crossing her arms over her chest, she stared deeply into Walter's eyes.

His lips parted as he inhaled before speaking. "I haven't taken the other job," he said. "I'm listening and here to consider."

"I don't care." She stepped toward him and heat immediately enveloped her body. "I don't need an enemy in my camp."

Walter stared at the floor.

"He already helped us, Alma," Bob said, irritation filtering between his words. "Judith Drake's whole life history has just been laid before me, as well as the reason why they're after you."

Alma turned away, stared into a mirror and was startled to see that she looked like a frightened child. She vowed to make sure her words corrected that expression. "There's not much of a reason I can think of for believing anything he has to say."

"He didn't make this up," Bob said, slapping a Louisville newspaper down in front of her. "What Mr. Gentry has provided is the thread—the link—that pulls all this together." He pointed at a story about the governor and the attorney general suing each other for slander. Then he pulled a Lexington paper from underneath it and showed her an article about several out-of-state millionaires who had contributed to the attorney general's re-election campaign in exchange for favorable rulings on their in-state business interests. The governor has asked for his resignation. If the attorney general isn't forced into resigning, he'll go after the governor. This state is about to go to war with itself and you are the first skirmish. That's why Judith Drake was sent here. It is necessary to discredit anyone who might be deemed competition."

"It's not necessarily even you," Walter said. "Commonwealth attorneys in several counties are facing IRS audits and FBI investigations based on anonymous tips. A half dozen other well-respected attorneys are under similar scrutiny. He's after anyone who might replace him." Walter bit his bottom lip in apparent hesitancy. "He has an army of wealthy out-of-state supporters, so the only way to save yourself is to destroy Judith Drake."

"None of that matters," Alma said. She reached into her pocket and pulled out the wood shavings. "There's a man—Grady saw him—a man who tried to kill me . . . who knows about . . . I met him through a . . . " Her heart pounded and she found herself sinking into a chair as she hyperventilated. The presence of Walter Gentry wound through her and all she could manage to say was, "Get him out of here."

Instead he went to the sink, brought back a glass of water, and patted her shoulders. Alma stared at the floor and tried to calm down, hating it that the two men spoke to each other as if she were not in the room.

"This man . . . " Walter said. "Did Grady recently arrest anybody fitting his description?"

"No," she said, clamming up more and more as she sensed that they were patronizing her.

"We can try and find him," Bob said, his voice soft and indulging.

"Oh, I will find him." She pointed at the shavings she had put on the desk. "He dropped wood flakes at the same place where I met him, Allafair Adair's grave. These were at Isham Thunderheart's cabin. This man was there."

"Even if it was him," Bob said, "that doesn't mean he shot those men. He could have been out there at any time. Or it could be the remains of somebody else's whittling." He touched her shoulder. "That's what the prosecution will argue."

"It's the only common thread," she said. "Yes, he could have been there by chance, but until I question him, my money is on the card that reads he's the killer."

"What's the motive?"

"You know," she huffed, frustration leaking through, "that's for the police to figure out."

"Let's think about this logically," Bob said. "If we go at it from the angle of a state turf battle . . . "

"The attorney general of this state may be a dishonest sleaze, but he's not going to kill Grady and Jefferson to get me!" Alma complained. "All I have to do is prove my innocence and that will handle the state and take care of Judith Drake."

"I have one suggestion." Walter sat down to write on a notepad on Bob's desk. "Here's the name of an artist at Kingsley University. When I was commonwealth attorney, the department often used him to draw suspect sketches. He's much stronger than a police artist, and uses a particular method to elicit information that results in a more realistic portrait. Tell him everything you can about this stranger and get a picture, then we can decide where to go from there."

Alma leaned toward him. "I haven't hired you."

He smiled and pushed the paper in front of her. "I haven't decided if I'll take the job." He stood, stepped back, nodded to excuse himself, and left the room.

She turned to Bob. "I'm begging you not to consult with that man again."

His questioning expression bored into her. "Why?" He let out a huff of frustration when she gave him no explanation. "Tell me why you two hate each other so much."

She had trouble speaking; the words that came out were disjointed and even she realized they made no sense. "He'll sabotage us," she managed to say coherently.

Bob stood and pushed his hands into his pockets, then spoke slowly and deliberately. "Alma, the state not only brought in a special prosecutor, but Judge Dulaney has excused herself. The attorney general has authorized bussing in a grand jury from Fayette County. We need Gentry's influence. Battle lines are being drawn. The governor has endorsed you for the next election. The slaughter is about to begin. You'll be a forgotten footnote. We need Walter to counteract that."

Alma sat there shaking her head, unable to provide an argument.

"If we don't hire him, they will," he said definitively. His gaze bored into her. "Give me one good reason not to do this."

She stared into the mirror, into her own eyes, into a past she was unable forget—an explanation she could never give him. A single image invaded her brain—that of a young Walter's face hovering over hers—*"Are you cold, Alma?"*

27

Alma hid amid circular hedges of azalea bushes. A bench in the center allowed her to watch the entrance to her office building. Judith Drake had to come out for lunch soon. When she did, it was time for a come-to-Jesus talk. *There has to be a way to end this,* Alma thought. She couldn't let her future lie in the hands of Walter Gentry. Whatever political incentives motivated Judith Drake couldn't possibly take precedence over the truth.

Finally, the regal, older woman left the building with her assistant. A surge of energy jolted through Alma when Ms. Drake walked directly toward the circle of azalea bushes—alone. Alma held her breath, then turned her back as she waited to see which direction Judith would go.

When Judith passed, Alma exhaled and watched her nemesis walk along a sidewalk leading to a seldom-visited city memorial. Intrigued by the choice, she decided to follow her.

The winding sidewalk meandered through an immaculately kept garden planted with pink, yellow, and red roses, purple irises, and orange wood lilies all tended with great care by the local Woman's Club. The wilder section, close to a shaded creek, was full of sun yellow dandelions, egg-colored daisies, baby blue chicory, and red clover flowers. Wooden benches faced a monument made of coal. Behind it stood a heart-shaped amphitheater about twenty feet wide. A plaque listed the names of those killed in a 1930s mining accident. The mine was in the hills above Contrary before it was even a town and nearly fifty men from Quinntown and Liberty had lost their lives. Judith sat down on a front bench and stared at the names.

Alma came up behind her. The slight jerk of Judith's shoulder told her that she had seen Alma's reflection on the shiny surface of the monument.

"I don't appreciate you following me here," Ms. Drake said.

Alma moved around the bench and sat beside her. Only then did she notice that Judith held a red rose. "You and I need to talk."

Judith stared at the memorial.

"It should be no surprise that I've investigated you as much as you have me," Alma said.

"Have you?" Judith responded.

"You're not a stupid woman. You see what's going on here."

"Why don't you tell me?"

Alma recognized the attempt to try and draw her out and decided to cut to the chase. "You know I'm being set up."

"Do I?"

"It's obvious to even you that Elaine Bartholomew had the museum rifle mailed to you."

"Is it?

"Will you stop it!" Alma bit her bottom lip in an attempt to control her temper. "Look," she added, "I'm about to tell you something, and you need to listen."

Judith's eyebrows arched and her lips pressed into the slightest smile reminiscent of a teacher awaiting a student's lie. "I'm listening."

"A few nights ago I was attacked in the Rose Hill Cemetery by a man who stole ten thousand dollars from me. Check the local papers; you'll find an ad offering that amount of money for information about an individual named Allafair Adair. This woman is connected to my father, who disappeared years ago."

"Is all this going somewhere, anywhere?" Judith asked in exasperation.

"The old man who stole the money is involved in Jefferson's and Grady's shootings." She stopped and inhaled. She didn't want to sound hysterical or give away information she wasn't ready to let go of—such as the possibility of the stranger being her father.

"What did this man look like?"

She held a small breath. "I didn't see him that well. He had a worn, gray hat pulled down low over his eyes."

"Convenient, a man you can't identify."

"But I can," she said. "That night, the old man was whittling. Grady found a strangulation device the old guy was making, probably to use on me. I found some of the same whittling remnants at the crime scene."

"A place you are not authorized to visit. I haven't released the crime scene."

Alma ignored her and continued. "We can work on this together. That's what I'm trying to get across to you. We have the same goal. If we can find this man, we have the murderer. You can go back wherever you came from and take all the credit with you."

"And you're sure of where I came from, aren't you?" Judith shifted away from Alma, crossing her legs to the opposite side. "You see that name there?" She pointed at the monument. "Third from the bottom, forth column."

Alma focused on it. "Killian Drake," she read aloud.

"My grandfather," Judith said. "What a wise man my father was to get us out of these godforsaken mountains."

"Judith," Alma said softly with as much empathy as she could muster, "you need to do the right thing. You know I'm innocent."

Waving the rose like a pointer, she stood up. "What I know is that you are trying to harass the prosecutor." She tossed the rose at the base of the monument and walked away.

"What you might not be aware of—" Alma said as she stood. She used such a commanding voice that Judith stopped and turned around. "—is that the names in the last two columns didn't die in the original accident. They died when they went into the mine and tried to save their friends."

Judith looked at the five columns of names. Her features twisted in unsettled emotions that she struggled to conceal. "Then," she said quietly, "Killian Drake was a bigger fool than I'd been told."

Alma watched as the prosecutor continued down the path. She understood Judith Drake better now. She was a woman who had masqueraded her way through life as a Bluegrass belle. Yet deep inside, her ancestry embarrassed her. Something else was clear, as well. There would be no sympathy, no help, no justice from Judith Drake.

28

Orange posters attached to the base of a statue of Kingsley University's founder proclaimed the presence of alien spaceships visiting the mountains, and invited readers to a seminar. Alma shook her head, half-amused and half-surprised that the university would open its conference rooms to such nonsense. A man wearing a baseball cap and dark sunglasses came around the statue, then turned abruptly the other direction. She looked after him—*maybe he thinks I'm an alien,* she chuckled to herself.

She studied the sketch drawn by the Kingsley University art professor and ignored her annoyance that Walter had been right, even helpful. From her vague memory of the sinister stranger's profile, the Professor extrapolated a full face that looked as real as any person crossing the campus. She sat on a bench in the shadow of a statue to escape the hot afternoon sun. Staring into the eyes of the drawing, she could hear the old man's gravely voice in her mind and tried to imagine what his motives might have been.

Replaying the scene over and over again, she examined what she knew for certain. He purposely hid his face to prevent identification and ran when Grady arrived. Grady said the old man intended strangling her. A memory of the wire flashed in her mind. "Now, wait a minute," she said aloud. Grady wouldn't let something like that go; he would try and find that guy, and start by looking for that truck.

Could Grady have found him? If this man was running from the law, he might have killed to escape capture. Maybe Grady confronted him at the lake.

Oh no, she thought. *Grady and Jefferson were both right. The whole thing had been a scam. That old man was going to kill her to take her money, but Grady tracked him down and died because of it.*

She flipped open her cell phone and dialed Henry Moody. When he answered, she said, "I have a favor to ask."

He was silent as if turning away from anyone who might hear him. "Alma, I should be interrogating you, not helping you."

"It has nothing to do with my case. I promise you."

"I don't know," he said, self-doubt filtering through his words.

"Henry, you know in your heart I didn't do this. Please, I need one piece of information." She waited, listening to his breath. "Grady ran the plates of a truck the day he was killed. I need to know if he discovered the name of the registered owner."

"Hold on," Henry said.

She waited, eyes closed, teeth clenched. The sound of a nearby choir floated from a classroom. Her fingers sweated and stained the edge of the sketch. "You said you knew me," she said to the drawing of the old man. "I will find you."

"Alma?"

"Yes," she said expectantly.

"I don't think I should tell you this."

"Please," she begged.

"Let me handle it. It might be connected."

"Who is it?" she demanded.

He paused and huffed out a frustrated breath. "Isham Thunderheart. The 1980 Chevy truck was registered to Isham Thunderheart."

Alma disconnected the phone. The shock settled into her. The old man stole Isham's truck. Did he kill Isham? Had he returned to the scene of the crime and shot Grady and Jefferson? Now, the whittling shavings she found at Isham's cabin couldn't be a coincidence. But this old man . . . did she know him?

Copies, she thought, studying the picture, *going to need lots of copies.* She headed across a courtyard toward the library. As she entered the building, she noticed a reflection of a man in the window. He wore a baseball hat and sunglasses. She turned to look at him, but he dropped some books and leaned down to get them. Inside she made several right and left turns, watching to see if he followed her. *Getting paranoid in your old age,* she thought.

When no one appeared she found a copier, wrote a phone number and request for information across the bottom of the picture of the old man and slid it in. After making a hundred copies, she left through a wing of the library with a museum filled with Appalachian art. She waited in a line of students exiting the building and idly looked at the work of an artist named Delta Wade.

Her drawings were raw, and probably of places near where she lived, Alma figured. A mountainous setting surrounded by huge trees; portraits of a sad-looking man named Henry, an intense younger man with a leonine mane of hair named Lafette, and a self-portrait showing a handsome woman with delicate, pretty features. Her eyes were mysterious and as sad as Henry's but Lafette held Alma's attention, the depth of his expression somehow familiar but impenetrable. She crossed over to the opposite wall to look at more of the woman's work. She was drawn to one sketch of a deep watering hole in a volcano-shaped rock from which ran several streams of water. A range of mountains lined the horizon as if this place was near the top of a mountain. Looking down at the title, she read: *The Streams of Tyme.*

29

"The witch of Shadow Mountain," the librarian said, smiling as she nodded her head. "Just an old legend. Delta Wade is the great-grandmother of the University's president, Arthur Kingsley. And of course, the other twelve Kingsleys who populate our faculty from physics to archaeology."

"What I need to know is—"

"Not to mention their children, who fill out the other twenty or so departments as various professors—"

"This place, the Streams of Tyme, where would I find it?"

"The place of the Watchers, of course."

"Watchers?"

"Another old legend." She pointed to a bookcase. "The Watchers protected the mountains in ways that normal folk might not understand. They lived on Shadow Mountain, which fed the streams of Tyme." She motioned for Alma to follow her. "I have a book of folklore—"

"We can skip that. The location?"

"I don't know—only the Kingsleys know that, and I've never known one to give the place away . . . you see, the legend says that the mountain is found only when it needs to be. You see—"

"Thank you," Alma said, and hurried off through the library. She found a computer terminal and put in the word "Tyme." All that came up was the drawing she had just seen, and a short biography of Delta Wade, who died during the birth of her son, Elisha. She never married his father, Henry Kingsley, who also died around the same time. His half-brother Lafette raised Elisha, and both took the name Kingsley. Alma thought back to the drawings of them as young men. "Fascinating," she said to herself, but I've got to have more information than this.'

She typed in the name "Shadow Mountain" and came up with a *Crimson County Sun* article: "The Melungeons of Shadow Mountain" by Vera Cleary. She leaned back in the chair, stunned by the connections—Melungeons, Shadow Mountain, and Vera Cleary, who that bossy little reporter considered to be such an icon. This was fitting together tighter than a jigsaw puzzle. She clicked to download the article but came up with an error message. As many times as she tried, she was unable to access the site.

Her mind ticked like a processing computer. The old man's words whirled in her mind. *Allafair's children,* she thought—*they're Melungeons—spawn of a shadow.*

She looked at the stack of copies of the drawing. The old man's expression was vacant but was traced with a kind of ignorance, an empty facial cast she recognized. Since becoming commonwealth attorney she prosecuted a handful of murders and a half-dozen more attempted murder charges. She stared into the eyes of these people. Killers like this always cried and professed their sorrow, but she knew better. Their tears weren't for their victims, but for themselves. Their only regret was being caught. She looked again into the eyes of the drawing—they were a killer's eyes. *But were they her father's eyes? Esau Bashears who whittled the little wooden what-nots for Mamaw's house?* By the end of the day, she would have that face plastered all over this valley. Now, all she needed to do was find a Kingsley and make him or her reveal the location of Shadow Mountain. She decided to start at the top with the university's president.

Alma found the administration building and got as far as his private secretary then waited while he was in a meeting. Before long the door opened. A tall man with salt-and-pepper hair and a wide smile said, "You're Ursula Bashears' granddaughter."

Alma was astonished. "How do you know my grandmother?"

He reached out and shook her hand, squeezing it with the strength of a connection he was trying to communicate. "It's a lengthy yarn. She did my family a favor a long time ago."

He invited her inside his office.

"I don't have a lot of time," she said, "and I don't want to take up yours. I need you to tell me how to find Shadow Mountain, and the location of the Streams of Tyme."

He brought his right hand to his chin and stared at her with less friendly and more scrutinizing eyes. "Please," he said, indicating two chairs in front of his desk. He sat in one of them.

Just as she started to join him, the outer door burst open and three officers rushed in and surrounded her. "Alma Bashears," said a state trooper. "You're to come with us."

The man in the baseball cap and sunglasses followed the troopers into the office. He walked up to Alma and removed his cap. Philip, Judith Drake's investigator. She hadn't recognized him earlier, and realized that he had been behind her all day. "Am I under arrest?" she asked.

"You have the right to remain silent," was the answer.

30

"She was re-Mirandized, your Honor," Judith Drake told Judge Martin Hatcher. "Nothing improper was done."

"I would never suggest that arresting my client for the death of a man who happens to be alive is improper," Bob Krauss argued with smiling sarcasm. "I'd call it stupid."

Alma sat behind the defense table, handcuffed and doubly frustrated at having to keep her mouth shut. The regional chief judge appointed Martin Hatcher to replace Mary Dulaney. Alma knew of him only by reputation as a prosecution's judge, someone she might have wanted to preside over her less compelling cases, but only because he wasn't the brightest bulb on the block and thus easy to manipulate. She glanced behind her and could see Walter Gentry sitting in the rear of the courtroom. *At least he's not at the prosecution table,* she thought. The only other person she recognized was Maggie Armstrong, so mesmerized with the drama that her pen hung loosely in her hand and her reporter's notebook had slid off her lap.

"Jefferson Bingham was clinically dead." Judith's face colored the palest shade of crimson. "That he was revived was a snafu that was simply lost in the translation."

"A snafu that the doctors saved him," Bob interjected with a dose of sarcasm, "or a snafu that you arrested Alma Bashears? We've already argued this before Judge Dulaney. She released Ms. Bashears."

"Had he stayed dead," Judith spit out the words without the least bit of compassion, "I'd have done whatever was necessary to put this double murderer in prison."

"This is pure harassment!" Bob clenched his fists in front of him. "This prosecutor is on a witch hunt!"

Alma wrote in large words so he could see them clearly—*THEY WERE FOLLOWING ME.* Instead of charging forward, he stepped back, leaned against the table, and looked down at the floor. *What's wrong with him,* she thought.

He glanced up and spoke quietly, making an awkward juxtaposition against the forward-leaning prosecutor. "I must also protest Ms. Drake having her own special investigator follow . . . " He stopped and the silence allowed Judith to intervene.

"Fine," she said, "since we are making protestations, this would be an opportunity for the court to put this woman into custody as a flight risk."

"Absurd!" Bob called out, but didn't move from his position against the table.

"This is exactly why I had her watched." Judith handed some papers to the judge. "I submit to this court an open-ended airline ticket in the name of Alma Bashears to Barbados. From there it is an easy step to South America and a new identity."

Alma's mouth dropped open. Bob's hand clenched onto the edge of the table. "What the hell does she have?" she whispered.

Standing up, she saw the pasty color of Bob's face and the sweat beading on his neck as he held his left arm. "My God! He needs a doctor."

An uproar of voices followed. Alma swung herself across the table, Judith stepped back as the court reporter screamed. The strike of the Judge's gavel was a continuous knock through the pandemonium. Two state troopers pounced on Alma, dragging her out of the room as she tried to help Bob Krauss before he slowly collapsed to the floor.

* * *

Alma paced the holding room while two Contrary police officers nervously glanced at each other. "I'm not under arrest," she said. "You can let me go."

The tall officer shook his head. "Until the judge tells us what to do, you have to wait here, Ms. Bashears."

"Can one of you go see what is going on?"

"The paramedics are with him," the female officer said with sympathy in her voice.

"Sit down or I'll have to put the handcuffs back on," the other officer warned, and positioned himself in front of the door.

Alma slowly lowered herself into a chair, continuing to stare hard at him. "I thought we were better than this. Grady worked so hard to make this a police force to be proud of, and I hope you remember that." Realizing there was little she could do except wait, she tapped her fingers on the metal chair frame and hoped the young officer would hear the sound in his dreams.

Twenty minutes passed then a knock on the door brought in the Judge and Judith Drake, her investigator, Philip, and a court stenographer. Judge Hatcher pulled at his robe and brought his gavel from beneath it, laying it in front of himself. "Ms. Drake has convinced me to come here and make my ruling since the courtroom is still filled with emergency personnel."

"Is Bob okay?"

"He's being attended to." Judge Hatcher stood at the head of the table and touched the tips of his fingers to the wood. "Those people are doing their job and I need to do mine."

"You're going to continue without my being represented by counsel?" Alma asked incredulously.

"All that was going to be said had been said." He spoke slowly, his drooping eyes glassy and the odor of alcohol wafting from him. "And after all, you are an attorney. Now, regarding the flight risk, I agree—"

Another knock on the door stopped the ruling. The smile that started to fill Judith's face froze when she saw Walter Gentry. They exchanged greetings like two professionals, then her expression turned to stone as Walter moved toward Alma.

"I'll be taking over the defense of this case," he said with a guarded stare that warned her not to argue, and a nod as if making an agreement with her. "Until Mr. Krauss can return."

"Fine," Judge Hatcher impatiently whined, "I'm about to rule."

"Before you do that," Walter interjected. "I have something to ask."

"Your Honor was going to rule," Judith interrupted. "Do we need to be in this cramped, hot room all day? Rule, and let's move on."

Walter leaned toward Judge Hatcher in a familiar we're-both-men-and-know-better kind of way. "I'm sure Ms. Drake enjoys pushing Your Honor into rulings but the evidence she put before you was only partial and presented in a misleading way."

"Explain," the Judge said.

"Where did you get the plane ticket?" he asked Judith.

Judith's mouth was a thin line. "We found it in Grady Forester's desk."

"And was there only one?"

"No," she said, acting unimpressed. "There were two."

"Ah, so all we know is that Mr. Forester planned to take Ms. Bashears on a trip at some future date." Walter chuckled, bringing a similar reaction from the judge. "This is hardly the flight risk Ms. Drake has presented. There isn't even any evidence that she knew about the tickets."

Alma watched Walter's old-boy methods work their magic. Judith Drake shifted from foot to foot as if unsure what to do next.

The judge nodded. "Well spoken, Mr. Gentry. I'm seeing the logic of your argument, however, I'm also not one to put a criminal in a position to escape justice." He turned toward the court reporter.

"I haven't been convicted of anything," Alma blurted, but was ignored by all of them.

"Your Honor, may I speak off the record with Ms. Drake?" Walker asked.

The judge waved a hand for him to proceed.

Walter took Judith's arm just above the elbow and turned her toward the door. Alma leaned back in her chair to listen.

"I'll have a federal judge looking at your actions by the end of the day," Walter threatened.

"You forget," Judith said. "I worked twenty years in Washington, I can pull more strings."

"If you don't mind federal officials looking into your procedures, examining every decision, every piece of paper." Walter paused to dip his head.

"I've always thought we could handle things ourselves in our own little patch of woods."

Judith Drake appeared to be biting the inside of her jaw. She turned to Judge Hatcher. "Given Mr. Gentry's argument," she said as if the words were poison, "I won't oppose Ms. Bashears' release."

Judge Hatcher scratched his head and mumbled something incoherent. "I'll release Ms. Bashers but will stipulate that she not leave Crimson County until the grand jury investigation has concluded." He looked directly at Alma. "If I find you've stepped one foot over the county line, young lady, I'll leave you in jail 'til the grand jury makes their call."

Part of her rebelled against his patronizing tone and wanted to argue the ridiculous ruling, but she knew it was a break and obediently thanked the judge then waited for him to leave.

Judith turned to Walter, her features molding into a perplexed expression. "I'm surprised," she said. "I'd thought—"

"I know," he replied. "I learned a long time ago to avoid predicting the future."

Judith glanced out the window. "How did you know about the other ticket?"

Alma edged toward them, eager to hear the answer.

"I bluffed you," he said. "What I did know is that Alma Bashears would never run away."

Judith's gaze dropped to the floor. "You've joined the wrong side."

"By the way," Alma interrupted. "I want all the evidence you have from Mr. Forester's desk."

Walter continued, "I sense that those plane tickets say something important about my client's relationship with him—something like they were closer than you want anyone to know."

"I trust I'll have no problem getting it," Alma said, challenging

"I thought that was your attorney's job," Judith retorted with a condescending sneer.

"You haven't taken on just another attorney, Ms. Drake. You've taken on me." Alma stared into the special prosecutor's eyes without blinking and with all the force of her being. Judith looked down, and Alma knew she had gotten under her skin.

"Of course, your discovery requests will be accommodated," Judith said and nodded. She was no fool. Walter was just as well connected and if she attempted to hide evidence, he'd find out about it. Judith backed from the room, her frustration evident in her squinting eyes and tight posture.

Alma waited until the door closed. "I can't let you do this," she told Walter.

"I always knew you were good at intimidation," he said and smiled, "but you have the nuances of threat management right down to the details."

"Thank you for this help today, but neither of us can see this through."

He motioned for her to sit down and followed her in the seat opposite. "Bob's had a major heart attack."

Alma covered her face with the palms of her hands. She squeezed her eyes closed, wishing this hadn't happened. When she looked back at Walter, his determined expression was a comfort she hated admitting.

"They're not going to wait," Walter said. "You have to come out fighting, now, and that means more than staring down a shill like Judith Drake. She has immense political power behind her." He paused, the crease between his eyes deepening the longer she remained silent. "Alma, you don't have a choice."

She held her hands behind her back, squeezing them together. "I have a choice," she said. "And it can't be you."

"Stop fighting me," he spat out, rapping his knuckles on the table, and then laid his hands open, palms up. "Let me do this for you." His voice softened. "If I do anything you wouldn't have done, I'll step down. I'll step down the minute you say or if you find someone better, but please, let me . . . let me . . ." He hesitated, reached out to touch Alma's chin and turned her face toward his. The watering in his eyes glistened. "Let me do this to make up for the past."

The facts weighed against her deepest feeling—there was no one better and there was no one she trusted less. She looked into his eyes, staring as deep as she could penetrate the brown pupils. *Ambition,* she thought, and it repeated in her mind over and over as if someone whispered the word in her ear. The one thing she could trust was his ambition. He hated to lose, and he would especially want to win against Judith Drake. This could put his failing career back on track and position him as a major player in the coming political battle. Just where he needed to be. The words struggled from her lips and part of her felt like she was falling.

"All right," she said. "I'll let you represent me."

31

Walter studied the drawing of the old man while Alma paced in front of a glass table with chrome legs that served as his desk. His office in the Daniel Boone Complex faced the intersection of Contrary's main street. Alma watched as cars stopped and started with the green and red lights.

"I've made a hundred copies at the university library," she said, "but I can have 5,000 printed and put up all over the county. I think we should also have it published in all the state newspapers, maybe even Knoxville and Kingsport."

"Let's wait," Walter suggested, raising a finger and then thoughtfully touching it to his lips.

"Why?" she asked. "This is my only lead."

"Exactly." He patted a hand in the air to calm her down. "And as such, we need to preserve it."

She hesitated, intuiting some logic in his words, but unwilling to completely trust his assessment.

"Two things," he continued. "One, it'll tip Ms. Drake to our case, or lack of it. More importantly, if this fella gets the idea that half the county is looking for him, he'll skip. We'll never see him in this part of the country again."

Alma bit the inside of her mouth. It made sense. She hated admitting it, but he was right. "I'm going find him," she said, determined to let Walter know she would guide the direction of this case.

"We will," he assured her. "Let's move our chess pieces so that Ms. Drake thinks we have little concern for her pitiful allegations." He stood up causing a creaking sound from his straight-back oak chair, picked up the phone, and buzzed his secretary. "Send him in."

Alma turned toward the door. The younger man who had spirited Walter away from his luncheon entered. He extended his hand first to Walter and then to her.

"This is Orson Burke," Walter said. "He's a private investigator. In fact, his father, Cedric, used to work for mine, so I've known them both a long time and trust them. They recently handled a private family matter for me."

Alma recalled the day of the luncheon and figured that whatever was going on behind the scenes was handled by the Burke team. She picked up the sketch of the old man. "Do you think you can find him?"

He stared at it, his eyebrows rising. "How sure are you of this drawing?" he asked.

"Not very. I only saw him for a few minutes before he grabbed my money."

"How much?"

Alma glanced out the window at a long line of cars waiting at the stoplight. She fought the urge to escape, feeling foolish in front of these men. "Ten thousand."

Orson looked up at Walter, his lips parted as if drawing in a long, slow breath. "That's enough to get him out of the country."

She continued watching the cars until the light turned green. "Let me make one thing clear, Mr. Burke. If you take this case, you work for me, no one else."

He glanced at Walter, then nodded his head. "As it should be. I'm a professional, Ms. Bashears."

She hated having to explain her actions to a stranger who would never understand. Wiping a patch of sweat from the back of her neck, she cleared her throat, "It all started with a newspaper ad."

"I'll fill him in on the details," Walter interjected. "In the meantime, there is some advice I want you to take." He led her toward the door. "I know Bob Krauss told you to stay away from the press and out of the community. I think you need to do just the opposite. Don't hide as if you're a guilty person."

His disregard of Bob's advice raised a knot of doubt inside her. Being social was the last thing she felt like doing. "Flaunting myself is only going to make the other half of the town hate me."

"Even I know it's your mother's annual half-birthday party in two days. Make sure you attend. Letting everyone else know your family supports you is very important."

"That information will flow through this community like baby pictures," she said, unsure of what he was trying to prove.

"Exactly."

"The grand jurors will hear about it."

"Exactly." He opened the door and pressed a hand on her shoulder. "Drake begins calling her first witnesses tomorrow."

"A ruse like that could backfire."

"Only on an outsider—like Judith Drake. You'll look like a family member supported by her clan."

"I'll think about it," she said, more to conclude the subject than agree with him.

Walter stared off to the side as if to indicate there was more.

"Okay," she said, "and the bad news?"

"Elaine Bartholomew is her first witness."

32

"**I** just don't understand it," Vernon said, staring out the window of Mamaw's kitchen as he sipped from a cup of coffee.

"I can explain why I hired Walter Gentry." For the last hour Alma anticipated an uproar in her family. Aunt Joyce had already flagged down her car and expressed concern, so Alma decided it was best to come to her grandmother's house where everyone usually gathered, and face the firestorm.

Vernon looked at her, his lips pressed to one side in an aggravated grimace. "That's only the second thing I don't understand." He looked out the window again. Using his coffee cup, he indicated the barn. "There's a horse in the barn."

"A horse?"

"Why's there a horse in the barn?" He glanced at her, then back out the window, unable to sustain eye contact. "I leave town for one darn month and come back to find everything's changed."

"I don't know why there's a horse in the barn," she said. His furrowed brow showed his anger growing like a swelling phrase of music. "I can explain why I hired Walter Gentry."

"There's a damn horse in the barn." He set the mug on the table with a thud. "And you go and hire the rottenest son of a bitch in Midnight Valley. What is wrong with you?"

"It's my horse," Mamaw said, coming into the kitchen in her motorized wheelchair. She pulled up at the head of the table and reached for a pill bottle kept beside the salt and pepper shakers. "By the way, Alma. A man named Arthur Kingsley has left two messages for you."

"Thank you, Mamaw." She figured her arrest in his office had him wondering if he was about to be implicated in some crime.

Vernon pulled back. "I didn't mean to upset you, Mamaw."

"It's my barn, my field, and my horse." She swallowed one of the pills without water. "I don't have to explain myself." She waited for a response from her grandson. He sat there quietly and she continued. "And neither does Alma."

"Maybe in this case, I do, Mamaw. At least I need to explain to Vernon."

"You talking about that scuffle the two boys got into when they were teenagers," Mamaw said.

"I spent a year in Crimson County Juvenile Reform School because of that," Vernon sneered. He studied Alma, their eyes connecting in the knowledge of a secret the rest of the family would never know. Vernon had beaten Walter and put him in the hospital for his part in Alma's rape. The Gentrys made sure Vernon did some time.

"Poor Walter," Mamaw said. "He's got a shadow on his soul, not of his making." She backed up the wheelchair and maneuvered it toward the front of the house.

When Mamaw was out of hearing range, Vernon lowered his head and whispered. "You even got her feeling sorry for him."

"There are good reasons for why I did this," Alma said, staring after her grandmother and pondering her words.

"So he can stomp on this family one more time."

She took a deep breath. "He is better connected than anyone in eastern Kentucky. He can fight Judith Drake on levels that even I can't."

"And you can trust him?" Vernon stared into her eyes.

She paused and put her hand over his. "No, I don't trust him. But I need him."

"I hate this." Vernon pulled his hand away and slapped the table.

"I'll be watching him," she promised.

"He steps out of line, I'll be there."

The few seconds of quiet that followed hung like a mist that obscured the future. She wished there was another way out. The dice had been thrown, and now she must place her bet. She needed a lawyer who was a force to be dealt with, not simply another attorney.

"Alma," her grandmother called. "There's a reporter waiting to see you."

She groaned and rubbed her hands through her hair. "How'd anybody get up here?" she complained. "Vernon, can you—"

"It's that little blond-headed one." Mamaw poked her head into the kitchen. "I think you ought to talk to her."

Alma thought for a moment and decided this might be the right opportunity to make use of the press. "I'll leave you two to discuss horses," she said to Vernon.

* * *

Maggie Armstrong stood on the eastern slope of the property where the land lifted into a series of hills. Alma watched as she shielded her eyes to study a pair of beehives shelved into a ten-foot cliff.

"We used to have them over beside the barn," Alma said, coming up behind her. "They swarmed last summer and stung two dogs to death." She led the way toward a well-worn footpath up to the square white bee houses. As they walked, she noticed that the young reporter was unusually quiet. "Moving them up here is no guarantee the same thing won't happen again, but I guess a shift in position made everybody feel better."

Maggie opened her mouth to speak, then stopped. She looked away, her eyes narrowing in thought.

The steady hum of the bees comforted Alma. They took flight from the hives, swinging around the two women like precision divers. "Step carefully," Alma said, pointing down at dandelions where the bees hovered. Maggie bit her lower lip and the troubled expression in her eyes struggled to find release in her voice. "I'm glad you came up here," Alma said, deciding to take the lead. "I was going to call you and ask a favor."

"What kind of favor?" Maggie's inflection was soft, almost vulnerable.

"There's a *Crimson County Sun* article called "The Melungeons of Shadow Mountain" by your mentor, Vera Cleary, published in the mid-70s, probably '75 or so. I can't find a copy, not online, not in the Kingsley University Library, and of late, I've been a bit too preoccupied to go make a request of the paper's archivists. I'm hoping you might—"

"I'll find it for you." Maggie turned away with a deliberate twirl. "Everybody," she blurted, gesturing emphatically, "everybody has a past." She tried smoothing her hair, but the insistent curls sprung back. "I understand that." She shifted her weight to one leg and shook her head as if confused by an internal monologue.

"Why don't you say what you're thinking?" Alma asked in an encouraging tone.

"In . . . " Maggie paused and turned toward her. "In researching Walter Gentry, I came across articles from 1980 about a case of assault by your brother, Vernon."

"That's no secret. He and Walter got into a fight as teenagers, and Vernon served a year in a juvenile facility."

"There were two other names linked to this case, Earl Roscoe and Rudy Delmar. It seems Vernon made threats against those two boys as well."

An icy coldness filled Alma even though the sun beat directly on her from above. "Car wreck," she said, walking toward the hives and scooping up a handful of drones. "Those two men are dead."

"But their families aren't. I talked to Colleen Roscoe, Earl's sister." Maggie stood silent for several seconds, and then looked deeply into Alma's eyes. "She and her brother were close . . . they talked a lot."

"Just what are you saying?" Alma asked, determined to act unconcerned. She cupped one hand over the other and concentrated on the vibration of the drone's wings on her skin.

"I interviewed Earl's sister," Maggie said, more insistently. "You probably know what she told me." She reached out and clasped Alma's forearm. "But I've also researched you." Her eyes roamed over Alma's face. "I've studied you backward and forward. I know your strategies, your weaknesses, your strengths, but there were patterns I didn't understand until now." She paused and swallowed. "I've learned enough about your character as an adult to know deep in my gut that you are not the kind of woman—" She stopped and sucked in a deep breath as she struggled for words. "You were never the kind of teenager who'd have sex with three boys under a bridge."

Alma stepped back, her breath caught like an insect in a web, and realized that Maggie still held onto her arm. "Bet you didn't know you could hold bees without being stung," she said, opening her palms to show her the handful of drones. Most flew back toward the hive, while three stayed to inspect her hand.

"I have a sister who was raped. I know the scars it leaves, and I see them all over you."

"You, you're, you're wrong." Alma stared down to avoid eye contact then pulled back, breaking Maggie's grip, and turned aside but could not step away. It took all her strength to speak with a level voice. "You don't know what you're talking about."

"That's not all." Maggie's voice quivered. "Judith Drake's investigators were there before me."

Alma felt her very life drain out of her. She fought to keep from dropping to her knees. "The Cleary article," she said, keeping her voice distant and unwavering. "It's important." She moved away from the hives and went back down the footpath, concentrating on one step at a time. For now, that's all she could manage.

Instead of returning to Mamaw's kitchen she walked up the gravel road toward her own house. Near the turn in the path, she realized that her hands were still clasped tightly in front of her. She loosened her grip and felt a soft lump. She had killed the bees.

33

"There is nothing Judith Drake can do with that information," Walter assured Alma. A single desk lamp illuminated the office. His secretary was at lunch and the emptiness of the rooms gave his voice a slight echo.

"Why would she have talked to Colleen Roscoe if she wasn't going to use that story?" Alma paced like an unfed cat.

"Hearsay," Walter reminded her. "Earl's sister is not material to this case, and calling her before the grand jury to smear your character will backfire."

"We need a preemptive strike. I've thought about it all night long." She picked up the phone. What are you doing?"

"Calling the *Crimson County Sun*," she said as she dialed. "I'm going to tell what happened—the rape, your fight with Vernon—everything. I'm going to tell my side of the story."

Walter pressed the disconnect button, took the receiver from her hand and lay it back in the cradle. "Are you crazy? You can't do that."

"The hell I can't." She picked up the phone again. "It's already out there. I don't have a choice."

"Alma, wait."

There was just enough pleading in his voice to make her freeze, but she couldn't look into his eyes. "What can you say? You, of all people, what can you say?"

"I haven't been named." He opened his palms outward as if in a plea. "I'll be ruined."

"I *am* ruined," she said in a slow, deliberate voice. "Since that day, not a week has gone by that I haven't found myself in a rage at thinking that I could have killed you any number of ways." She stepped closer, suppressing every other emotion in order to do what she knew she must. "If I had my choice, I'd go to my grave with this, but it's too late."

"I promise you, if one word leaks out about what happened, I'll make Judith Drake pay for it." His hands formed into fists. "But, please, don't tell this story. Think strategically. From Colleen's lips, it sounds like gossip. If you confirm the facts, her spin will sound truthful."

The phone rang, breaking the tension like a shattering of glass. Since Alma still held the receiver, she answered. "Walter Gentry's office."

"Alma, it's Val," said her assistant. "Elaine Bartholomew is about to come out of the grand jury and she's expected to give a statement to reporters."

"I'll turn on the TV." She motioned to Walter, who pressed the button on a small remote he kept on his desk.

The front of the courthouse appeared on the screen. The local station's logos faded in at the bottom. Elaine Bartholomew stepped through the main door, flanked by her attorney and her father, and approached a cluster of microphones. Her eyes were red-rimmed and puffy.

"I have just . . . " She paused and blew her nose into a hanky, " . . . given testimony to the grand jury relating my relationship to Grady Forester, as well as my heartfelt belief that Alma Bashears is his killer."

A shiver coursed its way up Alma's back. Her muscles trembled with anger. She knew what the little rich twit was about to say.

"I know I wasn't there when he died. I didn't see the murderer, and I have no proof of my allegations, but what I do know is how much Grady loved me."

"We have people who can derail that testimony," Walter said. "Lou Mills, for one."

"And I do know," Elaine continued, "that he'd recently discovered Miss Bashears' character was not as upright as he believed. My close and dear friend, Colleen Roscoe, knows all too well the kind of woman Alma is; Miss Bashears seduced Colleen's brother and his friend, Rudy Delmar, when they were only teenagers. In fact, she was with both of them on the same night. Miss Bashears' own attorney can confirm these facts. He was there, as well."

"My God," Walter said, his mouth dropping open. "Drake is responsible for this."

"What were you telling me," Alma snapped, "about the special prosecutor not being able to use this information? Seems to me she's tied it right in with a motive." She clutched the arms of the chair and collapsed backward. "I can't believe this. I can't believe that horrible day is finally out." Part of her was horrified and another part almost relieved. Her voice trembled. "It's out of my hands now."

Elaine swiped a wisp of brown hair from her forehead and continued. "When Grady found out about Alma's promiscuity, he decided that he could not stay in a relationship with a woman who possessed such low morals. This is the reason Grady died. I believe this with all my heart. Grady rejected her, and she killed him. And now I alone must fight for the man I loved. The man who would have married me. I have it on good authority that there was a diamond engagement ring in his pocket on the night he was killed. I believe he planned on giving it to me later that night."

For several seconds, sound and sight seemed to have vanished. When Alma came back to herself, she was covering her mouth with one hand. Walter turned off the TV. She rose and poured a glass of water to give her trembling hands something to do. Unsure that words would even form on her lips, she swallowed until the glass was empty, then stared out the window at the busy intersection. "You know what I hate most about this," she said, hardly recognizing the sound of her own voice. "I hate needing you."

"We didn't make this situation, Alma." He leaned his head back against the wall and closed his eyes. "We're just two people who try to fix things and, the more we try, the more some evil crops out of the woodwork like mold that won't wash away." He rubbed his face with both hands, then stood beside her at the window. "I think that, after this is over, we should both leave town. You go back to San Francisco. I'm going to New York and try to put things back together with my wife and kids."

"Quincy Pollard told me that the past could strangle the future." She placed a hand on the window, strength draining from her body. In the reflection, she could see Walter watching her, his arms hanging limply at his sides. His shoulders were slumped in defeat. "There was never a way to escape what happened. It flows though our lives like the blood in our veins. We've just been fooling ourselves all these years."

He gripped both sides of his head and massaged his temples, looking downward to avoid her eyes when she glanced toward him. "I have no more tricks in my bag. I've only got what brute force is left within me to bulldoze my way through this. I promise you, I'll get you off, and I will not let Judith Drake walk away unscathed."

Alma leaned her forehead against the glass pane. She could care less about Drake at the moment. Her thoughts whirled like a spinning top. Considering. Rejecting. Never wanting her family to know. All the years she had kept the secret crashed in on her. The information would stain her career. No matter how much people would profess to understand, some would always blame her. Worse than that, they would pity her.

She turned, her eyes narrowing in forced concentration, and took firm hold of Walter's jacket sleeve. Slowly, his gaze came to meet hers. With iron-like precision, she faced him full on and spoke as an instruction, a mandate, an order he dared not disobey. "I'm not going to tell the story of what happened all those years ago, but you are."

34

Was it Judgment Day or the Apocalypse? The answer to this secret formed the outline of how Alma lived; now its revelation would change her life forever. It took an hour for the family to gather at Sue's house. Alma sat in her car, watching the house. She saw her mother impatiently pacing in front of the living room window.

She got out of the car and walked toward Larry Joe and Eddie, where they stood near a patch of trees. Her stomach churned and, as she moved to stand behind them, she wished for childhood simplicity. The boys looked so innocent and, for a few seconds, in Alma's mind, like strangers.

"We got sent outside," Eddie said, turning toward her.

Alma stroked his head. "We adults have to talk for a little while."

"Not because of that," Larry Joe added. "Momma says on account of we play with the computer too much. She said we had to go out and play with the trees like you and Uncle Vernon used to do."

Alma chuckled, a crowd of childhood memories filled her thoughts.

"But we don't rightly see the point." Eddie eyed her with a perplexed expression.

Alma knelt down and put an arm around each of them. "Now, look at that ash tree with the crooked limb. Doesn't it look like a dragon? What about that viney bittersweet; it's kind of like a spidery octopus. You could save Cindy Jane Collier from a monster like that."

Both boys drew back, their eyes narrowed with disbelief. "A dragon?" Eddie asked.

"Just use your imagination," she said.

"There's no octopus out there," Larry Joe insisted, his tone astounded by her suggestions. The boys walked to the edge of the thicket, staring at the trees and speaking softly to each other. "I still wouldn't take ten million dollars for Cindy Jane," Larry Joe sighed with all the intensity of puppy love.

Alma went into Sue's house and found the family gathered around the television set just as she had asked. Vernon was the only one not present. Her sister, mother, Aunt Joyce, Uncle George, Uncle Ames, and Mamaw all looked at her. Their confused and disturbed expressions said that they had heard about Elaine's statement. Alma thanked them for coming but found herself deliberately avoiding eye contact with her grandmother. She was the hardest person to face. Mamaw sat in the corner embroidering a blanket that lay across her lap. She looked up at Alma. "Arthur Kingsley called three more times for you, honey. It seemed real important."

Alma nodded and turned on the television. "In a few minutes," she said, "Walter Gentry is going to hold a press conference. It will explain everything." She turned up the sound and moved back toward the door, cracking it to breathe in the fresh air. Outside, she could see the boys attacking the dragon tree. Larry Joe swung at it with a stick and yelled, "In the name of Cindy Jane Collier!" Alma wished that fighting her own dragons was as simple.

Walter appeared on the TV screen, standing at a podium in front of a roomful of reporters. He looked down at a script, then up at the crowd. He met each gaze directly. "I have a statement to make regarding Elaine Bartholomew's comments earlier today. I, Walter Gentry, have firsthand knowledge that the story told by Ms. Bartholomew is completely untrue. That she would repeat such an outrageous lie shows the lengths that Prosecutor Judith Drake will go to smear Alma Bashears' good name."

Merl broke into applause. Gleeful comments from the rest of the family overlapped. Alma motioned for them to wait.

Walter continued. "The reason I know Ms. Bartholomew's testimony to be a lie is because . . . what happened that day, many years ago . . . " He coughed and paused. A reporter shouted a question that he ignored. "The only thing about this story that is true is that I was there. I was there when Earl Roscoe and Rudy Delmar savagely and viciously raped Alma Bashears. I hardly knew those boys. They ordered me to hold her down . . . and I did. I was a young, inexperienced, and naive teenager. This in no way abrogates my responsibility for what happened to Ms. Bashears. I simply didn't know how to stop it. My inaction has haunted me and will torture me for the rest of my life. Ms. Bashears and I chose to handle this matter privately, but Judith Drake has now made that impossible. She has shifted from being a prosecutor to a persecutor. As a boy, I could not find the courage to do what I must do today . . . set right a wrong. I will not allow Judith Drake to destroy a woman because of my failure."

The questioning expressions invaded the silence with disquiet louder than speech. Alma tried to speak, but her voice failed her. One by one, her family looked at her, then turned away. She knew the uncomfortable feelings they must be struggling against; as much guilt as pity. Finally Sue put her arms around Alma.

"You should have told me," she whispered in her ear.

"So much makes sense now," Merl said. Her hands tightened into fists. "If I'd only known, I'd have . . . "

Her uncles stood up, the fact of being men making their movements awkward. "Think I'll go outside and talk to the boys," Uncle George said. Uncle Ames followed him without a word, but his firm jaw pulsed with what appeared to be consuming anger.

Alma leaned against the arm of a couch, still clinging to the fresh air from the open door. "I'm going to go home now," she said.

"We're coming with you," her mother said.

"For now, I'd rather be alone."

"You're thinking of leaving Contrary, aren't you?" Mamaw said from the across the room where she sat in an overstuffed chair, her hands busy with the embroidery. "When this is over."

Alma started to answer, but what could she say? She looked down, and then away.

"No," Merl said. "Don't let these fools run you off." She pushed the door closed, as if that would keep Alma from leaving. "I'm gonna cancel my party and move in with you until—"

"This is exactly what I don't want to happen," Alma said. "All of you changing your lives for me because of what happened years ago. I can fight these people. If you try to do it for me, they'll go after you, and I couldn't stand that!"

Only her grandmother's gentle hand movements as she pulled a long piece of thread through the eye of a needle kept Alma from fleeing out the door. The gesture looked like the wide arms of a parent opening to await the running child. Mamaw brought the needle back to the material, inserted it into a temporary position, and then rested her hands on both sides of the chair as if it were a throne. "You've forged yourself a place here," she said, "and now, Alma, you need to remake yourself again. You can do it with a hammer, or with a needle and thread. If you use a hammer, don't expect it to look like this." She unrolled the blanket to reveal a richly colored tapestry in shades of red, blue, green, purple, and yellow. Up close they were merely colors, but standing back, using imagination, the various hues and textures appeared to be a mountain range. On the left were summer images with bees lighting on purple irises, on the right a rainbow of fall leaves fell from a tree; the top showed a wintry snow scene and from the bottom sprang forth all the brilliant varieties of spring flora. Slowly Mamaw regarded each remaining family member, letting her words soak into them. "Merl's not going to cancel her party. Me and Ames are gonna babysit the boys. Sue and Jack, Joyce, and George and, naturally, Vernon will be there. Remember, Granddaughter, that we're here and the wall that we form is not so weak as to crumble from a little hammering. Remember that truth can always stand the light of day."

35

Female friends and family members had come and gone. *Sent away,* Alma thought. *I sent them all away when I needed them the most.*

She hated herself for not reaching out. She needed them, but could no longer look at their guilt-filled expressions, or listen to the sorrowful regards as they talked around a tragedy from over twenty years ago as if it had just happened. "Better to right this wrong now than not at all," Aunt Joyce had said. "You should have told me, I am your mother," Merl kept repeating. Their faces faded in and out of her memory, their words ringing like school bells. She squeezed her eyes closed, fighting down the loss of control that wanted to overtake her.

The men, even Vernon, stayed away. Probably too embarrassed to see her, she decided. It was a common reaction. She saw it many times as a prosecutor, the families of crime victims often having as difficult a time dealing with the circumstances as the person who had been hurt. Despite their words—and as much as they wanted to be supportive, she rationalized—they now struggled with the guilt that the knowledge inflicted on them.

Val had offered to spend the night, but Alma assured her she needed time alone. After cleaning up from all the visitors and pouring Alma a glass of Merlot, even she reluctantly left. Strewn around the rooms were books, skiing equipment usually stored in the hall closet, and other remnants of Judith Drake's search yet to be reorganized. Sitting on the couch, staring into the deep red color of the wine, the stillness of the room ticked like a clock. The only sound was a blue jay, which landed on the side porch and bravely hopped toward the open sliding glass door.

"Hey," Alma said. "Cats live under that porch, you better . . . " The phone rang and the bird flew away.

She had unplugged the living room phone after several obscene messages, and it took several seconds for her to realize it was the cell phone in her purse. She hesitated. So few people knew that number that she expected Val was calling to check on her. "Yes?" she said.

"Get another lawyer," came Bob Krauss's weak but insistent voice.

"How are you?" she asked.

"Dying," he said, flatly, "but not until I see Walter Gentry fired from this case." He told her to hold on while he fussed at people in the room, ordered a nurse to lock the door on her way out, then said, "Alma, why didn't you ever tell me what happened all those years ago?"

"I didn't tell anybody, not even Grady. Vernon and Jefferson were the only people who knew."

"And Walter," he fumed. "He should never have come near this case. He knew better."

"Don't get yourself upset," she said, concerned for Bob's condition.

"Judith Drake must be needling Walter's ego?"

"Let's just say that, for him, now it's very personal."

For a moment Bob didn't speak and seemed to be considering. "George Lincoln could take over your defense, or Griffin MacKay . . . "

"Bob," she said sincerely, "you concentrate on getting better—"

"This is not the time to think about anyone but yourself," he yelled. "If I weren't scheduled for a double bypass tomorrow morning, I'd kick that scoundrel's butt myself!"

"Calm down," she said.

"I tell you, with all the legal knowledge I have, Alma, get another attorney. This man is now too invested for his own good to look out for yours." He argued again with a nurse. "I have to hang up now. Think about what I've said."

Outside, dusk began to settle. Alma picked up her wine glass and swallowed a gulp as she went out into the warm evening air. One of the relatives took the time to fill the pet's food troughs but so far none of the dogs or cats had appeared. She picked at a bowl of grapes left on the picnic table, but the tart taste spread through her mouth like pain. Finishing the wine, she stepped over to the edge of the porch and stared into a wrap of mountains—the valley of Midnight.

A train whistle blew as the rumble of the locomotive jarred the ground. She could see the top of it passing by. How easy it might be to pick up and leave. Never looking back on all this adversity. She fingered a topaz birthstone ring on her right hand, then gripped the porch railing as the wine loosened her mental hold on all the things she wanted to avoid thinking about. *What if Grady had been about to propose to Elaine? What if he had simply not found a way to tell me that Elaine was whom he really loved?* It would explain why he started the fights with her that week. He might have been trying to get her to break off with him.

"No!" she said out loud. "Someone else killed him. I didn't cause this."

A sob filled her throat. She fell back into a lawn chair, pulling a towel off the table and squeezing it to her eyes. "I didn't want to have sex with those boys. I didn't want that to happen. I couldn't stop it. I didn't hurt Jefferson. I wanted to love him. I couldn't. I'm not to blame for this." Her muscles trembled and contracted her body into a fetal position as she shook and shook, trying to defend her life to a court that would not rule in her favor and a jury with little sympathy—her own conscience.

* * *

It was dark when Alma opened her eyes. She was unsure how long she had slept. The moon was a slice away from full. A smoky fog wound through the woods and spilled over the slope. A movement caught her attention. She sat up, alarm shooting through her body. People stood in a half circle about twenty feet from her porch. She wondered if the effects of the wine fuzzed her thoughts. No, she had drunk only one glass. The people were familiar, but their names didn't surface in her memory.

A man with black hair stepped into the center of the semicircle and spoke toward the house. "There is lore in these mountains of a Watcher who protects. Not in the way of the law, not in the way of religion, not in the way that any human being can understand."

Alma rose from her chair and moved toward the edge of the porch. They were far enough away so that their features were indistinct. But she knew these people. And they were real—it was not a dream. The man was Arthur Kingsley, but that a university president would come to her at this time of night with a strange story about Watchers was unlikely. The others were dark-haired like him and, the more she looked at them, the more she realized they looked alike. They were the twelve Kingsley children, but one was missing.

"Thirteen of us were told in parts the directions to Shadow Mountain. Our promise was never to give them out unless a soul crossed our threshold in search of it. In all these years, no one has ever asked us, until you."

He stepped back and a woman stepped forward. She spoke with a clear voice. "Start where the Warrior's Path . . . "

One by one, they stepped forward and recited. " . . . crosses the back of the falcon."

"Down the creek where no water runs."

"Follow the moonlit path."

"The smell of pine will lead you . . . "

" . . . through the tunnel where no light shines."

"The panther's scream opens the way . . . "

" . . . and wolves howl from the bowels of the earth."

"Trust the crows, the crows will protect you."

"From the hand of Orion . . . "

" . . . springs the origin of tears. As above, so below."

The twelfth stood there for several seconds, looking at the ground, then up at Alma. "The thirteenth of us, a sister, followed the trail to Shadow Mountain nearly twenty-five years ago. We have not set eyes on her since."

Arthur stepped forward again. "We do not know the meaning or the consequences of telling you this information. We cannot tell you how to use it. We are aware of current circumstances and gave our actions here tonight serious consideration. Sometimes all you can do is speak the truth and let happen what will." A river of fog circled around them, causing half of them to disappear. "What was told to us by elders of our clan was that the seeker of Shadow Mountain would bring back the means to change life as we know it." He hesitated, then raised his hand. "We do not know what that means. I cannot tell you what to do. What happens now is up to you."

Alma looked away, not knowing how to respond to the strange visit. When she looked up, they were gone. She walked out into the yard, turning in a circle several times to try and figure out how they had gotten there and how they had disappeared. The fog was thick and blew down the mountainside like a river. *They probably used it as cover,* she figured. They could walk down the hill and follow the railroad tracks to the main road and, from there, be within walking distance of the university.

But why, she wondered, *would a trip to Shadow Mountain be so important to them or to her?*

36

The next morning, the mysterious visit from the Kingsleys weighed on Alma's mind as heavily as the press conference. Strangers speaking like ancient oracles. Whatever mystery they might be involved in, she was in no shape to solve it for them. She couldn't even help herself right now, and it would be impossible to take part in their troubles. Yet she was struck by Arthur Kingsley's words, so reminiscent of her grandmother's—*sometimes all you can do is speak the truth and let happen what will.*

Alma lay in bed and stared at the ceiling, wishing to be awakened from a bad dream, wondering if she would ever be able to face anyone in the town again. The clock read 11:00 a.m. She closed her eyes and, when she opened them again, it read 3:00 p.m. She sat up in bed, blood rushing from her head, leaving her disoriented. The bedside phone rang. She picked it up but, before she could speak, a woman's voice said, "Is this the slut from under the bridge?" Alma hung up and pulled the cord out of the wall.

Train whistles came and went. Dogs barked as they hunted in the surrounding woods. She held still, every movement as painful as her thoughts. She wished her memories would fade away. She wished she lived far from these suffocating mountains. One realization came to her over and over again: she was completely and totally alone. Her family might sympathize, might try to protect her, but they couldn't fight for her. There were only two people who could have done that—Jefferson and Grady. She closed her eyes again until the clock read 6:00 p.m. Part of her wanted to die.

The sound of a car coming up the hill sent a wave of dread through her. She was surprised no dog barked, then remembered that she hadn't fed them today, and figured they had wandered to other houses in the hollow. The engine was switched off and, before long, someone was knocking on the door.

Alma just lay there. *They'll go away,* she decided. Right now, she needed to think. There were too many plans she needed to work out if she was going to face the world again. In spite of herself, she sat up. *Lousy job I'm doing,* she thought.

Whoever was downstairs came in through the broken patio door. Footsteps sounded inside the house. She stepped out of the bedroom and met Val on the staircase. The receptionist was so excited that she panted out the words, "Ballistics . . . no match!"

Alma touched her arm, wanting to make sure she understood. "Are you saying what I think you are?"

Val gulped for air. "The tests are back. The gun that shot Jefferson and Grady is not the one with your fingerprints on it."

"Has Judith—"

"She doesn't intend on telling you," Val said, sneering off to the side.

"But, she has to. It's the law."

"She doesn't care. She thinks she can convict you on gossip." Alma leaned against the wall, trying to figure what Drake's strategy might be. "When this gets out, her case is over." A flood of relief washed through her, but the concern on Val's face said that there was more.

"I did something I shouldn't have done."

Alma sat down on the top step. "If you're in more trouble than me, I don't know if I can help you."

From her pocket, Val pulled out the micro-pen flashlight/recorder Merl brought her from Hollywood. "I was in the office taking notes for the umpteenth stupid Judith Drake memo, and she took a phone call."

"You didn't," Alma said.

"Not on purpose."

"Val, I shouldn't hear this."

"You need to hear this." She clicked on the recorder. Judith's voice made small talk about the Frankfort weather and state politics. It became obvious that she was speaking to the attorney general. "Her mother is having some silly half-birthday tonight," the prosecutor said. "I've got two agents sitting at the bar and our undercover guy ready to provoke her. I may make an appearance myself. We'll have such a presence there that even her relatives won't want to stand beside her."

"Is she out of her mind?" Alma wanted to laugh and cry at the same time. "That stupid woman thinks she can intimidate me, as well as all the Bashears."

"I hope you're not mad," Val said.

Alma shook her head. "It might have been the one thing I needed to hear today. And you know what's odd? She didn't tell the attorney general that she no longer has a murder weapon."

Val leaned against the stairwell wall and jacked one foot on an upper step. "Judith Drake scares me."

Alma stared at her feet. "There's a stack of brand new books on the desk in the study. Why don't you pick one out that you think Momma would like, and wrap it up while I take a shower."

Before Alma left the house, she made a quick call to Walter, explained Judith Drake's plan, then asked, "Did she tell you about the ballistics?"

"No," he said, calmly, "but that's not surprising. She'll try and hide it as long as she can."

"I'm going to make this a party she'll remember."

"I can have some of my people run interference," he said. "She won't get away with this."

"The more the merrier." Alma couldn't help but smile after she hung up. Part of her felt enriched with the sensation of being slightly out of control. She wondered if criminals felt this way before committing a crime. "Time to party," she said aloud. She snapped on her *The Young and Restless* fanny pack and inserted her cell phone and Val's recorder pen. *In case Judith Drake wants to make a confession.*

She chuckled.

37

Outside the Hog's Wallow, a Garth Brooks song blasted from every open window. Alma and Val stood on the side of the road and watched two of Merl's ex-boyfriends enter. "You go on in," she told Val, knowing she needed some time to build up her courage.

The receptionist sensed her apprehension and spoke gently, "You know, there're friends inside, too."

Above them the star-speckled evening sky overshot a mountain of kudzu-vined trees behind the bar. Alma stared up at the peak, where a rock formation rose higher than the trees. "Quinntown's on the other side, isn't it?" she asked.

"Yeah, but we're on the Tennessee side." Val pointed at the peak. "That's the marker, Falcon Rock."

"The back of the falcon," Alma said to herself, remembering the Kingsley's directions. She stared up at the massive formation. Coincidence, she decided. "Let's go," she said, shaking off a shiver and pulling open the door for Val.

Inside they joined in a round of applause for two legal secretaries who sang "Walkaway Joe" with a tinny-sounding karaoke machine. Alma glanced over at the bar and noticed Judith Drake and Philip on one end, martinis in front of them. They were a strange sight, surrounded by all the Budweiser and Schlitz drinkers. She noticed two other men drinking Heinekens—they had to be Drake's henchmen.

There were about fifty people in the seating area, with another twenty on the dance floor. In front of the small stage Merl sat at a table filled with brightly wrapped presents. Val whispered in Alma's ear. "I just told the bartender to double the liquor in Judy and Phil's drinks. In fifteen minutes they'll be zipped out of their minds."

"Then I better get in my jabs now so they remember them." She strolled in Judith's direction. The special prosecutor didn't look at her and acted as if she were in deep conversation with her assistant.

"You pick interesting places to get drunk," Alma said, leaning against the bar. She motioned for a bottle of Michelob.

Judith turned only slightly and spoke toward the bartender. "I'll have another." She finished the martini, letting her fingers toy with the stem of the empty glass.

"I was wondering," Alma said. "Ballistics back from the state lab?"

The hard glaze over the special prosecutor's face spoke more than her lack of words. She took a healthy gulp of the fresh drink. "Um, strong," she murmured, then took another sip.

"Because I've been thinking about how a rifle with my fingerprints made its way out of the Appalachian Museum and got delivered right to the police department with a note that it was connected to this case."

"I think she's a little nervous," Judith said to Philip.

"It had to be someone who knew that I'd fired it, or saw the picture in the newspaper, or is slightly obsessed with everything I do." She hummed loud enough to be annoying. "Did you know the Bartholomew family matched the state grant that operates the museum?" Alma touched the tip of a beer bottle to the edge of the martini glass. "But then, that wouldn't matter if the ballistics did match." She waited, delighting in the moment as Judith twisted on the stool. "Enjoy yourself tonight . . . while you can."

As Alma moved sideways through the crowd, she saw a man shaped like a huge football stumble into Philip's back, then edge up beside Judith. "How 'bout a tumble, Tulip?" He leered over the special prosecutor, letting his belly bump against her. *Must be one of Walter's men,* Alma figured.

Vernon rushed up to her, a serious expression on his face. His voice was a plea when he spoke. "I looked everywhere—"

"You did this last year." Alma pointed her finger at his face. "I'm not sharing again."

"Please, please, please, please, please," he begged. "She'll think I don't love her."

Alma laughed, appreciating his attempts to bring her into the group. "Okay, but next year you do your own shopping."

Val shot over and steered them toward a table where Merl was holding court, a myriad of fanciful packaged gifts in front of her. She slipped a wrapped book into Alma's hand.

"Glad to see you dressed for the occasion," her mother said, pointing at the Los Angeles T-shirt and *The Young and Restless* fanny pack that Alma wore.

"Here's mine and Vernon's present," she said, sliding the package across the table.

"I'll open it next." Merl ripped into the wrapping like a cat shredding carpet. She held up the book, looking over the top of it at Vernon, then Alma, and blinked several times. Alma had no clue what book Val had wrapped up and could only hope it didn't turn out to be a terrible blunder. The dim light, and Merl's hand sporting brightly painted pink nails, obscured the back cover so she couldn't see the title. "I had it gift wrapped at the store," she said quickly, hoping to make an excuse.

"*Flim-Flam! Psychics, ESP, Unicorns and other Delusions,*" Merl read aloud, "by James Randi, the Amazing Randi." She held the book aside and looked accusingly at Alma and Vernon.

He kicked Alma under the table. Merl's expression was as sour as curdled milk. "It was Alma's idea," he said. "I suggested a gift certificate to your beauty shop."

"I . . . I thought a different perspective on Aunt Hester might be interesting for you," Alma explained. *Man, am I in big trouble.*

"Well," Merl said, laying the book down and casually sliding it off to the side. "I think it's time for my Hollywood story." She stood, tapping her glass with a spoon to get everyone's attention, then walked toward the stage.

"Brilliant, Alma," Vernon said, shaking his head. "Maybe I'll go jump off the top of the roof without the bungee cord. This means socks for my next five birthdays."

"I thought it was great," Sue piped up. "It's made my curler set look like the best present ever." She giggled as she rose and took her husband's hand to go to the dance floor and await the return of the music.

A spotlight fastened on Merl as she told the audience about a dream she dreamt before going on vacation. "I was in this terrible car wreck, couldn't get out, and who comes to my rescue but the man I have loved with all my heart since I was twelve years old." She paused and put a hand on her heart. "Bobby Sherman." The crowd roared in laughter. "But I woke up and it was a dream, only a dream, so I do what we all do. I go on with my life. So here I am in Hollywood, California, walking up Sunset Boulevard, actually stepping over a lot of bums and no-accounts." That brought another chuckle from the crowd.

Alma turned to see what Judith and Philip were doing. He was trying to disengage yet another drunk from his boss's leg. The two other men at the bar dealt with an equally intoxicated woman trying to start a fight, and a waitress who spilled every drink she brought by, finally losing one into the crotch of Drake's henchmen. Alma raised her bottle in a toast. Judith glared at her. Turning away, Alma felt a measure of satisfaction that the night wasn't turning out as the special prosecutor hoped.

"The next thing I know," Merl continued her story, "I am flat on my back and seeing stars like the movie industry could never invent. They told me I was out for two minutes, but it seemed like twenty. When I popped open my eyes, I gazed into a pair of the most beautiful blue puddles of color I'd ever seen in my life, and then I think to myself, 'I know those eyes. I've looked into those eyes. I'd done things I wouldn't tell my momma when looking into those baby-blues.' Then my focus starts to come back to me and there before me is the familiar, but now slightly wrinkled, face of Bobby Sherman!"

The crowd broke into a stampede of applause. Merl ate it up. "Lord have mercy, I thought I died and was on my way to heaven! Turns out he's a paramedic and has just saved my life! So for Bobby Sherman and all of you who have come to celebrate my half-birthday, here's my own version of 'Easy Come, Easy Go.' " The karaoke machine blasted the introduction. Merl began to sing in a slightly quivery voice, but by the second bar, a church choir sweetness emerged. The audience went wild when three gospel singers from the Junction Baptist Church came up behind her and sang background. Before long, the whole room was shaking to "Easy Come, Easy Go."

Alma's cell phone rang and she unzipped the fanny pack and answered.

"It's Sheila," Jefferson's sister said. "I have something important to tell you about Jefferson."

38

Alma steeled herself for bad news. "Yes?" Trying not to draw attention to herself, she made her way toward the back of the room where she could hear over the music. Judith and her cronies glared in Alma's direction, but were immediately distracted by a contrived disturbance by a hefty man who pinched Judith's butt. Alma turned her back on them and held her breath as she asked, "What's the word on Jefferson?"

"I wanted you to know," Sheila said, "the doctors just told us it doesn't look as if there's any brain damage, and the biggest challenge is to continue getting the swelling to go down."

"Has he regained consciousness?" Alma held her breath and said a silent prayer.

"Off and on. Alma, I know you could never have done this to him." Sheila paused and sniffed, obviously holding back a rush of feelings. "The doctors say in cases like this, the person hardly ever remembers the event, so even when he does come to, don't expect too much."

Alma could hardly contain her relief and her joy. "That he's alive is enough for me. Everything else will take care of itself."

"I'm sorry for all my anger toward you. I know he wouldn't want me to treat you the way I did."

Regardless of the grateful emotions bursting in her chest, Alma knew that now, more than ever, vigilance and stealth would be their greatest protection.

"Sheila," she said, lowering her voice and taking as serious a tone as she could, "this is very important. Do not let anyone know of his improving condition. If the person who did this finds out, then Jefferson's life is in danger."

"Two of our brothers are here, twenty-four hours a day," she said, understanding at once. "Both are armed. And the nurse is a ringer for George Foreman."

After Sheila hung up, Alma slipped into the restroom. She needed a moment alone and expected the vultures wouldn't follow her there. She leaned over the sink and splashed water on her face. *Good news,* she thought. *Finally, some good news.* The ballistics didn't implicate her, and Jefferson was getting better.

The door behind her opened and someone disappeared into the first stall. Judith Drake, she decided. She wiped water out of her eyes, taking a moment to pull out a paper towel and blot it against her cheeks. For the first time in days she felt like she could really breathe. Now, nothing the special prosecutor did would disturb her.

She looked at herself in the mirror. Even the color of her face seemed to perk up under the greenish glare. The walls of the room vibrated from the music, louder than ever with the audience singing along with Merl. The door on the bathroom stall remained ajar. Alma looked at the reflection of it in the mirror. Someone was holding the door in that position. "You can come out, Ms. Drake," she said.

No one answered. She turned and faced a man dressed in black, a dark ski mask covering his face. He pointed a revolver at her chest.

"What do you want?" she asked.

He motioned her over toward the low window.

She took one step, then realized that if he got her out the window, she was dead. Refusing to take another step, she decided to fight and not make it easy for him. "Is it money you want? I didn't bring much." She tugged at some bills in her pocket, pretending to have difficulty pulling them free. He banged on a stall door to get her attention and waved the gun for her to go out the open window. "Talk to me," she said. "Tell me what you want." Outside someone called her name.

"Alma, Alma, are you in here?" Val asked, swinging through the door.

"Val, get out of here!" She threw her body at the man and they slammed into a stall door. He brought the gun down on the top of her head and she dropped to the floor. An army boot caught her under the chin. Stunned, she looked up and his movements seemed to be in slow motion. Val's scream stretched out. Alma reached for his arm, but not fast enough. The barrel flashed. The sharp crack exploded in her ears. Val's body smashed against the door and a spray of blood spattered the wall.

The man grabbed Alma by the hair, dragging her toward the window. She scratched at him, but he managed to hold her down. A loud knocking on the door was followed by the bartender shouting, "Everything okay in there?" He banged again and tried to open the door. Val's body blocked entry. "Oh, my God!" he groaned. "Ma'am are you all right?"

The masked stranger tightened his grip on Alma. Others joined the bartender and beat against the door and yelled. They pushed but were blocked by the body. Alma looked up and saw panic in the eyes of her attacker. He had been caught, and he knew it. He jerked her head back, pressing the barrel of the gun into her forehead. With all her strength she shoved herself up, grabbed his arm, and bit into the flesh of his hand. He screamed in agony, and she tasted blood. The weapon dropped and skidded across the floor.

Alma scrambled for it on her hands and knees, grabbed the gun, and turned around. The man was halfway out the window. "Stop or I'll shoot!" she yelled. A second later he disappeared, and she jumped up and followed him.

He stepped onto the top of a shed attached to the building, then climbed to the roof of the bar. Alma swung a leg out the window and crouched on the shed. A series of pops met her ears; another gun. She crept on her hands and knees across the roof of the shed, keeping close to the building until she felt safe enough to stand and peer onto the rooftop. At the far edge, she saw her attacker leap to the ground. She heaved herself up and sprinted across the roof of the bar; but, by the time she reached the other side, he had landed on a soft mound of dirt below. He aimed his pistol at her. She raised her gun. He scrambled up and ran, and she emptied the handgun into the darkness that swallowed him.

"Don't move or the next bullet goes right through your back," said a male voice behind her. "Drop the gun."

Alma lowered the pistol. She started to turn, but a woman's voice halted the movement. "He said don't move!"

Alma recognized Judith's voice; the man's voice must belong to Philip. They must have been alerted by the waiter and followed the trail out the open window onto the roof. "Did you get help tor Val?" she asked, turning toward them despite the order. Judith and her flunky stood on top of the shed. Philip anchored his arms on the edge of the adjoining roof, his pistol trained on her.

"As usual you don't listen well," Judith said. "Drop that gun, now."

Police lights swirled all over the ground below. Confused and distraught voices surrounded them as the party broke up and people began to realize what had happened. Several handheld spotlights swept across the roof, finally stopping on her.

"He ran that way!" She waved at several people on the ground and pointed toward the dark hills. "Didn't you see him?"

"I didn't see anybody," Judith replied as she struggled to climb up onto the roof of the bar. Philip assisted her, never losing his aim on Alma.

"Lower your weapon," another voice ordered.

This time she recognized Henry Moody's voice. "Thank God," she said, relief as mere breath as Henry climbed onto the roof. He would get the situation under control.

Henry faced Philip. "I said holster that gun."

Philip's eyes widened in disbelief. "She's the one who—"

Henry reached out and took the henchman's pistol.

"Get some men over there fast," Alma said, pointing the direction the man disappeared. "He's dressed in black, a mask over his head."

"Ah," said Judith Drake, "first a man in a hat and now a mask."

"Alma," Moody said firmly, "drop the gun and keep your hands high." He glared at Judith and Philip, aware that they were mentally taking notes of his every action. "Alma, very slowly, I want you to get down on your knees."

"He's getting away!" She continued pointing toward the mountain and called down to the police on the ground. "You men, get over there now! Look for a man about five-nine with army boots. You others look for footprints."

"I don't believe you're in a position to order anyone to do anything," Judith said. She motioned to her aides on the ground to ignore Alma's instructions.

Alma whirled toward her, taking a step so firm that Judith backed up. "Now is not the time for you to show how big a bitch you can be."

"Alma," Moody said, maintaining a calm voice, "no one saw another suspect."

"Why'd you shoot that girl?" Judith asked. "Seems to me she was one of the few people on your side."

"Please," Alma pleaded, ignoring Judith and Philip, "send some men over there to look for him. I might have hit him." She focused all her energy on Henry Moody. "You know me. You know I'd never do this. I have no reason to do this." She slowly lowered her right arm, bending enough to drop the gun on the rooftop.

"I don't know about that," Judith said. "You've already done it once."

"What better alibi than blaming some shadow," Philip said, unaware that Vernon had climbed onto the roof behind him. "That some innocent person has to die to get your sorry keister off the hook is a by-product."

"My sister doesn't shoot her friends," Vernon said, giving Philip such a scare that he dropped to one knee.

"Moody, get this man off the roof," Judith demanded.

"He has no business here." Philip rose and shoved Vernon toward the edge, indicating for him to step down onto the shed and away from them.

"He has as much reason to be here as a special prosecutor who's more versed in railroading than lawyering," Alma said.

Vernon braced, immobile. "Henry, if Alma says there was another man, there was. Listening to this jack-off is going to get people hurt."

"Is that a threat?" Philip asked edging in to confront Vernon.

"No, it's an invitation to use your common sense." Vernon paced, moving too close to Philip, then turning erratically and making Henry and Judith shift toward him. He shot glances at Alma with an intensity that held a message; he was trying to tell her something. Suddenly he stopped and stared at a corner of the roof directly behind her.

"This man is impeding the investigation," Judith said. "Either get him out of here or arrest him."

While Henry dealt with Vernon, Alma backed toward the corner. She looked it over as much as possible without drawing attention to herself. A vine was stacked like a coiled snake with one end attached to a thin birch tree overhanging a ravine that dropped at least sixty feet. This was the place Vernon used to bungee jump.

"Okay, Henry," Vernon said. "I'll get off the roof, but you promise me you won't shoot my sister."

"We're just going to take her in," Moody said. "She knows our procedure."

Vernon jumped from the roof onto the shed, then Henry turned his attention back to Alma. "Henry," she said, holding up her hands to keep everyone's eyes high. "Elaine Bartholomew said there was a diamond ring in Grady's possession. Is that true?" She slowly twisted off her birthstone ring. "This will blow the lid off Judith Drake's case." She pointed at Judith. "In fact, since the ballistics report clears me," she added, watching Henry's surprised look—the expression of a man completely in the dark. She held out the ring. "With this, their motive fails apart."

"We're wasting time," Judith said, a wisp of worry crossing her face. "But to make your efforts count, this woman was ordered by the court not to leave Crimson County, and I believe this establishment is in Tennessee. Now I am ordering you to arrest her."

"You don't order me to do anything," Moody said, then looked back at Alma. "There's time to sort out what happened. Alma, kick that gun my way, and we'll wait for the Tennessee authorities to get here."

"If it's true that I killed him out of unrequited love, then that ring will fit Elaine's finger and not mine, right?"

"What are you getting at?" Henry said.

"You're not buying this," Judith said. "As of this minute I am moving this case to Lexington where I hope to find civilization."

"As Henry just pointed out," Alma told her, "you have no authority in this state, Ms. Drake."

"As an officer of the court," she retorted, "I'm obligated to take whatever action necessary to protect the public."

Alma held out the ring to Henry. "Look at Elaine's hands. She must wear at least a size seven." She tossed the piece of jewelry and it landed with a distinct clatter on the tin rooftop in front of Detective Moody. "I'm a size five. If he was going to ask Elaine to marry him, the ring would fit her, not me. Go ahead, pick it up. See if Ms. Drake's theory holds true."

Judith stamped her foot, causing the tin roof to tremble. "Put her in custody and transport her to the Fayette County jail. Tonight!"

"Try it," Alma said, "and you'll get hit with a lawsuit for false arrest."

"Even I know you don't have the authority to take her out of the county, Miss Judy," Merl Bashears yelled from the ground below. "You need a judge and, while you're are it, you need a better haircut!"

"We want a killer, not a scapegoat!" someone yelled.

"Who runs this place, Henry," somebody else demanded, "us or them!"

Judith stared down at the crowd, stunned, and tried to ignore the catcalls as the party mood turned on the outsiders. All Alma could think was that the man who had shot Val was getting away and, if she was taken to Fayette County, she would be caught in a bureaucracy with no escape.

The detective looked at the ring that had landed in front of his shoes. The jewel glistened with a captured flash of moonlight. He bent to pick it up.

Just as his eyes came off her, Alma swung one leg backward, catching it in the loop of a vine, then took a running dive off the side of the building. Sailing through the air, she broke through branches of thick leaves that ripped her skin and filled her head with the grassy smell of green. She wrapped her arms around her head in case she smacked into a branch or something harder. The vine held. A jerk swung her far outward, then back, her face passing only inches from jagged stone. Above her, shouts from the crowd and the police intermixed in confusion. Searchlights spread down the ravine in stark beams of light that struck around her. She told herself that Moody knew she had no gun. He would never let them fire. In the next instant, she heard bullets whiz past. No one could control Drake's people.

She struggled to right herself, released her foot from the loop, and dropped down on a thick bed of moss. From there she sped up the bank, through thick ferns and scouring rush. One idea obsessed her: escape the law. Above all the commotion at the top of the ravine—screams, sirens, Drake and Moody fighting for jurisdiction—her mother's voice shouted, "Run, Alma! Run!"

39

Howls filled the night. Alma climbed, stumbled, and ran for almost thirty minutes before the dogs began tracking her. She knew the chilling yodels meant they had caught her scent. Sparingly, she used a penlight to follow the downward slope of a dry creek bed. It paralleled the direction the attacker had run. That, she decided was the best strategy. Follow him. The police would follow her. That way, Moody's men would be there as backup whether they liked it or not. Everything depended on catching the man who had shot Val.

As she scrambled over a table-sized boulder, she said a silent prayer for her assistant. An ambulance raced along the road above her. *Please let that mean she's alive,* Alma thought.

When the police got too close, she pocketed the penlight and let the full moon be her guide. Behind her, flashlights shifted through the thick forest. She followed broken twigs and mashed down ferns. She found blood spatters on a sandstone rock and an excited shiver shot up her spine. She was behind him. She still tasted his flesh in her mouth. Her head pounded from the blow of the gun butt, and she realized a line of blood was dripping down the side of her face. She wiped it on her bare arm.

Out of breath, she was suddenly aware of how much her muscles ached. The barking came closer. The police were catching up. Searchlights from the road above shined dangerously close to her. *That man has to be out here somewhere,* she thought.

Two policemen climbed down an embankment ahead of her. Again, she shut off the penlight and hid behind a boulder. They passed on the other side, then stopped to discuss which way to go. Alma inhaled slowly, clinging to the rock and wishing she could disappear inside it. They went the opposite direction. She exhaled, breathing hard. Her chest throbbed as she used one hand to apply pressure to the wound on her head. *Go,* a voice inside of her said, *go, go, go.* She ran down a narrow valley, then climbed a bank of briar patches, struggling to avoid the thorns. Finally, she pulled herself to the top of a cliff and collapsed. For a few seconds she lost consciousness. *Concussion,* she thought. *Doctor. Need help.*

Peering into the woods, the shapes amid the trees seemed sharper and distorted. Once more baying dogs picked up her trail. *Which way?* she wondered frantically. The two policemen had turned back in her direction. They broke through the brush to the right of her position. *No use,* she told herself.

They were going to catch her. Her chest burned and her side ached from running. She sucked in air; her head spun. She fell, slid down a ravine and lost the penlight. "Damn!" she gasped and felt around for it, but glimpsed the police above her and froze in place.

"This way," a child's voice whispered. "Follow the path of the moon."

Alma looked up at a little girl with long black hair pointing to a bluish glow that lit a path through a slope of waist-deep ferns. She ran onto it, then stopped after a few yards. *What is a child doing out here so far from anything?* She spun around. No one was there. She looked for a house or a cabin where a family might live. Had she imagined the girl? "Hurry," said a hushed voice. Alma spun in the other direction. Fifty feet farther down the path, she saw the faint outline of a person. Her attacker. "Over here!" she yelled toward the police, then plunged after him.

A voice echoed lightly around her. *"Hurry, we must save Helen Marie."*

Alma ran as fast as she could, but the figure stayed ahead of her, at times appearing as small as a child, other times like a man running with all his might to escape her. When the moon moved behind a ridge of trees, her only light was strips of illumination that filtered through the thick branches. She no longer heard the pursuing dogs or the policemen calling to each other but knew better than to think that they had given up the search.

She grabbed her cell phone from the fanny pack and dialed Walter's number. The call didn't go through. She tried Vernon, then realized the phone was dead. *Odd,* she thought. *I took it directly from the charger, where it had sat for nearly two days.* After several more attempts, she gave up trying to get a phone signal.

She slowed her pace to a walk, finally stopping to look around. Despite the full moon, she could hardly make out anything more than ten feet in front of her. From the hill above came chatter, "Chrrrrr-chrrrrr-chrrrrr-chrrrr." *A Carolina wren,* she thought. A small, perky bird that didn't like its territory invaded. *But not by me,* she realized. *I'm too far away.* The birds would follow whoever was up there until they moved out of their neck of the woods. She decided to circle around and see if she could come up in front of the person.

Near a flat plateau, she lost the path. Tripping around a tree root, she picked herself up and dusted off the knees of her jeans. She shivered, a T-shirt was hardly enough covering. Her stomach grumbled with hunger. She had no idea which direction to go and turned around in a circle, looking up at the sky, the stars, trying to get her bearings. Nothing came, no instinct or hint or sense of direction. She was lost.

From the left came a clacking sound, like someone hammering. She hid behind a tree and peered around. "Kak-kak-kak-kak-kak." A black shape flew at her, almost hitting her face. She ducked and then turned to look at a large pileated woodpecker, its wingspan almost two feet wide. Such a bird was only found in the deep woods. She was totally lost. Now, she wished the police *would* find her.

Soon the tree branches interlocked, forming a barrier with only a narrow tunnel to pass through. She could see barely a foot in front of her. Then, pitch black. Her apprehension bordered on panic. Subtlety, the smell of pine trees infused the air. She locked her feet in place—the smell of pine, the little girl telling her to run down the moonlit path—the same directions given to her by the Kingsleys.

My God, she thought. *I'm on Shadow Mountain.*

Fear and anger filled her. She had been tricked. Now was not the time to go on a fool's errand that no one, including the Kingsleys, understood. Lives were at stake. A killer was out here somewhere, and no one else was looking for him.

There had to be a way off the mountain. She tried the phone one more time. Still no service. As she walked through the pine grove, she heard footsteps. *Stop. Listen carefully. Is it the wind? Then,* a wail, as if someone had fallen a great distance. Was it the attacker? She listened again. No sound. *It's the wind,* she decided. Warily, she held a hand out in front of her, making her way among the scratchy tree limbs. A high-pitched scream shot through the air like an arrow.

"Oh, God!" she gasped, dropping to the ground in a crouch. What was that?! A woman's scream, a baby's cry—no, she realized, it was an animal. *The panther's scream will open the way.*

Alma shook her head. How could this be? There were no panthers in the Cumberland Mountains. She doubted if there had ever been many, if any, cougars north of Florida since the late 1700s. There had to be another explanation. She came to the end of the tree tunnel and held her arm up where the moon would light her wristwatch. It said 8:00 p.m, but that was impossible. She had arrived at the party around 7:00 p.m. The watch must be broken.

She leaned against a pile of rocks. Something about them felt strange, too orderly. She examined them and saw they were shaped into a pyramid that sat at the apex of three paths. The peak of the pile came almost to her waist. The more she looked at it, the more it looked man-made. A cool stream of air shot up from the top, causing an odd kind of howl from beneath the rocks. She peered into it; it opened into the earth. A cave. When her hand covered half the opening, the sound was higher pitched. It could have mimicked the panther's scream, she thought; and, if she covered it even more, the wind howled like a wolf. But if sounds were caused only by the degree of her hand covering it—that could mean only one thing. Someone else's hands had recently half-covered the opening.

She sat, anchoring her back on the rocks. The attacker had to be up there with her. From the silence all around, it was clear the police had lost her trail. She was alone with a killer. He still had a gun, and she had nothing with which to protect herself. The brisk air began to frost her breath. Scratches on her arms and face stung. She turned her head, leaning her cheek against the stone; her muscles shivered from exhaustion and cold, her stomach cramped from hunger. Her head drooped a little more, and she closed her eyes for a few seconds' rest.

The flapping of wings roused her. "Caw! Caw! Caw!" She jerked awake. A dozen crows were making a ruckus in a nearby tree, their usual cries when a hawk was sighted. They rarely shut up until the flock attacked their major predator. She held onto the ground. An awful premonition coursed through her; something was about to happen. She could feel it deep inside of her. Someone was coming up the hill. She crawled around the stone pyramid and crouched behind it.

A shadow passed over her. She held her breath. If it was the attacker, she had no way to defend herself. Steps padded on the ground around her. She clasped her hands over her head, squeezing her eyes closed. If he found her, he would kill her. Those words played like a song in her head. *If he finds me, he will kill me.*

The footsteps moved on. She looked over at the trees. The huge black birds were perched on its branches like stone statues. If they hadn't awakened her, whoever passed would have found her. She could be dead now.

Slowly, she pulled herself up and looked at the moon. The silhouette of a man stood on a craggy cliff jutting out above her. The hand of Orion cupped his back. He looked down at her. Their eyes linked like an ancient past pulling itself into the future. She heard the words in her mind—*as above, so below.* His body was lanky, but strong; a shadowy beard layered his jowls, large hands hung loose at his sides, a tattered gray hat was pulled low on his head. The old man!

40

Father? The word rang in her mind again and again. Was this old man Esau Bashears? She thought carefully. He couldn't be the same person who attacked her in the restroom. Too tall, shoulders squared, his movements slow with age. It must have taken all his strength to climb this mountain. The gunman was a younger, stronger man. Again, the question repeated—*is this man my father?*

He chuckled with a low, grim sound as he looked down at her. It was as if she no longer mattered, as if he had beaten her in a race of which she was unaware. He turned, ignoring her presence. When she climbed the slope up to him, she realized he was at the peak of the mountain. They were above the fog line. All around was a sea of white clouds.

She and the old man stood on top of Shadow Mountain, high above any other peak. Cautiously, she picked up a small branch from a fallen chestnut tree. Any kind of weapon would do. He was still facing away from her and was leaning over something. She couldn't tell what. Then she heard the ripple of water. A small waterfall fell over a large stone at the base of a hollowed-out black rock. The man splashed water on his face from a pool, before he spoke. She strained to hear his words.

"Where are ye?" he asked. He opened his arms, as if taking in the disk of the moon that loomed large in the sky beyond him. "Why?" he asked. "Why?"

"Hey," Alma called out. "You. Turn around." She tightened her grip on the branch, holding it like a baseball bat.

He didn't turn; instead, he repeated one word over and over again. "No, no, no, no, no, no, no, no."

Gingerly she stepped a foot closer. "Who are you?"

He emitted a low chuckle. "Spite."

"That's your name?" His voice sent chills up and down her spine.

"Never pays to bargain with Old Scratch. Death don't answer. Death don't answer." The old man whipped around, his eyes wild and ferocious, as if he saw another world, and not the one he was in. Tears gushed down his face as his breath heaved out in a guttural sob. He stared at her, then Alma realized it wasn't she who he saw, but someone or something beyond her. Suddenly he screamed. "Esau! Esau Bashears!" and charged forward. He knocked her down and plunged off the side of the mountain.

Alma struggled to her feet and stared in disbelief. He was sliding down an embankment and screaming out all the breath in his lungs. She started after him, but paused when a strange light whipped past her. She turned toward it. It came from the place where the old man had stood. She took a step forward, then another.

There it was—a moonbow over the pool of water that filled a round base of black rock. A rainbow only caused by the light of the moon when in contact with hazy mist rising from water. In the entire world, only a few moonbows were known to exist. The nearest one Alma knew of was at Cumberland Falls in Whitley County, just northwest of Crimson. As the moon fastened the color on the water, the reflection formed a mesmerizing kaleidoscope of iridescent colors.

Alma became aware of how much her head hurt. Every muscle in her body pulsed with pain. She dipped her hands into the water and came up with a flat stone. She let it go and dipped her hands again, but once more the stone floated onto her palm. She pressed it to her head; the cold rock was strangely comforting. Bending down low, she sipped the icy water, drinking it deeply and without restraint. As she swallowed, a voice whispered. "For whom do you live?"

Alma shot up and looked around. The voice was soft, but unmistakable. She saw no one. "Who's there?" she called out. Her mouth and chin began to tingle, like she had eaten a hot pepper. The only response was the high-pitched cry of a screech owl. She touched her cheek. It was numb, tingly. "Oh no," she whispered to herself. She, of all people, knew better than to drink untested mountain water. Parasites could make her sick for months or possibly kill her. The plants growing around it might be medicinal or even hallucinogenic.

"That was really stupid," she said. The flat stone still pressed to her head, she leaned against the base of the hollowed-out rock. The coldness of the stone seemed to alleviate the ache and throbbing in her skull, making her light-headed. She closed her eyes, resting; and, at the same time, telling herself to start moving again. Follow the old man. Her body wouldn't move. *Got to follow the old man,* she thought.

"Daughter," said someone behind her.

Alma froze. Even after all those years, she knew that voice. "Daddy?" *This is a trick,* she told herself. She was hallucinating.

The soft voice came from the direction of the moonbow. Its tone penetrated her like a whisper from the grave. She held out a hand out toward the moonbow. Her eyes blurred and her insides filled with sorrow she willed herself not to feel. "If you're there, show yourself."

"For whom do you live?"

The colors of the moonbow mixed with a fog steaming off the water. The black pool circled into a stream of images that showed her life—her hurts, her successes, her fears, her ambitions, and a deep pit of feelings no words could describe. She couldn't speak; her throat was parched, but in her mind she saw the breadth of her life.

"For whom do you live?" his voice asked again.

She stared into the water and the swirl of images gelled into a set of eyes. A reflection, she realized. But it was not human. A jolt of adrenaline shot through her body and she held as still as possible. She lifted her gaze above the waterfall to the top of the stone and stared into the face of a cougar. Its whiskers twitched and its mouth grinned, showing fangs. She slowly stepped back, heart beating wildly; if only she could drop below the top of the mountain, it might not chase her.

Her eyes and the cat's eyes linked like iron. It patted its fore paws and tightened its haunches, preparing to spring. Her breathing matched the feline's. Seconds seemed like an eternity. She was consumed by a white darkness so stark that the world no longer existed. White that drank in every trace of her being. Dark filled with terror that cut to the inner sanctums of her heart. Her breath panted out in white puffs, bringing her back to her reality.

The cougar screamed a howl so deafening that all other sound was obliterated. In that instant, she knew that everything she had done in life was for only one person. "For you, Daddy," she said. "Everything I've done, I did for you." The cougar screamed again, the sound like a freight train in her head. She had finally met an opponent she could not defeat.

The cat sprang and she raised her arms, knowing she was about to die. Her own scream mixed with the cougar's. They both fell to the ground. A wind whipped around her, through her, not one part of her being remaining untouched. Then . . . silence. She lifted her head. There was no animal. She looked in the direction it had jumped. Nothing. She listened. It was as if the cougar had disappeared inside of her.

She found herself staring at the stream that dripped over the pool of water, taking with it the colors of the moonbow. With every ounce of strength she possessed, she pushed herself to stand up, sobs heaving from her chest. Circling around and around, she tried to make out the terrain that stretched below her on all sides. Her forehead smacked into a low tree branch and she collapsed into a heap.

What had she been thinking, following something she had not even seen? Trying to move, she felt nauseous and dizzy. Pain hammered in her head again. The moonbow was gone. The cougar was gone. All that remained were the occasional caws of the crows and the sound of her own soulful wails. She was lost, out in the middle of a nowhere called Shadow Mountain, and she was losing her mind.

41

As the sun peeked over the eastern mountains, Alma opened her eyes to hundreds of small yellow butterflies fluttering in and out of an overhanging bank of mountain laurel. She put a hand to her head. Groggy from the lack of sleep, painful scrapes, bruises, and memories she didn't understand. Her stomach growled with hunger. The butterflies lilted around her, moving in different directions as she struggled to her feet.

A massive rock formation made up most of the mountaintop. Its pinnacle was sharp, as if an explosion had blasted off a rounder summit. The dark peak shadowed a deserted cabin that had collapsed from age. Floral vines, moss and animals had overtaken the house. A raccoon poked its head up through the porch floorboards, then scurried inside the open door. The murmur of hummingbirds mixed with the chirps of blue jays and cardinals. Dragonflies and honeybees darted in and out of dew-covered wild roses growing up a side wall. Only the drone of a faraway airplane intruded on their symphony.

Alma was woozy at first; but, as she took a few steps, her body felt stronger and her mind clearer. She studied the pool of water and the streams that trickled over the southern edge. It was almost identical to the picture she had seen in the Kingsley Library. The place where Delta Wade lived. The drawing called *The Streams of Tyme.*

Thoughtfully, Alma leaned on an ancient birch tree, pressing her cheek onto the peeling, silvery bark. She touched the top of her head. The wound produced by the gun butt was packed with a muddy mixture. She pulled some of it off; green, the texture more gritty than mud. It held together like dough and smelled of herbs. *A poultice,* she realized. Someone had taken care of her during the night. The Kingsleys? Maybe the Kingleys' elder sister who had gone to Shadow Mountain twenty-five years ago? She, the little girl, perhaps others . . . people who want to hide from the world like Isham Thunderheart.

Alma looked at the scope of the land . . . large enough to disappear. Enough game to hunt, fruit and berries grew wild and, if the Kingsley woman grew a garden and stored the food properly in a smokehouse or cellar, she could live a frontier life. Alma thought it odd that the woman hadn't stayed around. She might have gone for help, but looking out at the range of mountains as far as she could see, it seemed unlikely. A recluse, she decided, who probably wouldn't be much help finding the way home.

Circling around the mountaintop, Alma saw no sign of a town, road, or house, except for the dilapidated cabin. How in the world could she find her way back to civilization? She might last a week out there, maybe two if she found drinkable water, but she did not possess the skills to cope with such rough terrain.

Even worse, she couldn't explain what had happened to her last night. Anxiety, she rationalized, a concussion, stress of being pursued, the old man. Her mind had played tricks. One thing in particular bothered her—did the old man answer the same question as she? *For whom do you live?* All her life she had believed that the things she did—going to law school, becoming commonwealth attorney, coming home—had been to better herself, to help her family; a dozen reasons. But there was a deeper answer, an answer she had not known until last night. She could not quite formulate the logic, but now knew it was steeped in the love of a father she had lost.

When the old man called out the name Esau Bashears, there was no love. There was fear, hatred, and menace. The meaning of his words must hold the clues to his connection to her father and to Allafair.

Alma dipped her fingers into the cold water in the black rock pool. Somehow, she had managed to do everything she had tried to avoid. Yesterday, she coaxed her nephews into doing things that did not interest them. What was it she had told Larry Joe and Eddie about using their imaginations? *Of course,* she thought. *Find the dragon in the tree*—that is what would get her home.

Right. The idea made her laugh out loud. She was injured, famished, hopelessly lost, and some fairy-tale idea was going to rescue her—just like that! The childish hope made her wonder if she was losing it—losing it so badly that in an hour or so she would be dead of exposure or exhaustion or . . . but what else was there? "Damn," she said, choking down a sob. "Damn!"

She closed her eyes and visualized where Contrary was located on a map. Starting out south at the Hog's Wallow, running east, then up the mountain, home would be more or less . . .

"That way." She opened her eyes and pointed to the streams dripping over the black rock onto the ground below. The water that trickled over the side was little more than a drip from a faucet. She did not believe in psychics or ghosts or visions and sometimes even questioned the existence of God; but, after last night, she could only trust what her mind was making known to her, even if she didn't understand it. If destiny called for her to follow the Streams of Tyme, then she would follow it wherever it led.

Alma picked up the chestnut branch she had intended to use as a weapon and found it was a good walking stick. Pausing for a last look at the top of the mountain, she used the branch for support. "Delta Wade, you must have had some life story to tell," she said. Butterflies crisscrossed in the air, landing on the fallen frame of the house, and honeybees, dragonflies, and humming birds darted among the thick tangle of honeysuckle and wisteria vines dangling from the roof. Despite the ruggedness, she felt that the isolated kingdom had a kind of magic to it. She had been granted entry into a place few humans were ever blessed to see.

After a few of hours of walking, the stream merged into a bubbling creek that twisted around the mountainside. She rested and picked some blackberries, filling her mouth with the fruit until the juice seeped down her chin, then washed off in the stream. Following it until the flow became a cascading waterfall down onto a pallet of rock, she climbed down a stone staircase where the stream once again turned into a slow-moving creek as peaceful as those that ran through her hollow.

Alma thought she might be headed in the direction of Contrary. At any rate, when she found a road, she would still be a good twenty miles from a town. A misty fog steamed off the water and the cavernous trees were sixty to a hundred feet in height. She kept a lookout for another person, but no one crossed her path—not a Kingsley, a gunman, or an old man.

After a while, she looked at her watch and found the second hand ticking. "How about that?" she said, looking back at the distance she had covered. The entire mountain had disappeared behind a bank of thick fog. Quickly, she pulled out her cell phone, found that it was working, and called Walter. She got his voice mail. She didn't leave a message. She started to dial Vernon but paused when she caught sight of a building in the distance.

She clicked off the phone and peered through the trees. Several hundred yards away stood a cabin, outhouse off to the side, a garden in the front yard. She rushed down to within hollering distance. *Isham Thunderheart's cabin,* she realized. She studied the stream and the direction it flowed, down from the mountain, down this last hill, ahead through paths of slate and sandstone boulders into a marshy cove that she could see and, finally, emptying into Silver Lake.

Breathless, Alma trudged up to the cabin and sank onto the porch steps. She sat and stared, knowing she had to think this out clearly. What were all the clues leading to—Quincy Pollard telling her to seek out Isham; Isham being killed before she could talk to him; the old man telling her Allafair's children were the spawn of a Shadow; Grady and Jefferson coming to this place. They were all very real events, but what connected them? Her mind spun, giving her no answers. There was only one event that seemed to be a link, but it was not based in reality, it was a dream: a hallucination of a little black-haired girl standing at the edge of the woods, clutching a doll. *The answer you seek is in the Streams of Tyme.*

Alma stared at the creek. Where did it lead? Only one place—into the depths of Silver Lake. Which meant what? Maybe nothing. Yet so many other pieces fit together. It wouldn't be simple to put the last piece in place. She needed help.

She took out her cell phone and dialed Vernon.

"Yep?" he answered.

"It's me," she said.

"Howdy there, Anna Ruth," he said quickly.

Alma smiled. Either the phone was tapped or policemen were nearby. She said the first thing that came into her mind. "I've been calling you for several days." Frantically, she reorganized her thoughts and fought to keep a cool, businesslike tone. "That scuba diving equipment you ordered arrived today, and we're about to ship it to the fishing dock at Silver Lake, but I wasn't sure of the address."

"Send it to the house," he said. "There isn't a good address out there."

"Okay, but make sure this stuff doesn't sit in the attic too long," she added, hinting at the equipment's location. "It's time sensitive."

"I won't."

"By the way, last time we talked you had a sick dog. Did it survive?" She hoped he realized she was asking about Val.

"Thanks for calling," he said. "I have to get off the phone."

She hung up. Val had died. She heard it in the tone of his voice. Tears filled her eyes. She blinked them back and silently cursed the killer. "I'll hunt him down," she promised, looking up at the sky. "He'll pay for your death with his life." A quick, hot heat rushed through her as she quelled the rage of wanting to kill this man.

She sat quietly, staring at the smooth surface of the lake and thinking about the many times she and Val had argued, laughed, and schemed. The memories brought her only a small measure of peace. So far, the deaths had multiplied and produced only ghosts that had not been avenged.

She hoped Vernon understood her message—get the scuba equipment from her attic and meet her at the dock at Silver Lake. She looked back at the stream, which was so obviously a shortcut to the mountain; a mountain that most regarded as a myth, a mystical place where people either lost their sanity or found it.

Okay, she thought, *I've lived too many years obsessed by the past.* The mountain revealed her heart and showed it to her in such a way that now she must embrace it or die. She would not be free until the mystery of her father was solved.

Now the Streams of Tyme had led her here. If the answer was in that lake, then that was where she was going.

She hid among the trees, waiting for Vernon. In her mind she kept hearing the words, *hurry, hurry, we must save Helen Marie.*

42

"It was thoughtful of you to remember my wet suit," Alma told Vernon. She ducked behind the opposite side of the truck and peeled off her clothes while alternately wolfing down a ham sandwich. "I wasn't relishing doing this in my underwear or on an empty stomach." She aimed a can of antibiotic spray at several cuts and scrapes and winced through the sting.

Nervously, he watched the road. "I can't be sure Drake's people didn't figure out what was going on." He nodded at the paper sack containing tennis shoes, overalls, and a cap sporting a logo for Marcum's Garage. "If you shave your head, maybe they won't recognize you."

She chuckled and pointed at the vehicle. "Vernon, you hot-wired—"

"Borrowed," he corrected. "I left a note."

"*Borrowed* Gary Marcum's tow truck, took it in and out of the hollow loaded with my scuba equipment, got the doctor at the emergency room to fill the air tank, and drove out here without them following you. I'd call that a talent."

"I didn't bring this truck so I wouldn't be noticed."

"It's a perfect foil," she said, strapping a forty-pound weight belt around her waist. "Anyone sees you, they'll think you're towing abandoned cars from the lakeshore."

"I brought it because it's got a thousand feet of rope in the back."

"A thousand?" She hesitated, then realized his meaning. "Oh no, I'm not tying myself to that truck."

"Alma, people don't generally dive in these waters. You don't know what you'll run into."

"I was certified in Monterey, California. Those are among the most difficult waters to learn in."

"But aren't scuba divers supposed to buddy-up?"

She paused, afraid the conversation was about to turn into a fight. "Well, yes, but that's not an option here."

"Then," he said, looping the end of the rope around her waist, "I might have to tow you in."

"That's something a big sister does to a little brother." She dropped an underwater light into a collecting bag and inserted her diving knife in a sheath strapped around her calf.

"You want some help with that tank?"

Alma realized she would get nowhere trying to convince him, so she zipped her boots and stepped into the water to put on the flippers. "Yeah, come on out," she said. "Might as well get your shoes wet."

He stared at her for several seconds. "Alma, are you all right?"

"Yeah," she said, "for somebody who spent last night in a T-shirt and a pair of wet jeans."

"Something about you seems different."

"What?"

"Don't know yet."

Alma spit in the mask, wiping the plastic to keep it from fogging, then turned away from shore. Vernon was right. There was something different about her, but she couldn't name it either. Her eyes stared harder, her mind calculated the consequences of each move, a vast stillness rocked inside of her, edged with whispers that she couldn't quite hear. She couldn't risk getting locked in a psychiatric ward so, for now, she had to keep quiet about what had happened on Shadow Mountain.

She dipped into the water and swam out, breathing through the snorkel for about a hundred feet from shore. The weight of the equipment was heavy on her chest and she hungrily sucked in air. The water beneath her had good visibility, at least thirty feet, but at the bottom she didn't see anything more than mossy rocks, beer cans and a few large carp that streaked away from her. She righted herself and bit down on the regulator, blowing out a stream of bubbles to test it, then she deflated the buoyancy control device, piked in the water, and began a descent.

Once completely underwater, she could breathe easier. She cleared her ears several times on the way down, holding her nose through the mask and blowing. At the bottom of the lake she touched solid ground and read twenty feet on the digital depth gauge. She had been as deep as sixty and wasn't confident about going beyond that.

The surrounding rocks were an olive green, slimy to the touch but firmly entrenched. A snapping turtle crawled out of a black stump and onto a hollow log that sheltered two long-whiskered catfish. The ground hadn't changed since the water covered it. A school of silvery shad swam closer and then jetted quickly in the opposite direction. She pulled herself along the bottom, coming to the approximate place where Isham's creek entered Silver Lake.

Vernon's rope caught on barbwire twisted around the rusted frame of a submerged car. She untangled the rope with a jerk and the trunk popped open, releasing a dozen pancake-shaped bluegills. Slowly, she swam in circles without really knowing what she was looking for. The lake was at least half a mile across. The clear water had a strangeness, a spookiness that she refused to let shake her.

Checking the depth gauge, she reckoned about thirty more minutes at her current depth before she had to surface. The dive could end up a wild goose chase. Even if something was in the lake, how could she hope to find it in one dive? A sunken boat, dropped fishing reels, and snarled lines wrapped around rocks—nothing else. She was running out of time.

Drifting toward an underwater cliff, she looked over the edge and felt an electrical charge rush through her. About sixty feet down sat a house. The water was murkier than the shallower part of the lake and gave off a silvery sheen. Alma cleared her ears again. If she tried to explore the house she would be almost a hundred feet down by the time she reached it. She had only been that deep once before and had gotten such a bad case of nitrogen narcosis that she spent the rest of the day in the hospital emergency room. She checked her gauge: about ten minutes to explore and ten more to decompress.

She kicked forward and was jerked back. "No!" she said, through a stream of bubbles. She had run out of line.

Holding onto a stick jutting from the cliff edge, she stared down at the clapboard house. She had come too far to turn back. Whatever she was looking for had to be in that house. *Sorry, Vernon,* she thought as she reached for the diving knife, cut the rope, and plunged downward.

She had to clear her ears about every ten feet. Steadily, she sank toward the back porch of the house, then was amazed to see that the stillness of the water had maintained a swing tied to the rafters, a tin tub, and a flower pot. A raccoon skin was still tacked to the outside wall, though much of it had been pecked away by fish. She swam up to a doorframe, mired in a foot of gray sediment. Pushing on the door did no good. It wouldn't budge. She floated over to a crumbled window, aimed her light at the hole, and slipped into the murky darkness of the house.

Without the illumination of the penetrating sun, the black water became a night dive. She covered as much ground as possible with the single beam— picture frames on a wall where the photos had faded, coal stove, kettle on a burner, overturned chairs, washboard tipped against the wall, a razor strop hanging on a nail. Suddenly, glowing disks appeared and disappeared. Alma held as still as she could. The luminescent specks shot off in different directions as her light chased them. A dozen cylindrical shapes darted around her, mouths opening and closing, showing needlelike teeth as a school of wall-eyed pike tried to escape.

She ducked under the fish and came out the other side of the house to a living room. There was less sediment there. She held up a hand and felt a current. Part of the wall had collapsed and sunlight from above allowed a clearer view of a potbellied stove, several handmade chairs held together with strips of bark, half-burned candles in saucers, and wallpaper hand decorated with hummingbirds.

A couch hung on the edge of a partially shattered floor. A blanket covered a long lump on the couch. Alma pulled it off, sending up a flurry of flaky sediment that covered a pile of bones. Human bones. She tumbled backward in shock until she bumped the wall. On second glance she saw that there were two skeletons. A wild exhale of bubbles exploded from her mask in an underwater scream.

Regaining her composure, she swept a hand through the snowy particles. One was an adult, the other, a child. She was sure it wasn't an infant, but also not older than ten. The adult's arm bones were wrapped around the child, whose own arms had either disintegrated or been carried away by lake creatures. Alma picked up the adult hand and measured it against her own. It was large, a man's. Between the man and the child lay something gray and wrinkled.

Alma hesitated, partly in distaste at reaching among the bones, partly an aversion to invading their resting place. The skeletons had been protected by the blanket and preserved by the sediment on top. She could even see the red color of the couch underneath them. Slowly she picked up what was embedded in the bones and let it float toward her: two porcelain legs, two porcelain arms, and a small mane of black curls that expanded in the water. She gasped at the faceless doll as it gently danced in front of her.

Swimming backward, she retreated to the porch and held onto one of the rails. What did it mean? Her mind said coincidence, but her heart knew that word no longer fit her world. She went into the house again to retrieve the doll, clasped it to her chest with one hand, pulled the blanket back over the two skeletons, then swam upward toward the cliff.

It took time to decompress. In fifteen feet of water, she waited out three minutes but could see Vernon watching up above. The sight of someone standing beside him sent a jolt through her. There was no mistaking that mass of blond, unruly curls that wouldn't hold a style. She emerged in six feet of water, swam until she could stand, and spit out the regulator. "How," she asked Vernon, "did that woman find you?" Even though Maggie Armstrong was a reporter, Alma was a fugitive and could be turned in by anyone.

"I let her follow me," he said.

"Why?"

"I figured if Drake's people found me, I'd turn around and kiss her."

"What?" Maggie stared at him incredulously.

"Neckin' at the lake is always a good alibi."

The two women looked at each other as Vernon leaned on the back of the truck with a goofy grin on his face. Maggie whispered to him, "In your dreams, cowboy," then she stepped forward and offered Alma a hand out of the water.

"She's got something to tell you" Vernon said to Alma, acting as if he didn't know the meaning of insult. Then, noticing that the rope he held in his hands was no longer attached to his sister's waist, he let loose a string of cuss words.

"This is more important," Alma said, patting his shoulder to calm him down. "Go back to town and call the state police. Tell them there are two skeletons about a hundred feet down, inside a house." She pointed at a line of bald cypress trees. "Go straight out from there, almost mid lake. They'll find them." She put the doll in the collecting bag and gave it to him. "Take this to my house, fill the sink with water, and leave it there. Better it stays wet until I can dry it properly." She turned to Maggie. "Well, here's the story I promised you, but I don't know what it means yet."

Maggie pushed back a mass of her hair and swallowed hard.

Alma watched her, curiously realizing how serious her mood was. "You must have found the Vera Cleary article."

"No," Maggie said. "Better."

Alma waited.

"I found Vera Cleary." She looked down, and then back to Alma. "I spoke with her, and she wants to talk with you as fast as water can boil."

43

Sirens wailed behind Maggie's Honda. Alma held her breath. *Let them pass,* she prayed, crouched on the backseat floor. Gravel crunched under the wheels as the car swerved onto the side of the road. She figured every law enforcement unit in the Southeast was on the lookout for her.

"Don't worry," Maggie said without turning around. "I have a sister who always gets into trouble. I'm experienced at this sort of thing."

"Hiding fugitives?" Alma asked.

"Covering for her. And when that didn't work, Daddy paid her way out of it."

"You sound a bit proud."

"I hate admitting it, but money does buy power." The siren was almost upon them. Maggie hummed, and then began nervously singing the *Gilligan's Island* theme song.

Alma scrunched lower. No matter who was in the pursuing police car—Drake or Moody's people—she knew they wouldn't let her walk. Back to Contrary jail she'd go. What railed through her mind was, whenever she got near to important information, the key person was killed. Quincy Pollard. Isham Thunderheart. She had to talk to Vera Cleary today and hoped no one else would find her. Her nails dug into the seat fabric as the siren came up directly behind them, and then passed. She let out a huff of relief.

They drove on. Alma used the time to find out as much as she could about the young woman so intent on being part of this investigation. Maggie grew up in Washington DC, one of four daughters of lobbyists. Alma suspected her upbringing instilled a need to convince—a need of which she was probably unaware. Maggie knew the ins and outs of government, as well as most of the insider gossip. Yet, savvy as she was, the young woman's choice to come to Appalachia must fit either a politically correct agenda, which spiced up her resume, or some rich girl's sense of guilt. *Time will tell,* she decided.

Thunder's Trace Retirement Home was located near Tazewell, Tennessee, in the graceful, rolling hills of Powell Valley. It had the look of a school dormitory; a one-story, long rectangle with shutterless windows and individual patios off the backside. Cushioned into a grove of dogwood and maple trees that shaded wrought iron benches, the building's hunter green paint almost made it disappear into the scenery. As Maggie led Alma down the main corridor, she glanced into the shared rooms. Elderly people lay in beds, some conscious, some not. Parts of the retirement home appeared more like a depository for forgotten family members rather than a place for retirees.

They entered a midsized recreation room filled with active men and women, some playing cards, others ping pong. One gravelly, smoke-scarred voice rose above the rest— "Get your cotton-pickin' hands away from my cigarettes!"

"Let me guess," Alma said toward Maggie. "That is the voice of the senior citizen who unofficially runs the place, whether the staff likes it or not."

Vera Cleary was a thin woman of about five feet six inches; her snow-colored hair was pulled back into a braid that shot down past her waist. Thick wire-framed glasses sat on her nose and she had a habit of punching them up with her pinkie finger. Leaning against an open door, she flicked ashes and blew smoke outside. She caught sight of Alma and Maggie immediately but didn't come over to them.

Alma took the opportunity to study her. She was dressed in blue jeans and a tank top. Perhaps eighty, she looked flexible and active, as if age were an inconvenience rather than a reality. As a journalist, she had dressed as a man and gone to the DMZ during the Vietnam conflict, so Vera Cleary was as tough a bird as there was. Alma decided a direct approach would work best, but she'd have to move at Ms. Cleary's pace. A reporter with her experience would sense anyone trying to get at information circuitously.

Maggie waved at Vera to get her attention. The elderly woman gave them a look of indifference, apparently not ready to talk.

"I think she knows we're here," Alma said, growing impatient with being deliberately ignored while Ms. Cleary finished her cigarette.

Finally, she mashed out the half-smoked stub on the doorframe and approached them. "Somebody named Judith Drake was here this morning looking for you," she said.

Alma and Maggie exchanged a glance, both fighting a spear of adrenaline that quickly fed a dozen fears. Judith Drake had people watching everyone. Maggie's expression turned to anger, but she instantly concealed her feelings, as if she had learned the talent from her politically connected parents.

"She quacked about being a friend." Vera chuckled and nodded her head for Alma and Maggie to follow. "I wanted to make sure she'd gone."

They entered a room as small as a college dormitory single containing a bed and table and a sliding glass door that led to a patio. Vera stepped into the closet and pulled down a box. With a dismissive glance, she turned to Maggie. "Close that door on your way out, will ya, honey?"

"But I—" Maggie stuttered, caught off guard. Then she reminded them, "This is my story."

Vera let the dusty box hit her bed with a bounce and smiled at the younger reporter. "Honey, when you're as old as me, you'll learn that a story comes in its own time, but right now, I need to speak to this lady alone."

Maggie scowled, realizing she had no choice. After she left, Vera opened the box and shuffled through it until she found a large manila envelope stuffed full of papers. The face of it was unmarked. Alma stayed deliberately quiet, noting that this was a woman who liked directing the show. Vera held the envelope to her chest and motioned for Alma to go outside and sit at a table on the patio.

Alma did so, and Vera stood in the frame of the sliding glass door and looked out at a partially tended flower garden and a tiny lawn that needed mowing. Her expression became hesitant; even regretful. For an admitted curmudgeon, Alma wondered why Vera was unable to stare her down. Such reticence didn't mesh with the legends the journalist had inspired. "You asked to see me," Alma finally said.

Vera stared at her, eyes dead, a challenge. "You're Ursula Bashears' grand-daughter?"

Alma stared straight back. "Yes."

"She did me a favor once." Vera took out another cigarette but left it unlit. "I want to make sure I'm talking to the right person."

Alma maintained eye contact without speaking. *Time to try a little intimidation myself,* she thought.

"I've been dreading this meeting for the last twenty-eight years." Vera took the opposite chair and laid the envelope between them. "Here it is. What you've come for." As Alma reached for the envelope, Vera's hand came down on top of hers. "I only ask that you not judge me too harshly."

Alma pulled the envelope toward her and took out a half-inch thick manuscript titled "The Melungeons of Shadow Mountain."

She turned over the title page and read the first paragraph:

Shadow Mountain is a folktale. No such place is officially registered in Kentucky, Tennessee, or Virginia. The mountain is a mythical place said to hold riches of silver, copper and, perhaps, an undiscovered mineral more precious than gold. Likely it also contained a rich vein of ore, possibly coal, which its overseers wanted to protect from speculators in the early 1900s. The legend behind the mountain states that it is only found when it needs to be, and that makes some people question if it really exists. It is said to be the spiritual home to a group of Melungeons, a people whose curious genetic makeup has made them a local mystery. Some of their descendants now live in a glen called Pollyhollow. If Shadow Mountain has not come into this century, the Melungeons have, because Pollyhollow is halfway to civilization, This cove was recently destroyed to create Midnight Valley's water source. Silver Lake. What the people of Midnight Valley don't know is that, not only was a hollow destroyed and its Melungeons forced to flee for their lives when the ridge holding back a dozen creeks was blown up prematurely, but Silver Lake is a grave. A sepulcher containing the greed of a man and the pride of a woman—Walt and Charlotte Gentry.

Alma looked up after reading the names. Vera seemed to know exactly where she had stopped reading, as if the manuscript was memorized. "You're not the only one who made enemies of the Gentrys," she said. "And your father is perhaps the only person on this earth who ever outfoxed them."

"What does he have to do with this story?" Alma asked, too curious to read on.

"Walt, Sr. needed your father."

"Walter Gentry, Sr. fired my father and kept him from getting employment in the entire valley. He had to go to Detroit to get a job so our family would have money for Christmas. He was killed. His body was never found."

Vera kept shaking her head as Alma spoke. "Walt sent your father to Detroit."

"What? Why?"

"To find Allafair Adair."

Alma leaned back in the chair, one hand pressing her forehead. "That doesn't make sense. My father was a working man. The Gentrys had money, contacts that could have—"

"Walt searched everywhere for her, hired every private detective in the Southeast. No one could find her. She always had a way of staying hidden when she wanted. Finally, in desperation I believe, he caught on to the old legends of how one Melungeon always knows another no matter how distant the bloodline."

"But my father wasn't a Melungeon. How would he know about Shadow Mountain or Pollyhollow or Melungeons?"

Vera held her hands up in a "who-knows" gesture. "He found her, didn't he?"

"Did he?" Alma asked rhetorically. "My mother received letters from Daddy for months after he went missing."

Vera nodded her head as if familiar with the information. "In researching this story, I traced Allafair's tracks—as well as anybody could ever follow her. To throw Walt off the track, your father wrote the letters and predated them. He gave them to a trusted neighbor, who mailed them from Detroit faithfully every week. Walt had people watching your mother, your whole family. This gave Esau and Allafair the time they needed to get safely to Pollyhollow, or so they thought."

Alma considered each detail of the older woman's story. If her father went to Detroit to do Gentry's dirty work, he must have had a good reason. "But somewhere along the way he had too much conscience to return her to Walt Gentry." She closed her eyes and could see the story unfolding. "Was Walt the father of Allafair's children? Is that their connection?"

"I don't know," Vera said. "I entered this story much later, through his wife, Charlotte." She lit the cigarette and laughed a slight, cynical chuckle through puffs of smoke. "You'll find this hard to believe, but there was a time when she was young and beautiful and very kind."

"Excuse me if I do find that impossible to accept."

Vera looked away, her eyes focused on a patch of orange tiger lilies, and moved back and forth as if another lifetime were springing up before her. "Charlotte wanted me to write an article on the water project at Silver Lake, and I was more than happy to. It was to be this Valley's finest accomplishment to date. Charlotte made it all possible. Silver Lake is on Federal land that was leased to Crimson County for one hundred years." Vera shifted in her chair and looked away. "Little did either of us know that we were about to walk into the middle of a war."

Again Alma looked down at the manuscript and turned to the next page. Vera leaned back, chain-smoking with her eyes closed. As Alma read, Vera spoke occasionally as if following the manuscript in her own mind. "There was a fight. Allafair's child was knocked to the ground. I'll never forget it. Caught between her mother and Charlotte, she clutched a doll, which broke her fall. The doll's face struck a rock and came off in a perfect eyeless piece. Charlotte picked it up, clasping it so tightly, she cut her hand."

"That was my doll," Alma whispered. "My father must have let Allafair's child play with it." Alma kept reading, then gasped. "Charlotte blew up the ridge!" she said, one hand covering mouth. "But there were people in those houses."

Vera blinked back tears. "Charlotte wasn't thinking about that. She acted in impulse, in anger. If her husband was going to leave her, she would destroy the one thing he wanted."

"Which was what? Allafair?"

"He wanted Shadow Mountain. Those people knew how to get there. Through Allafair and her children, he'd control it."

A burning sensation filled Alma's insides. "What is on Shadow Mountain? It has to be more than mythic stories."

"Evidently, something more valuable than gold." Vera sniffed and inhaled on her cigarette.

The words on Charlotte Gentry's tombstone went through Alma's mind like an ironic taunt: *As above so below, come walk with me on streets of gold.* A dare to someone? A challenge, a sneer, dedicated to her deceased husband?

"With all of the adults standing there," Vera said in a distant, sad voice, "it was only the small child who seemed to understand the implications of the explosion. I will never forget the sight of her, struggling to her feet, clutching her faceless doll and screaming, *'Hurry, hurry, we must save Helen Marie.'* She believed her infant sister was still in the house."

It was a story larger than Alma could comprehend, but one that still didn't make sense. "Why wasn't that evil woman sent to jail? Why did you keep this a secret for so many years?" The blame in her voice etched pain into Vera's expression. Now she understood Vera's only request—*don't judge me too harshly.*

Vera's eyes closed for a moment as if remembering a terrible past, then she opened them and pointed at a picture on a shelf of herself, two children, and a man. "I wrote my story—too much a journalist to call the police before I did that. My failing. My fault. I wanted the story that bad. That same night, after my family ate dinner, my husband got violently ill." She paused and swallowed hard. "He died three days later after the most agonizing illness one can imagine. Then, the phone calls began. A voice repeating, 'Your children could be next.'" She bit her bottom lip and huffed out several distressed breaths. "The doctors said the mushrooms on our dinner table were poisonous. My God, my husband was a botanist. Do you think he couldn't tell a poison mushroom when he saw it? My children were sitting at that table. They could have been . . . " Her hand went to her throat and she stared at the concrete patio floor. "I pulled the article and held it all these years. Charlotte couldn't hurt my children as long as I held onto this story, and I couldn't risk their lives. We were at a stalemate. I quit my job at the *Crimson County Sun* and waited. I knew someday, someone would come looking for the truth."

"That's more trust than I would have had."

"And yet, here you are." She sat up and looked deeply into Alma's eyes. "That's something your grandmother taught me—the truth will always find the light of day. It was a secret I had to keep, a secret I was forced to keep."

"She's updated that a little." Alma shook her head as if she could hear Mamaw saying the words. "What happened to Allafair?"

216

Curiosity lit up Vera's eyes. "I heard that her other daughter was given up for adoption, so evidently the infant didn't die in the flood."

Alma felt the pain of that statement, but her own needs overrode any concern. "Tell me. What happened to my father?"

"He protected Allafair." Vera's expression grew hard, not the steeliness of hate, but the facade trauma victims assume in order to protect themselves. She bit the side of her lip, then said one word. "Read."

Alma turned her attention back to the remaining pages of the manuscript. She swept through the words, her breath caught in her throat. The entire world disappeared. "My father," she said after finishing the last page. "My father."

Vera's hands covered her mouth and chin and she spoke through spread fingers. "He ran back to the house after the little girl, who believed her baby sister was still in her crib." She hesitated, then spoke through a shivered breath. "The wave of water hit. I never saw him again."

44

"Well?" Maggie Armstrong squirmed in the front seat like an eager child who wanted candy.

In back, Alma focused on the ceiling light as she shifted into an uncomfortable crouch. Maggie cleared her throat. "Shhh," Alma said, needing silence to think. Hours ago, she had found her father's bones at the bottom of a lake. Charlotte had caused his death and someone was still protecting that woman's secrets. *Another journalist could be my answer,* she thought. *A young one.* She clutched the envelope tightly to her chest and pressed the strip of tape over the opening, resealing it loosely.

Maggie finally exploded. "If I don't get the story, I am not only in big trouble with my boss, but I am personally about to fall over and die in a fit of wiggles if you don't tell me something."

Yes, Alma said to herself. *Maggie Armstrong, you have exactly the qualities needed to become part of this story.* She sat up, causing Maggie to glance in the rearview mirror. The car swerved.

"We're in the middle of town," Maggie snapped, "as in Contrary, Kentucky. Get down! Anybody sees you, and we'll be sharing a stinky cell in county jail."

Alma tentatively held out the envelope. "This is what you want." She dangled it over the front seat. "I'm giving it to you on one condition." She waited. The poor woman was almost salivating. "You have to promise me you'll open it only if, by morning . . . I'm dead."

Maggie's mouth dropped open. "Are you okay? Ever since I picked you up, something about you seems different." Her eyes locked with Alma's in the rearview mirror. Neither spoke. Both knew that something had changed. Something words could not describe. Maggie steered with one hand and held out the other. "I . . . I . . . " She hesitated, her attention darting from the road to the envelope. "I promise."

Alma had Maggie drop her off at the train tracks on the south end of town. She could follow them to the edge of the Bashears' hollow, climb the hill and end up in her own backyard. As she walked, she made a mental list of what to do next. If her plan was going to work, she would have to get every detail right. The sun was sinking and, in another hour, and it would be dark. She stopped, held to a rough-barked locust tree and analyzed her own actions. She gauged the time by the sun instead of looking at her watch. Somehow she felt different, almost possessed, and yet she was the same. The effects of Shadow Mountain went deeper than she could admit—the night on its slopes ran through her like an infection, giving her a feverish sense of mission that required total concentration. There was an iron heart inside of her. There was a cougar fighting to get out.

She climbed up an embankment and reached the cliffs above her house. Two state troopers sat on the porch. Steadily, she crept down and hid within the thick branches of a pine tree. As the sky grew darker, she felt braver about her plan and accepted that, with all she knew now, there was no other choice. Whip-poor-wills trilled. In between their warbling, she whistled a low birdcall and waited. Again, and waited. A few minutes later, Willie was at her side. "Good dog," she whispered and scratched behind both his ears. He licked her hands, his mouth forming an excited smile. "You are Sir William from now on." She took off her belt and looped it around his neck, tying him to a tree.

The troopers smoked cigarettes and drank coffee from a thermos. She followed a path down behind her house, crept toward the kitchen door, and entered. She peered into the living room and saw that the patio door was open. A third trooper sat outside in a lawn chair. She squatted, took off her shoes, and crawled on her hands and knees along the hallway baseboard until she reached the staircase and twisted up around the corner. At the top of the steps, she paused to listen. No one was on the second floor. She stood and went into her bedroom.

In the closet, she knelt and moved two floorboards, then pulled out her bulletproof vest and her pistol. Pocketing the gun, she put on the vest and covered it with the same loose jacket she had worn to the cemetery to meet the old man. On her way back down the steps, a whining creak from below stopped her cold. A trooper stepped into her living room. She froze; she would make too much noise if she went back up the stairs. Flattening herself against the wall, she breathed slow and even. Suddenly the trooper laughed.

Alma reached for her gun. She would never be able to shoot him but might be able to bluff her way out. If she made it to the woods, they wouldn't be able to track her in the mountains; she knew the area better than them. Confidence gushed deep inside of her like a newly formed fountainhead.

The trooper stopped in front of the steps, his back toward her. He leaned down, reached underneath a chair, and pulled out the Chihuahua. It whimpered. Cradling it in his arms, he said, "Come on, girl. I bet you ain't eaten all day. There's a food bin out here on the deck." He went back out to the patio.

Alma waited until she heard the lid of the bin knock against the house wall, then breathed a sigh of relief and slipped down to the kitchen. She grabbed her shoes and crept back into the woods. She made her way to the tree where Willie was tied, rechecked her gun, and closed the clips on the vest. Inside her head, a voice kept repeating—*Hurry, hurry, we must save Helen Marie.*

She and Willie went down the train tracks and climbed up toward her grandmother's house. The land was flatter and the police could see her more easily. A garden, high with ripe corn, offered protection. She walked through the stalks all the way to the barn.

Behind it came muffled yelps and growls as her other dogs settled in for the evening. Vernon was no doubt taking good care of them. Alma looked over at the lighted kitchen window in Mamaw's house; she heard a TV in her brother's trailer. Part of her longed to run to any one of them. They would all give their lives to protect her, but she could never involve any of them in what she was about to do.

She went into the barn through a back door. The pack of dogs tensed and jumped in excitement. She knelt down and shushed them as Sadie licked her face. "Come on, boy," she called to Caesar. He and Bud wagged their tails, while the collie and bird-dog watched expectantly. The horse Mamaw was boarding shifted to and fro in her stall. Alma looked at the chestnut mare. Her moist eyes blinked, then she shook her head and snorted, but accepted the bridle. Alma led the animal out of the stall and reached for a saddle.

The barn door creaked. She froze, afraid to look behind her. *No,* she thought. *After all of this, I can't get caught.*

"Alma?" her grandmother's voice asked.

She exhaled in relief, but facing Mamaw was too painful. She had always wanted her family to be proud of her. Now she was a fugitive on a mission no one would understand. She couldn't turn around, so she stared straight ahead. "Mamaw," she said. "Are we Melungeons?"

The soft shuffle of her grandmother's feet as she came forward was like a cat walking over fallen leaves. There was no hesitation in her voice. "You have a Cherokee ancestor, a few German ones, French, Dutch and plenty of English. There were five sisters in my family. Four of us had blue eyes, fair skin, hair that curled unless we let it grow, but the fifth . . . the fifth showed her blood. Dark, dreamy eyes as black as coal; skin like a copper penny and straight black hair that hung down past her knees. She married a man from Savannah. You and me, we'll have to go see her one day soon." Mamaw came up on the other side of the horse, stroking its throat and opening her hand with a gift of sugar. When she looked into Alma's eyes, her concerned expression changed.

Alma couldn't quite read it—fear and iron, yet filled with a fever of destiny. "I keep meeting people you've done favors for," she said. The awkwardness of the situation bit into her humiliation. "You get around a lot more than I ever would have imagined."

Mamaw nodded and let go of the horse's bridle as if it was the hardest thing she had ever done. She touched her granddaughter's cheek, the smell of cane sugar scenting her skin, then turned away without speaking.

Alma saddled the horse and led it down to the train rails, with the dogs following. The track curved around the town to the cemetery. When they reached the edge of the graveyard, she tied up the horse and ordered the dogs to sit and stay. Hurrying over the hill, she pulled out her phone, hoping it had enough power left for one more call. She dialed her attorney and, when he answered, she murmured the words, "As above, so below, come walk with me on streets of gold."

45

A solitary figure leaned against the backside of a marble angel. It was grand and expensive compared to the other more moderate-sized granite grave markers. Alma had watched him for the last twenty minutes, letting him wait until she was sure he was alone. She stepped into a broad band of moonlight. When he caught sight of her at the top of the hill, he waved an arm over his head, signaling her to come down. "Smart to use a code I'd recognize," Walter Gentry said when she came within earshot. "I wouldn't put it past Judith Drake to monitor my phone."

"I didn't know where to turn," Alma said. "If you only knew what I've been through in the last forty-eight hours." She slumped against the base of the angel and rested her head in her hands. "Judith has been behind me at every turn."

"It's okay," he said. "I'm here now. Trust me. When I'm done with her, Miss Drake is going to regret the day she ever came to eastern Kentucky." He rubbed Alma's arm, letting his other hand push back her hair from her forehead. "It's okay now," he said again, softer and with more compassion.

"I suppose I'll have to turn myself in," Alma said.

"Let me take you to my house first. We'll get you a bath, some hot food. We'll do this when you're ready."

"I'm ready. I'm ready for whatever I need to face." She straightened her back and looked up at him. Genuine concern flowed through his eyes. "It's funny, though . . . " she paused and stared out at the graveyard.

He waited on her and, when she didn't continue speaking, he touched her shoulder. "There's something wrong?"

"I saw the old man again. I saw him on a place called Shadow Mountain. I think he followed me there. Don't ask how I knew the way; it's too long a story."

"Do you know where he is now?" Walter asked, softly.

In his voice she heard fear trying to disguise itself as interest. He was afraid of the old man. "He's out there." She nodded at the darkness. "Watching us. I think he's a ghost."

"Oh, good God."

"A ghost of the past, someone whose life was stolen, an angry spirit who knows our names. Spite." She chuckled, sensing it send a shiver up Walter's spine. "Someone who's come back to do destiny's bidding."

"We make our own destinies," Walter said. "I know you believe that."

"We can't escape the past. It runs in our blood."

"Alma, you need to rest."

She turned toward him and gripped the sleeve of his shirt. "Every ancestor you've ever had lived and died to bring you to this point. Most of them were buried on the land where we stand."

"I'll take you home." He leaned into her, steadying her with an arm around her shoulders.

"Don't you see? It's your father, my father, all the past finally catching up to us." Her hands rested on his chest, clutching his shirt, pulling him closer. "There was a moment last night when I believed I was losing my mind."

"Alma, please." He cushioned her cheeks in his palms. "Let it go. Everything that happened back then, let it go." His forehead dipped and rested against hers, their breath intermingling.

"What can we do? What can we do to escape it?"

His mouth closed over hers and he kissed her with an anguished reverence. When they broke apart, he caressed her face and neck. "I'm not sorry for that," he said.

She bit down on her lower lip. "You and I, we carry the blood of all those before us. Do you understand that?"

"I promise you, we'll get through this."

She brought her fingers to her lips, tasting him and, at the same time, fingering the pistol in her pocket. Behind them a vehicle door slammed. Startled, they jumped apart and looked out at a van parked on the road below Allafair's grave. Alma stood quietly watching.

"Don't worry," Walter said. "It's Cedric and Orson. They're here to help."

Alma clipped off the pistol's safety. The two men separated to cover more ground. They looked around, appearing unsure of what they would find. Walter stepped out and motioned to them. Both came toward him but stopped when they saw Alma. Orson stared at her, keeping his right hand in his jacket pocket, while his father glanced tentatively toward Walter. She followed Walter down the hill to them and stopped beside Allafair's grave.

"Alma saw the old man," Walter said. "She's been to Shadow Mountain."

"Always heard that place was a myth," Cedric said, glancing over at his son. "Anybody that tried to find it went crazy." He looked at her suspiciously and his hands spread slightly from his sides.

"I may very well be a little crazy," she said, "but then you're used to dealing with crazy people, aren't you, Mr. Burke?"

He held his silence. His son stepped to the left, trying to get behind Alma.

She moved sideways to counter him and found herself staring into the barrel of Orson's gun.

46

"This has gotten interesting," Alma said, glancing back at Walter.

"Put that away," he told Orson.

Cedric also drew a gun and pointed it at Alma. "She knows," he said. "Only one way left to deal with this."

"Burke!" Walter snapped and waved him away. "Remember who you work for."

"But I do know," Alma said, stepping backward to keep the men in view. She pointed to Orson's right hand, which was wrapped with a bandage. "Bet those are my teeth marks in your flesh."

His apprehensive eyes wavered, just enough to tell her he was guilty.

She whistled and the dogs came scrambling over the hill. Caesar pointed, waiting for instructions. The other hounds surrounded the men. Vernon had trained them well. "With that injured hand, you might not be as fast as Caesar." She indicated the bandage. "Why did you kill Val? I can understand killing me; get rid of me and this all goes away, but she—"

"Was in the wrong place at the wrong time," Orson said, the slightest regret filtering through his voice.

"Still, it yielded results," Cedric continued. "You're accused of her murder, fingerprints on an untraceable gun, couldn't have worked out better if I had planned it."

"I would never have let them hurt you," Walter interrupted. "Alma, you have to understand, I didn't know. I didn't know what they were doing."

"That's what's wrong!" Cedric exploded at him. "Your father would have handled this no matter what!"

"I am not my father!"

A hard silence followed. The lonely blinking of thousands of fireflies lit up the night like beacons calling for action and the moon stood witness for the light of day.

"That's for damn sure," the older man finally said, shaking his head as if Walter were a sad, degenerate species on the verge of extinction. "You're about as sorry a coward as your father always thought you'd be."

"I'll give you an hour head start." Walter stepped in front of Alma.

"We're not going down for this," Cedric said, alarm filled his voice. He reached for his gun.

"Caesar, *angriff!*" Alma hollered the German word for attack. The German shepherd leaped on Orson, taking him down in a dive, and his gun discharged into the ground as the dog bit into his arm. The collie and bird-dog were on him, as well. Orson screamed.

Alma whipped around Walter, aiming her gun at Cedric. Both fired at the same time. A bullet smashed into her chest, and she fell back over a gravestone and slammed into the ground. Crushing pain seared through her. She struggled to hold onto her weapon and focused on her body until she was sure of her condition. The snarling of the dogs told her that Caesar, Bud, Sadie, and the rest had Orson on the ground and he was going nowhere.

Walter leaned over her. "No, no, no, not now. You can't die now!" He lifted her by the shoulders, one hand caressing her cheek.

She pointed the gun in his face, twisted away and staggered to her knees, heaving in for air. The dogs had Orson under control. Cedric was also flat on the ground.

"Dad!" Orson yelled, but every time he moved, Caesar bit down on his arm and held him still.

Alma put a hand on her chest and breathed out heavily. Walter stared at her with an expression of relief and denial. The bulletproof vest had done its job.

In the distance shone red and blue police lights. Sirens wailed.

47

Judith Drake stepped from the back of a sedan. Her assistant, Philip, followed closely behind along with several state troopers. Alma's heart sank.

Walter came up behind her. "Keep quiet," he whispered. "If we work together, there is still a way out of this."

"But I haven't done anything other than defend my life," she scoffed.

"They won't believe you. I warned you about Judith Drake."

Judith surveyed Cedric Burke's corpse with the compassion of staring at a fish fry, then turned toward the injured man still held down by Caesar. "Call off your dogs, Ms. Bashears," she ordered.

Alma whistled. *"Kommen, sitzen,"* she muttered. The pack of hounds lined up behind her.

"Seems everywhere you go, dead bodies follow," Judith said.

"Even more interesting is that you're always right behind me," Alma replied. "Mind if I ask how you ended up here?"

Judith licked her lips as if calculating how to work the situation to her advantage. "A phone tip."

Alma looked at Cedric. "I don't think you've found what the tipster intended."

"And what would that be?"

"My dead body." She turned her pistol around, holding the barrel, and handed it to one of the troopers. "I have a permit for that gun." She pointed at Orson Burke. "He killed Val Durwood,"

"Who killed that one?" Judith pointed at the older man on the ground.

Alma hesitated before answering. "I did."

"A confession." Judith nodded at Philip, who made notes, then turned to one of the troopers. "Arrest her."

"What?" Alma exclaimed. "It was self-defense! Look in his hand. He's holding a .22." She pointed to her own chest, at the bulletproof vest. "Here's a slug that will match that gun."

Judith looked in the direction of the splayed body, then stepped between the legs of the corpse. "I don't see anything."

Alma lunged forward. Philip moved in front of his boss, but that didn't keep Alma from speaking loud enough so the troopers would hear. "You would do this, knowing I'm telling the truth," she said. "Can you even look me in the eye?"

"You heard me!" Judith shouted at the nearest trooper. He reluctantly took out a pair of handcuffs.

Just as Alma's arms were pulled behind her back, another cluster of law enforcement lights sparkled down the dark road and the wail of sirens broke the night. Seconds later, Maggie Armstrong jumped from a squad car with Detective Moody and a half dozen Contrary policemen in tow. She clasped the envelope Alma had given her against her chest. It had been ripped open.

Officer Moody stormed toward Judith. "You're supposed to coordinate any law enforcement actions through me," he snapped.

"If I waited on your rinky-dink crew," she retorted, "half the criminals in eastern Kentucky would be in the North Carolina mountains."

"Don't make the mistake of thinking I report to you," Moody shot back.

"That's quite an insult," Maggie said, taking notes at a furious pace.

"This is a local matter!" Moody warned Judith.

"And as a representative of the attorney general, I claim jurisdiction. These events are germane to my investigation."

"You haven't investigated," Alma said. "There are more people here than me. What questions have you asked? Or is justice beyond your jurisdiction?"

"So far, Ms. Bashears," Judith said, "all you have is allegations. No proof."

"Are you saying I must prove my innocence?"

Judith focused her wrath on Alma. "You admitted shooting this man. The gun was in your possession. Ballistics, this time, will undoubtedly prove it the murder weapon. Your reign in Crimson County has come to an end."

Maggie pulled on Detective Moody's arm. "Walter Gentry saw what happened." She pointed up the hill to where he stood in front of his parent's graves, as if willing himself into invisibility.

"You've turned into such a disappointment," Judith told the young reporter.

The scowl on Maggie's face showed a nerve had been scratched. "You are so much like my mother," she huffed under her breath.

Slowly, Walter turned toward everyone below. His expression was one of stunned realization. He looked incapable of reasonable action, but Alma figured he was waiting to see how things played out. Judith was right. She had no proof of anything she claimed. And, if everything she had set out to prove tonight was true, Walter would be as tight-lipped as a clam. "All right," she said, knowing that for now, she was defeated. "I'll go with you."

"Wait," said a voice behind the line of Contrary policemen. A man in a dark blue suit stepped out of the shadows and held up an identification badge. "Agent Ron Cantalupo. The FBI will be assuming jurisdiction of this case."

"No," Judith objected, then looked at Maggie. "You stupid little blond twit!"

"It always helps having connections," she sneered.

Agent Cantalupo pointed to the envelope Maggie held. "If the contents of the papers Miss Armstrong presented me with tonight are true, then crimes have been committed on federal property and it is now our investigation. I'd like to hear what these people know about what happened twenty-eight years ago at Silver Lake and how it's connected with what went on here tonight."

Alma smiled slightly at Maggie.

"You counted on my opening this envelope, didn't you?" she whispered to Alma.

"Let's just say I was pretty sure your curiosity would get the best of you."

The FBI agent glanced around at the troopers and the Contrary police, then looked directly at Philip. "Anyone here have any problems taking my direction?" Even Judith's flunky nodded that he would comply. "Okay, everyone standing, I'd like you all to accompany me to the local police station. Officer Moody, get the coroner and a forensics team out here to deal with this body."

"There's one more person you'll want to talk to," Alma said. She slowly turned around and looked up the hill, then put her hands to each side of her mouth, and called out. "Come on out now . . . come on." The night was still, except for the sounds of a whip-poor-will.

"Alma," Walter said from where he stood uphill, "there's no one here."

"He's there," she said.

Walter strode back down to level ground to explain to the FBI agent. "My client hasn't been well. Perhaps she should be taken to the hospital."

"If you don't come out now, I'll send the dogs to get you," Alma said toward the gravestones.

The old man peered from behind the towering marble angel, his hat still pulled low on his head.

"Shine a light up there," Agent Cantalupo ordered.

The elderly man held up his hand to shield his eyes, looking down at them as if searching the crowd for a friend. His hands trembled as he stepped around to the front of the angel.

"My God," Detective Moody breathed. "It's Walt Gentry." His eyes, like many others' in the crowd who as children had known the larger-than-life man as he shoved his way around town, fixed on the carved lettering of his name on the tombstone. *Walter Gentry, Sr.* "He's alive."

48

"Allafair?" he called out in a thin, unsure voice. "Is that you, honey?" The lumbering figure used the base of the angel to steady himself. "I been following ye, been trying to get to you for so long." He paused, standing on his own grave. "You kept running away from me. You didn't need to do that. I'd've never hurt you none."

Horrified, Alma looked at Walter for some explanation, then realized that in the darkness, her black hair and stature must be similar to Allafair's. She stepped forward and raised a hand, motioning the elderly man to come down the hill. "I'm not Allafair, Mr. Gentry."

Walter let out an anguished gasp as he moved to Alma's side. "He thinks it's 1975," he said.

Orson held his arm, which now had a dog bite in addition to the one Alma had given him. "You're a sorry son of a bitch," he told Walter. "My father and I took care of your mother's dirty work since the old man lost his mind."

"You're the one who called me," Alma said to Orson. "Warned me against trying to find Allafair's children."

"No reason to deny it now," he replied. "We couldn't risk what was hidden finding the light of day."

"Orson!" Walter snapped.

"I think I want to hear this," Detective Moody said. The FBI agent and Judith Drake also moved closer to listen.

"The old man saw the ad you put in the paper," Orson explained. "Sent him off the deep end. I don't know what Allafair Adair was to him, but he'd sat in a room staring at a wall for fifteen years and, that night, he escaped." Orson looked at the agent. "We were just following orders." He glared at Walter, blaming him. "All we've done these past weeks was try to find a sick, old man. Look what's come of us."

"And when you couldn't find him, you needed to make sure I didn't," Alma said. Part of her wanted to grab a gun and give him some swift justice. "If I wasn't looking for him, no one else would be either, but poor Val ruined your plan."

The old man held up a paper and waved it. "I got it, Allafair. I finally found it."

"What do you have?" Alma asked, squinting into the darkness to see what he held.

"This is too painful," Walter interrupted. "I have to get him to a hospital."

Alma grabbed one of Walter's arms and nodded harshly at Henry. He sent a policeman to block the path between Walter and his father.

"The will," the old man said. "I got Isham Thunderheart's will."

Her insides twisted like a dishrag. "He hid it at his house?"

Walter jumped in again. "I am his attorney and you will not say another word to him."

"You found it when the two men were there?" Alma asked. "The policeman and the other—"

"Cedric'll handle the clean up," the old man croaked as if still a powerful patriarch ruling his mountain kingdom unchallenged. "They always do." He snickered. "I snuck up on 'em. The blond feller found the will hid 'neath the steps. They was reading how Shadow Mountain is yourn. But now, it's mine, 'cause I'll take care of ye. Me and you, we'll . . . " He looked around, suddenly realizing there were people all about. Turning toward Alma, he blinked his eyes several times. "You ain't Allafair."

"This is inadmissible in any court of law," Walter interrupted. "Father, shut up!"

Alma turned and faced the FBI agent. "I think Mr. Gentry needs to be taken to a hospital and put in protective custody. It's my belief that he's been held for many years against his will, first by his wife, and then by his son." She glanced over at Walter, who appeared stunned by her accusation. "Until his competence can be assessed, I don't want anyone, family or otherwise, near him."

The agent nodded, then motioned for two policemen to assist the elderly man the rest of the way down the hill. As they brought him closer, he walked between Walter and Alma, but did not glance at his son. He stared at Alma, his expression turning to confusion. "You're not her," he said, agitated by the discovery. "You're not my daughter."

"Daughter?" Walter looked as if questions he had probably wondered about all his life had been suddenly answered. "She wasn't his mistress," he said as much to himself as anyone. "She was his daughter . . . my sister."

"And your mother caused the death of his grandchild," Alma said.

"He never got over the grief." Walter reached out and put a hand on his father's shoulder. The old man didn't acknowledge him, and the pain in Walter's expression festered. "Her death was what ate at him until his mind couldn't handle it anymore." He turned to the FBI agent as if already calculating his father's defense. "That's what you need to understand. Let me take him home."

"Do as Ms. Bashears says," Cantalupo replied. "Stand back."

Alma looked down at Allafair's grave. The old man followed her gaze, then dropped to his knees, tearing away the honeysuckle vines wrapped around the stone. He embraced the headstone. "My Allafair can't be dead . . . can't be gone." He stared at Orson, a look of recognition that turned to hatred for the man who had held him hostage all these years. "I had to get some money—" he looked at Alma "—your money," he added, seeming to remember their last meeting here, "so I could find my daughter, start a new life. She and me'd own Shadow Mountain. We'll make so much money, that old witch Charlotte could never separate us again. We're family. Nobody should separate a family."

Alma took the will and opened it. It included a deed to a plot of land called Shadow Mountain and listed the previous owners going back for generations and into the future. After Isham Thunderheart's name was Allafair and her descendants up to the last of the Adair line, listed as Adair 1, Adair 2, Adair 3. When there were no more of them left, Kingsley University was to assume guardianship.

This is the Maltese Falcon, she realized. The prize that Jefferson anticipated was more valuable than gold. Alma felt sick looking at Walt Gentry, this old man who had gone mad from grief and obsession still hung onto his greed. Willie looked up at her and moaned. Caesar licked her hand. Even the animals sensed the human misery around them.

49

Alma and Walter watched as his father was seated in the back of a cruiser. The elderly Gentry stared out at her, sprinklings of recognition alternately lighting his eyes with the confusion of two dozen years. His lips began to move and Alma asked the policeman to open the door.

"I know you," he said with the coherence of a man navigating his own memory. "You belong to Esau Bashears."

She nodded once, unsure of what her expression gave away.

"He could've saved hisself, you know," the old man said, his lips trembling and almost unable to form words. He stared forward and blinked several times. "He could have swam for it when the water broke. A man could have survived crossing from the house to the dry land, but . . . "

"The little girl wouldn't have made it," Alma finished for him. "She ran back to the house to save her infant sister. My father ran back to save her."

"He made his own fortunes." The old man had cunning in his tone and Alma realized just what kind of amoral force her father had been up against.

"Should have swam for it," the old man said. "That's what any sane man would have done."

"My father lost his life because he wouldn't let a child die alone." She turned away sharply, no longer able to look at the man, and stood apart from the rest. Answers to questions that had haunted her soaked into her bones. The cruiser pulled away and, a minute later, she felt a presence behind her.

"I didn't find out until Mother died," Walter said, coming to her side. "I was trapped. He'd been dead to the public for so long . . . I couldn't destroy her legacy. All I could do was make him comfortable for the rest of his life."

"I understand," Alma said quietly, with a measure of control.

"You are right." Slowly he sucked in a deep breath. "The past can . . . terrorize the future. I've tried so hard to make up for the past and I'm exhausted." He wiped his face with both hands, the weariness of his burden making deep lines in his forehead. "Tomorrow morning, I'm going to get my father an attorney, and then I'm leaving. I'm putting a *'For Sale'* sign in front yard, packing everything I own, and leaving these mountains forever." He glanced at her, but not directly; another quick look as if to surmise her mood. "I want you to know I am sorry about Grady. If there was something I could have done to stop it, I would have. I was doing all I could to find him."

Alma stared at the ground and blinked several times. Her gaze wandered to his mother's gravestone, with its imposing angel looking down on them, and then to Allafair's simple stone wrapped in honeysuckle vines, their sweet scent flavoring the air along with the acrid smell of gunpowder.

Walter touched her shoulder, his hand lingering for a moment, then he stepped away. "If you ever need anything, anything . . . " he said and began to walk away.

"Wait." The word stopped him like the turning of a key. Her eyes flipped up and, without moving her head, she said what she hoped would fill him with more terror than he had ever known. "Do you think that, after what you did to Val Durward and Isham Thunderheart, I'd let you walk away?"

Walter stood like a statue. "It was Orson," he said, his voice flat. "You heard him. You saw the bite mark on his hand."

"Oh, yes." She straightened her back and walked toward him. "He did the dirty work, but it was your idea."

"Never." He turned to face her. "You know me. I'm not capable of that, and I'd never do anything like that to you."

"You've been doing it to me from the beginning," she accused him. "The only reason you got involved in my case was to keep an eye on me. When you saw that ad about Allafair, when you saw the picture of the old man in Krauss's office, you knew that I'd eventually find him and figure it out. You involved yourself so you could control what was going on. But, more than any of that, the most damning evidence—you were in my office the day I first heard of Isham Thunderheart. You, Grady, and Jefferson were the only people who knew I'd be trying to find him, and that night he ended up dead."

"My father had nothing to do with that."

"I believe you," she said and watched his surprised reaction. "But Isham knew things you didn't want me to find out. Someone had to get there first—and you're the only one who knew. What did you do? Have Orson steal the truck, so when Isham's body was found it looked like he was killed for it? Then when your father escaped, he took it."

"After all I've done to defend you." He stepped toward her, looking deeply into her eyes, his tone almost begging. "I would never have let Judith Drake send you to jail." He reached out to touch her arm and she jerked away. "If you believe anything, believe that."

"Of course, as long as it was to your benefit, but then you couldn't find your father. The risk was getting greater every day that I'd locate him first." She circled around him, feeling like an eagle bearing down on its prey. "Kill Isham Thunderheart and it all goes away. Kill me and it all goes away and, but for Val, I'd be dead. All the problems disappear with a single act that became a justified choice. You just got tired, Walter. Murder was the easy way to rewrite history."

"It was not my idea." His voice was a grave whisper. He patted his hands in the air, urging her to be silent, then stared at her, trying to read her face. "I tried everything else. I even thought we might . . . I'd hoped we could . . . " He reached up and touched her cheek, then his expression iced over as he reached a conclusion. "Alma, seems we've reached a stalemate once again. You can't prove anything you just said." He crossed his arms, his head tilting toward the side. "We can work this out."

She smirked at his arrogance. "I've got Orson Burke. After I'm done piling charges on him, do you really think he won't give you up for a deal?"

Fear flooded Walter's face and he turned away. "I told you," he said, barely glancing back. "I'll leave town tomorrow morning. You'll never see me again. It's all yours." He spread his arms to indicate the entire valley. "You win. I lose." He took a step, seeming to wait for her decision, then took another and, as his confidence returned, stepped again toward his car. "You know this is as good for you as it is for me. Think about it before you act."

"Detective Moody," Alma called loudly. "Arrest Mr. Gentry on the charge of conspiracy to commit murder."

Walter wheeled around to face her. His expression was incredulous, but he did not speak. He knew well his right to remain silent.

50

Judith Drake argued with Agent Cantalupo, although he was getting the best of her. She rolled her eyes and glared at Alma over his shoulder.

Alma walked directly up to her. "I'll be coming to my office first thing tomorrow morning," she said. "Be gone."

"This isn't over—"

"You are so right about that," Alma interrupted. "A number of state troopers watched as you instructed their brethren to ignore evidence. That little story is going to be in the hands of every newspaper in the state by tomorrow."

"Misunderstandings happen," she smirked. "No one will believe it was malicious."

"The attorney general isn't going to be pleased with you."

Her sarcastic grin vanished and she glanced aside. "As I said, this isn't over."

"It's over." Alma inhaled, enjoying the moment as she watched the woman squirm. "More than you realize. What is truly sad is that a woman like you could have used all your knowledge and talent for something important, something that mattered. And look at you." She paused to let the message sink in. "You're pathetic."

Judith straightened her shoulders but didn't look directly at Alma. Her lips were pursed to one side and one eyebrow was arched. "When the attorney general is elected governor, he'll be forming a commission for the investigation of rampant corruption in eastern Kentucky. Someone who isn't intimidated by the local powers-that-be has to head it. Someone who understands how this place works." She turned, opened a car door, and only then did she look at Alma. "I'm going, but I'll be back."

Her sedan screeched away onto the main road, and Alma and Moody watched it turn north toward the freeway rather than back to Contrary.

"I wonder if this means flunky boy will have to clean your office?" he asked.

"Either way," she said, "at least she's gone."

"Alma," Moody said, pulling something from his shirt pocket, "I've been carrying this around to give back to you." Carefully he put her birthstone ring in her hand. "I did check the size on the engagement ring."

She took a breath and looked away. "You can tell me."

"It's a size five. Technically, it'll belong to Grady's brother, who's coming down next week to pack up the apartment, but I have a feeling he'll give it to you."

A stillness washed over Alma, as if Grady's spirit had moved through her. She nodded to Moody and touched his arm as she stepped away. Staring up at the lines of graves, she considered the generations of mountain people that surrounded her. All of them had their stories, their lives making up the history of the land; not as sociology or caricature or stereotype, but as real, vital people who had fought and built and lived their lives. Someday she would lie among them and, when that rest came, she hoped her life would leave behind a story that mattered to someone.

Her cell phone rang and she dug it out of the fanny pack.

"I had to bribe the nurse," said a weak voice.

"Jefferson?" she gasped.

"She's only givin' me thirty-two and a half seconds."

"And I bet you really negotiated for those extra two and a half."

"As if before the Supreme Court," he said. "I learned that from you." He hesitated, the pause quiet, warm and full of meaning. "You know, Alma, I wouldn't take ten mil for you, either."

"I'm coming over," she said.

"You won't get two feet past Atilla; I mean, Arabella, the nurse." He lowered his voice to a whisper. "I think she has a crush on me. I may need rescuing."

A woman's voice came on the line. "Visiting hours are between ten and two and, yes, I'll be glad to get shed of this one. He keeps threatenin' to sue me for malpractice." The line disconnected and Alma held the phone to her chest as if she were clutching her old friend.

She turned to the FBI agent. "Agent Cantalupo, I have to take my dogs home, and I have a horse that's tied over the hill. Can I meet you in two hours?"

He gave her an odd look, but nodded, asking only that she leave her firearm. She readily agreed, then paused at Allafair's grave before leaving. She wondered about the baby her father had run back to save. Were other relatives able to get the infant out before the water rose? Was Vera Cleary right about the baby being put up for adoption? Had her father and the little girl died in vain? At least now the youngster would have a resting place beside her mother. And the other child, if alive, she could only hope had found peace in her life.

Alma walked up the hill, passing Charlotte Gentry's commanding angel that no longer sent a chill through her. The Gentry demons had been exorcised forever. Continuing on with the dogs and horse in tow, she made her way through the river of ancestors toward her own small hollow.

51

The troopers were gone when Alma arrived at her house. The hollow was quiet and as peaceful as she had ever seen it. A bright, full moon hung in the dip between two mountains, a dusting of stars glittering around it. She heaved off the bulletproof vest, as well as her jacket, and dropped them on the porch, then lowered herself onto the top step for a moment's rest. The fanny pack hung low and heavy and she unzipped it. Inside lay the black stone that had floated into her hands in the pool on top of Shadow Mountain.

She held up the rock to get a better look, letting the light of the moon illuminate it. The stone was as transparent as crystal against the beams of the moon. Inside it was an object she couldn't identify. It looked like a kernel of corn, fossilized like a gem. When she lowered the stone, the dark color returned and hid what it held. *Well,* she thought, *if this stone is supposed to change the world, it seems right for it to end up with descendants of Delta Wade. Soon enough, they'll know about their inheritance from Isham's will—the mysterious Shadow Mountain.*

Alma forced just a little more strength into her bones. There was only one thing left to do. She retrieved the doll's body from the sink and brought it out to the porch, along with the snow globe. One swift crack of a hammer shattered the glass. She lifted out the doll's face, holding it carefully in her palm. Gently, she fit it into the empty head socket. It snapped into place perfectly as if its violent past had never occurred. She blinked back tears as she remembered hiding the toy in her father's car all those years ago. This doll had been her best friend, and she had sent it out into the world with a father who would never return.

Alma raised the doll skyward. Its face was as round as the moon in the background. Gray orbs now peered though the eye sockets and long black hair hung over the shriveled red-checkered dress. The tiny teardrop that she had drawn on the cheek so long ago faded as the water dried. A flood of memories rolled through her mind, and the mountaintop seemed filled with the presence of Allafair's child who had played with the doll and loved it so much that she must have convinced her mother to name the baby sister after it.

Alma smiled. "Welcome home, Helen Marie."

THE END

Author's Note

Thank you, Reader, for joining Alma and me in the final book of The Appalachian Trilogy. Much has changed since the first printing in 2003 but I decided to leave the story set in the original time period rather than updating it as other books refer to events or people during these years. If you enjoyed *The Law of Betrayal*, I hope you'll consider catching up on Crimson County history in *The Law of Revenge* and *The Law of the Dead*.

To stay updated about these and other books by me, sign up for my newsletter at TessCollins.com or check in on the blog at BearCatPress.com.

Thanks again, and Happy Reading!

Photo by Lisa Keeting

About the Author

Tess Collins is a coal miner's granddaughter. According to a family legend she is descended from a mountain clan known as the Seven Big Sisters. Raised in the southeastern Kentucky town of Middlesboro, she spent her early years listening to mountain tales of haunted hollows, ghosts, moonshiners and unsolved murders. No doubt they influenced her writing. She is the author of THE LAW OF REVENGE, THE LAW OF THE DEAD, and THE LAW OF BETRAYAL, thrillers set in Appalachia; HELEN OF TROY, NOTOWN, and THE HUNTER OF HERTHA. Her non-fiction book HOW THEATER MANAGERS MANAGE is published by Rowman and Littlefield's Scarecrow Press. Miss Collins received a B.A. from the University of Kentucky and a Ph.D. from The Union Institute. Check out her web page at TessCollins.com.